I Love
Claire

I Love
Claire

Tracey Bateman

New York Boston Nashville

Copyright © 2007 by Tracey Bateman

All rights reserved. No part of this book may be reproduced in any form or by any electronic or mechanical means, including information storage and retrieval systems, without permission in writing from the publisher, except by a reviewer who may quote brief passages in a review.

FaithWords
Hachette Book Group USA
1271 Avenue of the Americas, New York, NY 10020
Visit our Web site at www.faithwords.com.

Printed in the United States of America
First Edition: January 2007
10 9 8 7 6 5 4 3 2 1

The FaithWords name and logo are trademarks of Hachette Book Group USA.

Library of Congress Cataloging-in-Publication Data
Bateman, Tracey Victoria.
  I love Claire / Tracey Bateman. — 1st ed.
      p. cm.
  Summary: "Claire Everett finally snagged a man, but how will she pay for the wedding when her writing career hits a snag of its own?" —Provided by the publisher.
  ISBN-13: 978-0-446-69607-4
  ISBN-10: 0-446-69607-2
  1. Women novelists—Fiction. 2. Weddings—Fiction. I. Title.
  PS3602.A854I15 2007
  813'.6—dc22   2006021644

To the "ladies" of Lebanon Family Church.
You make my heart sing.

Acknowledgments

Rusty, as always, I couldn't do what I love to do without your support, help at home, help with kids, and arm and back massages to get me through sixteen-hour days. Thank you for unwavering faithfulness and strength. I don't tell you enough how much I need you and how grateful I am that God brought you into my life and heart.

Cat, Mike, Stevan, and Will, sometimes having a mom who works as much as I do gets to be a pain. You've told me. I hear you. Thank you for allowing me this journey and for being the great kids you are even when you don't like deadline crunch. I marvel every day at the wonderful people God is making you to be.

My mother, Frances Devine. Thank you. I love you.

Once again Debra Ullrick (I spelled it right this time!) and Chris Lynxwiler, you read and reread over and over. How can I ever thank either of you enough?

Anne Goldsmith, this book marks our first journey together as editor and author. You're good. Really good. I'm stretching. Looking forward to traveling a long road with you.

Steve Laube, the best agent ever. You continue to amaze me with each next step in my career. Thanks for believing in me more than I believe in myself.

Jesus, my captain, lover of my soul. Words don't express my adoration for You. There are times I forget that this ministry/career is only because of You, and for You alone. Not for me. During those times, You wait patiently while I struggle. But when I give up, Your arms are always open and with gentle condescension You redirect me.

Create in me a clean heart, O God, and renew a right spirit within me. . . .

I Love
Claire

1

Every novelist dreams of being on *Oprah*. Catapulted to literary stardom with one simple TV appearance. I—Claire Everett, writer of novels—am no different from the hopeful masses. I mean, I don't *really* think I'll ever have enough "twinkle, twinkle" to be a true star. Still, a girl can hope. Well, not hope, really. Hope is the evidence of faith. And I don't really have any faith that I'm ever going to be on *Oprah*. I do dream about it, though.

Catty-cornered from me, Oprah sits with queenly confidence, holding a copy of my most recent novel. She peels back the cover, turns the first few pages to get past the dedication and acknowledgments—the pages we authors labor over, but only our proofreaders and best friends read. I relax for the first time, settling into the soft leather, anticipating the rush I'll get from hearing my words flow melodiously from the lips of the Divine Miss O. My pulse and respiration rise as her mouth opens.

In that wonderful, rich voice the world has loved for the past twenty years, she begins to read. "See Dick run. See Jane run. Dick and Jane run fast."

I suck in a lungful of air as shock rockets to my gut. "What? Wait! That's not my book!" But the words somehow don't make it to Oprah's ears. No one can hear me. I'm a dream ghost. I see my body on the couch, but I'm floating above the roaring crowd. They're laughing at me. And all I can do is sit helplessly with my jaw open, eyes wide like I've just opened the closet door and there's a rat staring at me.

Oprah smirks. *Oh, Lord, please wake me up! Oprah's smirking at me.* "Jane runs faster than Dick."

"Wait! Stop it, Oprah—uh, Miss Winfrey. Please. That's not the right book!"

Suddenly, as I look down at my body, every stitch of clothing is gone. Frantically I reach for a couch pillow. Great. Not only a bad book dream. A naked dream, too. Why can't this be a romantic Greg dream? Wake up, Claire—you slug! What kind of a person has a bad book dream and a naked dream at the same time? I need some major identity counseling.

But the dream just goes on and on, and it's apparent that Oprah is getting a real kick out of the whole thing. "Jane and Dick walk home."

Cut it out, already! Suddenly I reach out and snatch the book from Oprah's hands. My eyes go wide as I realize I just did a bad thing. Rudeness to Oprah doesn't go over anywhere! Not even in one's own dream. This nightmare is getting worse by the millisecond.

She frowns at me then. And because Oprah frowns, so does the audience. I think I'm in big honkin' trouble. To be dissed by Oprah would be worse than receiving a bad review, worse than being black-balled by an elite authors group, and yes, even worse than my book tanking in sales.

"Th-that's not my book, Oprah."

She points to the cover. "Your name is right there, girl."

I look down and, just below a picture of little Jane in a red dress and Dick in pleated blue shorts, is my name. Claire Everett.

I can't hold back a big dream groan.

"Mom?" I hear my daughter's voice far away.

Ari? I don't remember Ari being with me on the show.

The crowd's laughter rises to a feverish pitch and drowns my daughter's voice. As much as I try to keep tears at bay, they spring to my eyes and spill over, hot and fast. Oprah generously hands me a tissue. The crowd "ahs" at her kindness.

"Mom! Snap out of it."

My eyes fly open and I push at the hands stinging my face. "Stop slapping me!" Sheesh. I sit up and glance around. As clarity settles on my sleep-fuzzed brain, a relieved sigh escapes me. My living room. My couch. I flash my gaze downward. Oh, praise the Lord. No nudity. My body is fully clad in SpongeBob SquarePants jammie bottoms, a faded old blue T-shirt, and fuzzy leopard-spotted slippers. Which, at three o'clock on a weekday afternoon is, admittedly, pathetic. But at least my book isn't being mocked on *Oprah*.

Ari snatches the remote from my hand and clicks off the TV. She stands in front of the couch, obstructing my view of the now-blank screen.

"What do you think you're doing?" I demand of my almost-seventeen-year-old daughter. "I was watching that."

"You were not. You were sleeping. And, for the record, you were crying and groaning in your sleep."

"I was not."

"You were." She shakes her head and slips me a tissue. "Why do you watch *Oprah* when you know it makes you have that dream?"

Wiping my eyes and nose, I purse my lips for a second. "I don't know what you're talking about." Highly emotional dreaming always feeds my appetite. Highly emotional anything, really. I grab a half-empty box of Milk Duds from the coffee table and pop one in my mouth.

"Dick and Jane?" Ari's smug look is reminiscent of Dream Oprah. "I heard you telling Linda about it last week."

Linda is my best friend. Her daughter, Trish, is Ari's best friend, so between the four of us, no secret is safe.

Still, some things should be sacred. I scowl at my daughter. "Eavesdropper," I accuse around chewy caramel and chocolate. The phone chirps from the kitchen. I fling myself back on the couch, glad I'm about to be alone in my misery. "Go answer that. It's probably for you anyway."

Ari's roll of the eyes tells me she isn't the least bit concerned about my eavesdropping comment. "You need help." She tosses me the remote and stomps off.

The kid has a point. I do need help. But then again, in my defense, I really don't have a lot of reason to be optimistic as far as my career is concerned. My last book barely made a blip on the sales radar, and my publisher felt we would both be happier if I moved to another publishing house. Newsflash! *They* might be happier, but I'm the one sitting on my couch every day, aimlessly watching *Oprah*, *Dr. Phil*, and *Ellen*, trying to find some direction in my life (well, I watch *Ellen* purely for entertainment purposes, but the other two . . . definitely therapeutic).

To top it off, my agent dumped me, too. The little weasel. So at the moment, I'm a writer with no publisher and no agent. And all my Milk Duds are gone. I think I need pizza. Or maybe a power walk—get those better-than-happy-pills endorphins kicking in. Or—well, no . . . I definitely need pizza.

"Pick up, Mom," Ari calls from the kitchen. "It's Greg."

The truly happy news in my life revolves around my boyfriend, Greg. Correction. Fiancé. Yes, I have a fiancé. Can you hear me singing? "Goin' to the chapel . . ." I smile and snatch up the cordless from the table next to the couch.

"Hello?" I put on that sexy tone that I know drives him crazy.

"Hi," he growls back, and my heart flips. Touché. "I have news."

"Oh?" I stay guarded. He didn't say whether it's bad news or good, and that sort of ambiguity hasn't boded well for us in the past. "What is it?"

The doorbell rings.

"Let me in and I'll tell you."

I gasp. Holy Toledo. My house is a wreck. I'm a mess. I've gained five pounds this month, plus I'm retaining water from Doritos and PMS. My vanity wars with my need to see Greg. I take a quick look in the little diamond-shaped mirror in the foyer, just above the coat rack. Fat face, no makeup, *and* bad hair. I think not. Vanity wins. Now, how do I get out of this gracefully?

"Greg, you can't come in."

"Why not? Got another guy in there?"

I laugh, low and husky. I love it when Greg flirts. "Maybe."

"Is he better looking than I am?"

"Hmm. Not possible."

"Tell me the truth. It's Andy Garcia, isn't it?"

Greg knows I have a crush on the Latino actor. "Never, babe. I only have eyes for you."

"Then how about letting me in? Don't you want to see me?"

Oh, be still my heart. "You know I do. But I look terrible

right now. So does the house. Go down to Mom's for an hour and I'll call you when the coast is clear."

Mom and Greg have been playing musical mortgages. He bought the house down the street from her when she moved to Texas, and she bought it back a year later when she got sick of the Lone Star State and my brother Charley's whining kids. The timing was perfect, considering Greg was off to Bible school in Tulsa, Oklahoma. He won't need it when he finishes school and comes home to marry me. His mom is deeding her *Father of the Bride* dream house to us as soon as we say our "I do's." Is it any wonder I love my soon-to-be mother-in-law?

Anyway, now my incredible fiancé is home for his weekly visit and I can't even open the door and greet him properly. But there's no way I'm going to let him see me looking like this. I mean, a girl has her standards. "Okay?" I say. "One hour?"

"Fine, but this is setting a bad precedent for our marriage." Greg is pouting. I can hear it in his voice. Very cute. "Don't you know I'll expect you to be gorgeous and keep a perfect house all the time once we're married if you don't give me a dose of reality now?"

Nice try. No one can say the guy doesn't give it his all. "No, you won't. You'll see the real me the morning after the wedding. After it's too late for you to back out."

"The morning after the wedding," he says wickedly. "Let's talk about that."

Heat bursts across my cheeks. "Let's not."

He chuckles. "I'm headed down to your mother's. Maybe she'll let me in and give me food."

"I'll call you in an hour."

A frustrated breath hisses through the phone line. "Hurry up, woman. I miss you."

Amazing how those words from the right man, said in just the right tone of voice, can make a girl trip all over herself. From the wrong man . . . well, that's another story, isn't it?

I click off the phone and spring into action, dashing toward the stairs. Then I stop short. Darn it! There's no way I can make both the house and myself presentable in the time frame allowed. There's only one thing to do. Dig into the money jar.

"Kids! Ten bucks for each of you if the house is spotless in an hour!"

"I'm playing Xbox!" My eight-year-old, Jake, calls from the bedroom he shares with his twelve-year-old brother, Shawn. "I don't want to clean."

"I get his ten dollars!" My oldest son, Tommy. The money mogul. At not quite fifteen he has already won some cash prizes at local skate competitions. Skate. As in skateboarding. The kid's a regular hotshot on wheels. And my prayer life has increased tenfold just to avoid the potential bone breakage.

"Get moving, guys! I have to take a shower and get ready to see Greg. I need your help. All of you!" I try to sound more authoritative and less desperate.

"You don't clean my room for me when I have a date," Ari pipes in.

So much for authoritative.

In no mood for arguing, I start up the steps. "What dates?" I pause for effect. "Oh, you mean the ones you used to have before you were grounded until graduation—which, according to my calculation, is about seven months away?"

Ari opens her bedroom door and stands there with a quirky

grin on her face. The grin of defeated good humor. "Gee, Mom. I'd love to help clean the house." Defeated good humor *and* sarcastic wit. I'm so proud. "Thanks for the opportunity to serve you. And for not taking away my dating privileges for the rest of the year. Oh, yeah. And the ten bucks."

I reach out and pat her cheek as I pass. "Don't mention it. You have the kitchen."

Followed by the sound of her moan, I continue down the hall and peek into the younger boys' room. Jake's practically drooling over his controller, and his eyes are bugging. "Get off the Xbox, Jake."

I glance over the pigsty and feel a little guilty that I'm making them clean the house instead of their room. Shawn, the only child yet to voice his opinion about my request/command to tidy up for Greg, is sprawled out on his bed, reading.

"Let's go, Shawny, my boy. You and Jake go downstairs and pick up any clothes or toys that belong to you."

He looks at me, surprise lighting his eyes. "You mean I have to clean, too?"

Okay, he's been in one play and is currently starring in *The Lion, the Witch, and the Wardrobe* and he's a diva all of a sudden? Do you call male divas "divas"?

"Of course you have to help."

The outrage on his face would be comical if I hadn't just wasted seven and a half minutes coercing my children into doing what I told them to do. By my calculation, that leaves me fifty-two and a half minutes. I'm not in the mood to deal with this from him when I have magic to perform in order to capture the essence of my youth and vitality. All with the help of Clinique products.

"Mom, I'm studying my lines. Mr. Wells said I should know my whole part by tomorrow's rehearsal."

"Family stuff first—including chores. Acting second. Remember?"

Heaving a great sigh, the future Brad Pitt (minus questionable moral issues) sets his script aside and hauls himself up from the bed with a dramatic flair that would make his acting coach and play director so proud.

I glance back to Jake. Video Boy hasn't budged. "Jake, I mean it. Do you want to be grounded from that thing?"

"I'm going." He tosses the controller on the carpet and clumsily shoves himself up from the floor. And that's when I notice for the first time—Jake's sort of . . . chubby. I barely contain a gasp, but apparently my dismay shows in my expression. Jake cuts me a wary look as he passes. "I said I'm going."

Okay, time for an intervention. With childhood obesity on the rise, I do not want my boy to be a statistic.

Lord, please give me wisdom to handle this without lowering his self-esteem or starting him on a yo-yo dieting course.

I try to shake it off for now. Will deal with that later. Healthier meals, more exercise, less TV and video games. The boy is not going to be happy. Not one bit.

Just before I turn on the shower, I hear the kids downstairs arguing over who does what. Satisfied they're working on it, I focus my attention on preparing to meet my fiancé.

Approximately fifty minutes later and forty dollars poorer, I open the front door and there he is. My man. The true love of my life. My soon-to-be husband. I haven't seen Greg in a week and I'm more than ready to throw myself into his arms.

He doesn't wait for an invitation. His hand is already on the storm door and he yanks it open with John Wayne-ish machismo (yeah, baby!), takes one step inside, and snatches me around the waist, pulling me close. He pauses, his face so close to mine that I can feel his warm breath on my face. And by the way, I can tell by the minty freshness that he's recently popped a Tic Tac—what a guy.

He doesn't disappoint me and gives me the kind of kiss you'd expect from a man in love after a whole week of separation. My toes are curling by the time he lets me go.

"Want something to drink?" I ask, trying to steady my rubbery knees. "Coffee? Coke?"

He shakes his head and follows me into the living room. "Your mom plied me with chai latte. What is it with her and that stuff?"

I grin. "Newly acquired taste." Not to mention the newly acquired latte machine Charley bought for her. I think he's trying to lure her back to Texas with gifts. I wouldn't be a bit surprised if he ups the ante to satellite TV and Tivo. "She likes showing off her latte machine."

"I'll say. I must have slugged down three mugs in the last hour." He groans. "The woman was relentless. She wouldn't take no for an answer."

I curl my fingers through his and lead him to the couch. We sit, facing each other, knees touching comfortably. "So, what's this news?"

He swallows hard and shifts a bit. The guy's about as nervous as a horse at the starting gate. What's up with that? Dread begins to weave through me, because the last time he needed to have a heart-to-heart, he told me he was going to Bible school and—guess what?—he wanted to be a pastor to boot. Which, of course, means I am going to be a pastor's wife. Something I'm not crazy about. But I've stopped fighting it.

No, really—I came to terms with it . . . after a slight breakup, some soul-searching, and reconciliation. But it's a shaky sort of coming to terms. I'm not sure I'm emotionally stable enough for the other shoe to drop.

I brace myself as he takes a deep breath. The kind of breath that comes right before a big announcement. "Okay, you know how we talked about going to Hawaii for our honeymoon?"

Oh, no. Lord, please don't tell me he's taking away my Hawaii. My beautiful tropical tan. Making love in a bamboo hut while the moon shines through the straw roof. Oh, what a dreamer I am. "Greg . . ."

"Honey, we might need to postpone our trip."

Deep breaths. Breathe, one . . . two . . . three . . . *postpone* is better than *cancel*, but still, just to be clear . . . I stare at him. "Do you mean we need to postpone the wedding *and* the honeymoon?"

I suppose his oh-so-winning smile is meant to reassure me. Yeah. Not so much. "No. Just the honeymoon. We can still get married when we planned." He shifts on the cushion and sits up just a bit straighter. "Here's the thing. One of my instructors is moving his parents to Tulsa in June, right after the end of spring term at the Bible school."

"Okay . . . and he needs your help to move them?" This is noble. We can postpone a day or two. I can be gentle-spirited, start the marriage as a real Proverbs-Thirty-One woman.

"Um, no. Honey." He reaches forward and tucks my hair behind my ear. I love those little intimate touches that show I belong to him.

"Could you just get to it? You're starting to make me nervous." I raise my eyebrow and brace myself.

"My instructor's dad is the minister of a small-town church, and they need an interim pastor while they find someone to take Pastor Miller's place."

I don't even want to know what this has to do with my honeymoon, but suddenly I see my sleek Hawaiian tan fade to bumpy white thighs. I'm thinking maybe I'll go to the islands alone. Maybe get my groove back. Greg's looking a little scared.

"So what are you saying, Greg?"

"Professor Miller has asked me to take over his dad's church for a few months."

"Take over? What's that supposed to mean?"

"As pastor. Preach for them."

Wait. What? This doesn't make any sense.

"But you haven't graduated."

"I know. It's a small independent church. I don't have to have a degree for it. My ordination through our church is enough."

I know many churches work this way. Especially country churches and small-town independent churches. But what was the whole point of uprooting everyone if he doesn't plan to stick it out at Bible school? "I think it's important to finish something you start."

He nods and swipes his hand through his hair. "I agree. I plan to take correspondence courses. And the last couple of months are supposed to be spent on an internship anyway. Professor Miller spoke with the administration, and they're willing to consider my months there as an internship for my final grade."

"Which months are we talking about?"

"Early June through August, at least. I've already explained that I start back to teaching school in the fall, so they'll have to have a permanent replacement for Pastor Miller by then."

Suddenly a burst of light—more like an explosion—blasts through my foggy confusion, and I get it. I know exactly what he's saying and . . . I shoot up from the couch. No, no, no! Wedding . . . honeymoon . . . *me* time. Haven't we been apart enough over the last few months? "Didn't you tell him you had plans?" Like a perfect June wedding and a perfect two-week Hawaiian honeymoon? The rest of the summer decorating our perfect new home to our tastes? Do those things ring a bell at all?

His expression crashes. "I told him I had to discuss it with you."

My temper is starting to flare. Pace. I must pace. Why does Greg keep changing the plan? I wouldn't do that to him. Doesn't he even care how I feel? "You mean like you *discussed* going to Bible school in the first place? Like you *discussed* quitting your teaching job and becoming a pastor instead? You shared the information, but discounting my feelings doesn't constitute a discussion, Greg."

His head is moving side to side, following my frantic pacing. In direct contrast to my losing it, he is infuriatingly together. "It's not about feelings, Claire. I had to obey God's call to go to school and become a pastor. But I don't have to go to Shepherd Falls."

I know he's meeting me in the middle. But I can't help but think about all the history behind this whole Bible school issue. I know Greg's following God. And I'm really trying to surrender my will to God's. But I guess I'm still a little frazzled at how my life is falling outside of the neat little package I'd envisioned. Me: *New York Times* bestselling author. Greg:

schoolteacher (the noblest of professions, after motherhood) and part-time praise and worship leader/sometimes fill-in preacher. Us: living the all-American dream in our dream home with my four children and his one daughter (possibly the only fly in the ointment, but I'm working on that). Suddenly, I can't hold back my discontent. "You were supposed to work at our church as associate pastor after graduation. Remember? And you were going to go back to teaching school?"

"I know." He raises his hands and lets them drop back to his thighs. "I told you, this is only through August." He takes my hand and presses it against his heart. So not fair. He knows that gets me every time. Still, I love this man. Shouldn't I be willing to follow him anywhere?

"I've never even heard of Shepherd Falls," I grumble. But it does sound like a picturesque town, doesn't it? I'm envisioning Victorian Christmas carolers and town hall meetings. "Where is it?"

An indulgent smile tips the corner of his mouth and his shoulders relax noticeably. "It's a little town right at the Arkansas/Missouri border."

"And you couldn't wait just two weeks for our wedding and honeymoon?"

He shakes his head, and I see a cloud of regret pass over his face. "Pastor Miller is having health problems. But he's adamant about not leaving his flock without a pastor. If I don't promise to be there every Sunday, he won't leave."

"If his health is so bad, why is he waiting so long to pass the torch?"

"He wants to wait until the church's anniversary. He'll have been preaching in Shepherd Falls thirty years on the last Sunday in May. He wants to make it until then."

"And your first service there?"

He barely looks me in the eye. "I'll actually start preaching a couple of times a month until June. And then the first Sunday in June, I'll take over as interim pastor."

My heart drops. "The day after the wedding."

He nods. "I can say no."

Oh, sure. Let the old guy keel over some Sunday while he's preaching so I can hula dance in a grass skirt and drink tropical drinks with those little umbrellas. I rear back and kick the coffee table leg. "Darn it."

"Someone else can take the church." Greg mumbles this, and I can tell he's trying hard to be noble. "I mean it. I don't want to start off our marriage with something between us like this. If you have your heart set on Hawaii, we'll go. Professor Miller has a couple of other guys in mind, just in case I can't do it."

I cut my eyes to him. "Really?"

He swallows—hard. "Yes. I was honored that he gave me first dibs. But I'm definitely not the only qualified student." He stands and meets me in the center of the room. His hand is all warm when he takes mine and presses my fingers to his lips. "I love you. My biggest priorities right now are finishing school and marrying you. I know you need a vacation after the tornado last spring and being without a book contract right now. I don't know what I was thinking. You're right. I'll tell Professor Miller to ask someone else."

Now, see? I feel like a jerk. I really want to just lie on the beach for two weeks in June and soak up the sun with my new husband. But the question my heart raises is: Since when did two weeks in Hawaii become more important than Greg's chance to do what his heart is telling him to do? What would the Proverbs-Thirty-One woman do?

"And we'd still get married when we planned, right?"

"No question." He leans forward and presses his forehead to mine. "You're the most important thing to me right now. You and my daughter. But you have to understand that if I give the board my word, I'm not going back on it. So you need to decide if you can live without your honeymoon."

"You're giving me the choice? Really? And you won't be mad either way?"

"I won't be mad."

I know this is my out. My chance to take my man and run off to the islands to soak up sun and discover the intimacies only husbands and wives should share. But . . . this is Greg. And as much as I'd love to keep him all to myself, God has a purpose for his life. A purpose that apparently doesn't include a tropical paradise, for the time being.

Love isn't selfish (my paraphrase)—a little positive self-talk.

My shoulders rise and fall with my next quick breath. "So, this Shepherd Falls . . . any chance there's even one honeymoon suite in the whole town?"

2

The selection of wedding gowns at Tammy's Bridal is sparse at best. Well, maybe not sparse in numbers, but definitely sparse in dresses *I'm* interested in. I've spent the last two hours sitting next to Linda on a paisley upholstered couch, while a petite twentysomething salesgirl rolls out rack after rack of gowns for my perusal.

"What about that one?" Linda asks—only it sounds more like a plea. My best friend is all class and red hair. Normally, she's my biggest support. But I can tell by the way she's rubbing her temples (both of them, alternately) that her patience is wearing thin.

I am the worst friend in the world. Her migraine is proof of that.

I pause, trying to figure out how to tell her that this one won't do, either. Apparently, however, she takes the pause as consideration, because she drops her fingertips and her eyes widen with hope. "Well?" She prods, then puts on the pressure. "I think this one is gorgeous. Look at the beaded buttons all the way down the back. There are a million of them."

The salesgirl gives me a hopeful smile.

I cut a glance to Linda, preparing her for the disappointment that's seconds away from hitting her. "You know whose job it would be to button all those buttons? I couldn't do that to my best friend."

She gives me a short laugh. A little sarcastic, if you want to know the truth. "Believe me, it couldn't be worse than helping you pick out the gown in the first place."

I shake my head.

Her disappointment hits with a vengeance. "Oh, for crying out loud, Claire." Linda flops against the back of the couch like I slugged her. She slouches in a manner I've rarely seen from her. She's the Kathie Lee Gifford type. Straight-backed. Great table manners. Soccer mom. PTA. You know what I mean. The sort of mother to whom all the other overwhelmed, frazzled, cluttered-house soccer moms are glad to give over control of school party-planning and fund-raising. All we ask is that we aren't required to contribute anything more demanding than a couple dozen cupcakes and some Hawaiian Punch now and then.

Hawaiian. *Sigh.*

"Claire, give me a break!" Shock zips through me as Linda punches (*punches!*) the couch cushion. So unlike her to be out of control.

I fight back tears, knowing I've brought her to this indignity. "I can't help it. None of these gowns are right for me."

Linda gives me a huff. "This shop was good enough for me when I got married." Technically, she means when she and her husband, Mark, renewed their vows, so it wasn't as important to find the perfect dress. But I'm not about to alienate my matron of honor. If she backs out on me, I'll have to bump my daughter from bridesmaid to maid of honor, and that means Darcy would have to fill in as a bridesmaid.

Despite our eggshell friendship, the thought of my ex-husband's wife standing next to me as I become someone else's wife is just a bit too bizarre. But Darcy's been doing a lot of hinting around lately. So I'm giving her no opportunity to worm her way into my wedding party. Linda is not finished with her pressure tactics anyway. "If Tammy's gowns were good enough for me, then they're good enough for you."

"It's not that they're not good enough." I give her a condescending pat on the arm. "And you were gorgeous in your gown. But this has to be perfect, Linda. I didn't have a real wedding the first time around. And doggone it, if I can't have a great honeymoon in Hawaii, at least I deserve to have a wedding gown that makes me feel like I'm the luckiest woman in the world—which I am."

Linda stares at me for a second, and by the expression in her luminous green eyes I can see her wheels turning as she makes a quick attitude adjustment. "You're absolutely right. You deserve the most fabulous dress in the history of fabulous wedding dresses. None of these will do." She gives a dismissive wave to the salesgirl, who I can tell was hoping against hope that Linda would be able to talk sense into me. "Take them away and bring out the next rack."

Every girl needs a best friend like this.

The salesgirl sucks in the side of her cheek. She is definitely not happy as she pushes the rack toward the storeroom. I can tell by her deceptively forced smile that she's trying not to throw a temper tantrum. Her eyes, though . . . catlike slits of pure evil. I'm sure if I dared cast my gaze to her hands, I'd see claws unsheathed and ready to slice me to ribbons.

I swear, you'd think I could find at least one gown that calls to me. One gown that says, "This is the first day of the rest of your life. Choose me and you'll never regret that walk down the aisle to the man you love." Or, at the very least, "Pick me!

Pick me! Don't you think I'm pretty?" But nothing. Nada. No creation of bliss is crying out to me with poetry or pleading.

"Let's just go, Linda. I give up. Maybe I'll walk down the aisle in a gunnysack."

I jerk to my feet, bad attitude propelling me upward. With a near-growl, I yank up my purse, a JCPenney special I was so proud of four years ago. Unfortunately, four years of use has weakened the strap. And guess who never zips her purse? As I yank, the strap snaps off. A moment of dreamlike slow-mo follows. The contents of my purse fly about the room as if suddenly endowed with wings.

Oh. My. Gosh.

I make a mad scramble for my treasures, snatching up lipstick, emergency face powder for that four o'clock shine, emergency tampon for obvious reasons, eye drops in case my contacts start to feel like sand in my eyes. I'm just starting to collect the dollars' and dollars' worth of change that weighs down my purse and keeps my chiropractor in business when I feel Linda's hand on my head. Patting, tapping. I jerk my head away from her as she starts to tug on my spiky do. "Hang on a sec, Linda," I say with all manner of testiness. "I'm almost done. And it wouldn't hurt you to give me a hand, you know."

With uncharacteristic insistence, my friend spans my head with her fingers and forces me to look up.

Frustration explodes in my throat. "What? For the love of—"

My breath catches in my throat, choking back my indignant comment.

Because . . .

There it is. Bathed in a glow I can only attribute to the angelic host. My gown. *The* one. Envisioned, designed, and stitched together for none other than me, Claire Everett, bride-to-be.

Oh, Lord. I really am still on Your radar. If my spiritual ears were more in tune, I'm sure I'd hear the "Hallelujah Chorus" ringing all the way to the third heaven.

I drop my purse and the handful of quarters, nickels, and dimes. The salesgirl is smiling with victory and doesn't seem to notice the contents of my purse cluttering her floor.

"Oh, Claire." The words leave my friend in a soft Marilyn Monroe breath. And I couldn't agree more.

She helps me to my feet and, hand-in-hand, we approach the wonderment. If ever a gown was made for me, this is it.

"I don't know why I didn't see it before," Linda says, her eyes scanning the gown. "All those other gowns were too . . . I don't know . . . too fancy, I guess. You don't need bows and beads and lace. This dress is you. Simple and full of grace."

I'm a little too ecstatic to analyze the "simple" part, but I'll give her the benefit of the doubt and assume she means uncomplicated. Tentatively I trail my fingers along the silk folds of the exquisite gown. I picture myself walking down the aisle to my love wearing the tank-style top with a square neckline that I suspect will show cleavage. Especially if I wear a push-up bra. I smile. Watch out, Greg. Oh, come on. We're getting married. What's wrong with teasing his imagination a little on our wedding day?

As if reading my mind, Linda grins. "Greg is going to flip his lid when he gets a load of you in this baby."

I send her a cheeky grin of my own. "I know."

The salesgirl has finally stopped giving me that Scarlett O'Hara "I hate you, Melly" glare and is actually smiling. I half expect her to hold up two fingers in a V for "victory."

"Okay, go try it on," Linda says. "I'll pick up your purse."

My stomach jumps. Not with mere butterflies. Butterflies are child's play compared to what I'm feeling. I'm filled with exploding Roman candles. Fireworks of excitement are lighting up my insides.

I disrobe in the dressing room, fingers shaking like I've just won the lottery. Delicate stitching on the bodice provides a contrast to the simplicity of the straight white gown. I stare in the mirror, wonder shooting through me at the thought of Greg's smile.

I think back to my first wedding. Rick and I ran off to Miami, Oklahoma, and said "I do" in a little wedding chapel at two o'clock in the morning. I hate to admit it, but I've always kind of thought that if we'd worked a little harder at putting on a decent wedding, maybe we'd have worked harder on the actual marriage. Easy come, not-so-easy go. Divorce is demoralizing and hurts so many more people than just the couple who can't make it work. And I never, ever want to go through it again. Maybe this is why finding the perfect gown is so important to me. Everything about my wedding to Greg has to be perfect. And this gown definitely is.

"Claire? Are you coming out so we can see?"

Guiltily I force my gaze from my reflection and turn. Introspection and self-analysis have a way of making me lose track of time. I'd almost forgotten Linda was waiting.

I hesitate as I reach for the door. I know my emotions are evident in my face and watery eyes, and I'm not sure I want to put myself out there. Vulnerability isn't easy for me. A side effect of being a woman scorned. Baggage embedded into my personality. Jesus and I are working on it. But Rome wasn't built in a day. Or in six years, apparently, which is how long I've been divorced. Easier to pretend it's no big deal. That I'm not a bit worried about this marriage I'm about to embark upon. I draw a breath. This is silly. Linda is my best friend. She knows my bruised spots and is careful not to press on them.

Still, I'm shy as I step out of my sanctuary. But immediately I'm glad I bit the bullet and allowed Linda to share the moment with me. Tears spring to my eyes at the look of utter joy on my dear friend's face. "Oh, Claire. You're just beautiful. That gown is perfect. Come here and let me zip you."

Sandwiched between three mirrors, I have to admit, I look good from every angle—butt angle notwithstanding.

"Now we need to find the right veil," Linda breathes over my shoulder.

From who knows where, the salesgirl appears with a pile of veils draped over her arm. She gives me the once-over and a broad smile stretches her glossy lips. "Perfect." She lifts a long veil from across her skinny tanned arm and sets the rest down on a Victorian-style loveseat. "How about this?" she asks, standing behind me as Linda scooches. The salesgirl is so little that she hides easily behind my body. Only her head and arms are visible in the mirror, and by comparison, I suddenly don't feel so glamorous in my perfect gown.

A little bit of reality worms its way through my fantasy bride scenario. Just out of curiosity . . . I glance at the salesgirl. "How much?"

She points to the tag peeking out from the shoulder strap. Funny how emotions can go from "ooh-la-la" to "crapola" in half a second.

I raise and drop my arms in despair and force my gaze away from my reflection. I can't look.

"Claire?" Linda asks, her hand on my arm. "What's wrong?"

A shrug lifts my shoulders. I hold out the tag. "Take a look."

Her face blanches. "Ouch."

"I can't believe I didn't check the price before I put it on." I release a breath. "Unhook me, will you?"

Without saying a word, Linda complies. I can feel her searching gaze in the mirror, but I can't look. I refuse to see myself in this unattainable creation.

"Well," I say with a brave, shuddering breath. "That's that."

Linda clears her throat. "Yep." Like the true friend she is, Linda doesn't try to sugarcoat the situation with worthless diatribe about how we'll find another gown just as perfect but more affordable.

"Should I make up a sales receipt?" the clueless salesgirl asks, voice laden with hopeless hope.

"No. Thanks." I'm already closing the dressing room door by the time she processes the unexpected information.

"You mean you don't want the dress? But it's perfect." Poor child. I know she's envisioning her commission on five grand slipping through her fingers. She was so close. I almost feel compelled to apologize for my appalling lack of funds. All that commission, lost to my pitiful bank account.

I hear the sound of Linda's voice, low and sorrowful, as she explains to the salesgirl that we will not be buying the gown.

Slowly I remove the yards of silk from my body. Weakness, born of disappointment, slows my progress. A full fifteen minutes later, I exit the dressing room. The salesgirl averts her gaze as I walk past the counter, and I've never felt more like a slug in my life.

I make it all the way to Linda's little red Miata before I give in to my dismay and burst into tears.

Linda rubs my arm. "It was a Vera Wang," she says, as though that explains it all.

"Vera Wang is . . ." Words escape me, and I can't think what I want to call a person who gets someone's hopes up and then flashes a five-thousand-dollar price tag. FIVE THOUSAND DOLLARS. "Well, I don't know what she is, but it's bad."

Oprah's grin gives me the dreaded realization that I am about to hear Dick and Jane again. Only this time I will not be out of my body, nor will I be naked. Somehow I know I'm dreaming, and that gives me the upper hand in this particular Oprah dream.

"So this book of yours," says the divine Miss O. "A little simple, isn't it?"

I lean forward. "Well, Oprah, if your people would get you the right book to read, you'd realize that I'm a fabulous writer."

She sputters. (Okay, this is my dream. And if I say she sputters, then she does.)

"Mom?"

I'm pulled from my dream by Tommy, my fourteen-year-old son. Darn it. Just when I'm actually winning this time. I sit up slowly, trying to come fully awake.

"Shane's here. He wants to talk to you."

"Oh, great." The youth pastor. "Just what I need when I have bed head."

"Sorry, Claire." Not Tommy's voice. Shoot. Shoot. Shoot. I'm going to kill that kid for bringing company into the house without making sure I'm decent. What if I'd been in my undies, for heaven's sake? Or had a food stain on my shirt?

Which is highly possible any given day, considering my tendency to be klutzy with food.

My hair is out of control. That's the thing about the spiked look. It's okay if you make it stick up on purpose, but when you've been sleeping, there's no convincing anyone you meant it to look that way. Bed head is bed head. And when it's so full of gel and spray, I can't make it behave without wetting it down. I raise my brow as I lock eyes with the cute twenty-six-year-old. He looks at my hair, smirks, and quickly averts his gaze to my eyes. I can see a little damage control is in order. Setting my shoulders a bit straighter, I give him a Mama Knows Best stare-down. "All right, Shane. I'm going to have to have your promise to keep quiet about what my hair looks like when I first wake up." I click off the TV. "And that I watch *Oprah* during the day. And I'm going to have to have that promise before I can let you leave."

A boyish grin breaks out across his face. "I promise."

"Fine, then you may proceed into my living room and take a seat."

Laughter rumbles in his throat. "I can see where Tank gets his sense of humor."

Since when did we start calling Tommy "Tank" again? I thought those days were behind us. I glare at my son and raise my eyebrow, and he knows where I'm about to go.

"It's just a nickname," he says in that "lighten up" tone I hate. "We *all* have nicknames."

Shane's eyes shift between us. "Is everything okay?"

"Fine." I pout because, really, after I agonized over baby-name books, fought with my ex-husband over naming our firstborn son Rick Jr. or Gerald Hugh after his paternal grandfather, endured ten hours of excruciating labor—okay, two before the epidural—I am not happy that Tommy has so uncer-emoniously settled for a stupid nickname like Tank. *Tank*, for crying out loud. Why Tank, anyway? It's not like the kid is as big as a tank, nor as lethal as a tank, nor even green like a tank. He's just a skinny, long-haired skater with cute dimples just above his lips on either side of his mouth.

I sigh loudly and give Shane my attention before I start flashing back to breast-feeding, potty training, first haircut, first day of school. I swallow back tears. "What can I do for you?"

Shane clears his throat and retrieves a paper from his brief-case. "Tank—er, Tommy is slated to compete at regional level in two months. He's really improved since we started sponsor-ing him. I think he's good enough to place."

Pride shoots through me like a swift arrow, targeting my mother's heart, but stinging a little as I conjure up the image of how high he flies in the air with nothing to break his fall. I give a nod. "I have no doubt."

"What I need from you is permission for him to ramp up the practice schedule at The Board. And there are a couple of new moves he'll need to learn that could be dangerous."

Now there's a word that makes me uncomfortable. "How dangerous?"

"Mo-om," Tommy groans. "I'm not a baby. I know what I'm getting into."

"Yeah, well, you don't pay to fix the broken bones, *Tank*."

Now I see why Tommy brought Shane in. Reinforcement. I turn my attention to the youth pastor. "I appreciate your coming to discuss this with me personally. Leave the permis-sion slip. I'll talk it over with his dad and we'll get back to you, okay?"

Once more Shane flashes me his grin and stands. "No problem. We'll stick to the rest of the routine for now." He hands me several papers. "There are three new moves. There's a detailed description of each for you so you can make an informed decision."

I nod, impressed that Shane had the forethought to do this. As soon as the young minister closes the door behind him, Tommy whips around like he's ready for a fight.

"I'm not a baby, you know," he says, anger burning in his eyes, his face red with embarrassment.

"I know you're not, son. But baby or no, you're still my kid. I can't just sign your safety away because you're not concerned. Work with me here, okay? Let's get some videos, and you can show me the moves on these papers."

The way his eyes open a little, like he's surprised I'm really and truly serious about looking into it, pushes a little guilt through me. "What?" I say.

"You mean there's a chance you'll say yes?"

"I said so, didn't I?"

"Yeah. But I figured that was for Shane's benefit."

Sheesh.

"Thanks a lot."

"Hey, no offense."

Oh, gee. None taken.

"Can we go now?" He gives me an impish grin and melts my heart like he has since the very first time he smiled his toothless baby smile when he was a month old.

"Where?"

"To the video store to rent the skateboarding DVD. I know just which one to get."

I didn't exactly plan on spending this particular afternoon

doing that, but then it's not like I have anything else to do. Shawn is at drama practice down the street in his coach's attic studio, my youngest son, Jake, is with his father for a little one-on-one time, and Ari is volunteering this afternoon at the crisis pregnancy center—her new passion. I have no good excuse. Besides, maybe it'll be fun.

"Okay. We can go." I slide out of my leopard-spotted slippers and into a pair of flip-flops.

"You're the greatest!" The kid snatches the keys from the hook by the door. "Can I drive?"

"Oh, sure."

His eyes widen in excitement. "Really?" I didn't think he'd actually take me seriously! I reach out and yank the keys from his hand.

"Yeah, right!"

He jerks open the door and slinks into the passenger seat of the minivan. Then he punches the button to raise the garage door, still scowling at me. I click my seatbelt into place. "Oh, come on, Toms. You knew I was kidding."

"You treat me like a baby. You know I drive all the time when I'm with Dad."

"In hay fields and on country roads. And quite frankly, I'm not nuts about your dad letting you do that, either."

"I'll be turning fifteen in four months, and then I'll have my permit."

Heaven help us. "Well, when you get your permit, you can drive the van. Until then you'll have to be content to obey the law and sit over there."

"Whatever." He gives a heavy breath. "You know what I was thinking, Mom?"

Amazing how the kid can switch topics so quickly. "Don't say 'whatever' to me."

"Sorry," he mutters.

"Okay. So what were you thinking?"

"I think we should get a cooler car."

"You do, huh?"

"For sure." He nods. "I mean, do you know how bad it looks for someone like me to be driving a minivan?"

I can't help but laugh.

He turns to me with a frown. "I'm serious." His tone overflows with offense. I don't believe it. He really is serious.

"Did you fall on your head today at practice? First you want to drive and now you think I'm going to buy a new car just to up your coolness factor?"

"Can we at least talk about getting something better to drive?"

"Oh, sure."

For the second time, he completely misses the sarcasm and sends me a hopeful look. "I saw a great Hummer at the GM lot."

A Hummer, for the love of Pete. Is that long hair clogging important brainwaves? "We can't afford a new car right now. Let alone a Hummer. But, hey, if the van cramps your style, the solution is simple: you don't have to drive it."

A scowl mars his face. "Never mind."

I toss him a "good choice" look.

And just like that I go from being "the greatest" to being "Mom the jerk."

Kids. Sheesh.

3

The thing about finding *the* perfect anything is that suddenly nothing else will satisfy. Find the perfect seafood platter, and no other greasy piece of batter-fried fish will do. Find the perfect pizza place, and no substandard, pseudo-Italian franchise holds a candle—for instance, Chicago-style pizza vs. any other pizza (not that I'm going to turn down a Super Supreme Deep Pan from Pizza Hut). Find a steakhouse that serves a decent filet mignon . . . you get my point.

I don't know—maybe it's just me. But ever since I saw that Vera Wang vision of perfection, I can't be happy about any other gown. And yes, I know it's the marriage and not the wedding that matters. Still, I want my wedding to shine. And I defy any honest bride-to-be to convince me I'm alone in my Cinderella dreaming.

The question is, how do I go about getting what I want, with only enough money in the bank to cover my household expenses until Greg and I get married, and a little extra for a no-frills wedding? We've agreed that neither of us will come into the marriage with credit card debt. So even though I have credit cards with decent limits, I can't use them. I could kick myself for agreeing to that stupid suggestion. Actually, now that I think about it, it was my idea. Hey, and since it was my idea, don't I get some kind of finder's exemption? Maybe I could just charge the dress and . . . *no*, Claire. Don't even go there. There has to be another way.

My mind slides to the various bank accounts in my name. College funds? I mean, really, what are the chances of Tommy's getting into college anyway with his sorry grades? No, no, no. Stop it. Bad Claire. No pilfering the kids' college money. For any reason.

Shoot.

Okay, the moment has passed. Sanity has returned. But I'm still broke.

Oh, sheesh. So what am I going to do?

I'm still pondering this heady question, a week after my encounter with the gown from heaven with the price from you-know-where, when the phone rings. Normally I wouldn't answer a call when I don't recognize the number on caller ID, but *Oprah*'s not on for another two hours and there's nothing else to do, so I snatch it up.

"Hello?"

"Hello?" It's a crackling old voice. Like Grandma's.

"Yes, ma'am?"

"Can you walk my dog?"

In my whole life, no one has asked me that question. Ever. I'm taken aback.

"I'm sorry, but you must have the wrong number."

"Oh, dear." She sounds as though she might cry.

Call it concern. Call it nosiness. But I can't just hang up when a woman who could just as easily be my grandma sounds so frail and vulnerable. I mean, what would Jesus do? "Are you all right, ma'am?"

"I've been trying to get in touch with a new dog walker all day. I could have sworn this was the number from the classifieds. My eyes aren't what they used to be. I'm sorry to disturb you."

I'm about to generously tell her, "No problem. Anyone can make a mistake." You know, the your-wrong-number-disturbed-me-but-I'm-a-nice-person-so-don't-worry-about-it drill. Only before I can say a word, she speaks up again. "My last dog walker quit this morning, and poor Ollie is getting desperate. He's used to morning and afternoon walks. And besides, I don't think those eggs he had for breakfast agreed with him too much. He's passing you-know-what all over the house and I'm afraid he's going to make a number-two on the floor soon."

Ew. "I'm so sorry." I feel for her, really, but what can I do? I don't know any dog walkers. That still, small voice deep within me is getting louder. I try to squash it because this caller may be Norman Bates, for all I know. For a guy, Norman did a pretty good imitation of an old-lady voice.

"Oh, it's not your fault, honey. I just don't know what I'm going to do. Poor Ollie. It's not his fault I broke my hip and can't walk him anymore."

Her pitiful sigh reaches my ear and, all of a sudden, I see James 1:27 playing out in my mind's eye. What have I done for any widows or orphans lately? Still, I hesitate. Do I really want to go walk a stranger's dog? *I was a stranger and you walked not my dog.* All right, now I know it's my guilt talking. That is most definitely not Scripture.

Besides, God wouldn't ask me to walk a dog. He's fully aware that I'm not really an animal lover. And who knows if, indeed, this woman is a widow?

"You know, my late husband, Alfred, always took care of the animals. Of course, we didn't have Ollie back then. He's been gone now for, oh, ten years, I guess. Alfred, that is, not Ollie. Ollie's needin' walked awfully bad."

Aw, shoot. When God speaks, He really speaks.

"All right, ma'am. Where do you live?" Why can't I ever just mind my own business?

Fifteen minutes later I find myself standing on the threshold of a white two-story house with black shutters. I'm shaking from head to toe because, guess what? When I open the door, I see that Ollie is a two-hundred-pound mastiff with strong protective instincts, and he doesn't know me from Adam.

"Uh, hello?" I call out. Ollie takes a menacing step toward me. He doesn't growl, but I know darn well he's telling me to back off. Why would the old woman invite me just to "walk on in" if she had a killer dog on the loose in the house? I'm thinking this beast can just walk himself, and I'm *this* close to leaving the way I came, when a woman in a motorized wheelchair buzzes into the room from a hallway to my left.

"Get back, Ollie! For shame. Is this the thanks you show?"

I nearly pass out in relief as he loses the attitude. The mammoth dog sidles over to her. He obviously adores the old woman and will defend her at all costs from intruders. He rests his enormous head on the arm of the chair and she scratches him behind one ear.

"Now, Ollie, this nice young woman is here to take you for a walk," she says, as though speaking to a child. "Go get your leash, like a good boy."

I watch in astonishment and hold my breath just a little as the bear-dog walks toward me, lifts a leash from the table next to the door (with his mouth of course), and sits in front of me. He tilts his head as if to say, "The ball's in your court."

"That's some smart dog you've got there."

The elderly woman beams with maternal pride. "Isn't he, though? He's going to like you. I can tell."

Good. Then maybe I'll return home with all my limbs intact.

"My name's Claire Everett." Author-slash-dog-walker. I reach out my hand and step forward. The dog drops the leash, keeping himself between me and his mistress.

The elderly woman clucks her tongue. "Oh, Ollie. She's not going to hurt me." She reaches her wrinkled, veiny hand out toward me. "I'm Lou Calloway. Don't mind him. He'll warm up to you in no time."

I take another dubious peek at Ollie the Horrible, not sure I want to take the chance. I hold my breath and step forward again. Ollie plants himself, and keeps an eye on me, but he doesn't snap as I gently take the frail hand. "Nice to meet you, Miss Lou."

She smiles a gummy smile, and it's quite possibly the sweetest thing I've seen since my youngest baby used to smile the exact same way.

Still keeping an eye on Ollie, I let go of her hand and head toward his leash. I pick it up from where he dropped it during his protective priority moment, and he puts his head down like he's ashamed of himself. "It's okay, boy." I smile at him. "Come here. Let's go for a walk."

He lifts his head for me to hook his leash, and I swear he smiles right back. Not being a dog lover, my sudden surge of affection surprises me a great deal. I reach out and scratch the humongous head right behind the ears and he moans with pleasure.

Lou chuckles. "Yep. He's smitten."

I look into his soulful brown eyes. He does sort of look like he's smiling. Aren't I a lucky girl? The last woman to be the object of infatuation for a massive, overgrown animal was Fay Wray. "Do I just walk him around the neighborhood? Or is there a park nearby?"

"Well, he likes to stay close. I doubt he'd let you take him too far from home." Her gray eyes twinkle. "He's a homebody like me."

"Okay, we'll walk around the block a few times. How long?"

"He needs his hour of exercise. Otherwise his joints might get stiff, as big as he is."

"One hour, around the neighborhood. Gotcha." I look down at Ollie, who is salivating just a bit and clearly anxious to get going. "All right, King Kong. Let's hit the road." He thumps his tail.

"Oh, wait, dear."

I turn. "Yes, ma'am?"

"You forgot this."

A pooper-scooper. My heart sinks. Now I remember why I don't own animals.

I learn very quickly that Ollie doesn't have to mind me if he doesn't want to. But bless the Creator, He fashioned this particular breed of dog to be the needy, I-want-my-human-companion-to-be-pleased-with-me type. I mean, if this beast realized just how powerful he truly is, I swear he could gather all his mastiff brothers and sisters all over the world, organize into a scary dog army, and literally take over the planet. Like the apes.

But Ollie doesn't care. He's too happy to be outside, doing his business and getting some fresh air and sunshine. I find myself enjoying the walk, too. Ollie's a good listener, and it just so happens I need to talk. I start off telling him how Greg and I met when my son wrote perverted letters to the school secretary, and Greg, being his teacher, had to call me in for a consultation. I tell Ollie how we fell in love and then broke up when Greg decided he was called to be a pastor and not a schoolteacher. And how God showed me that I could be anything He called me to be, even a pastor's wife, and so we got back together and Greg asked me to marry him.

"Only now," I say to the dog, who looks back every so often just so I know he's listening, "Greg is postponing our Hawaiian honeymoon to preach at this church until they get a new pastor. So I really, really do deserve that gown." I sigh. "Except I'm just not sure how I'm going to come up with the money to get it and still buy a cake and flowers and all that other wedding stuff. What do you think, Ollie?"

You know you're desperate when you are asking a dog for advice. But he glances over his shoulder and gives me a look that says: *Duh. How about walking dogs?* And it makes sense.

A short gasp fills my throat. "Ollie, my boy, you are a genius. What if I advertise to walk dogs?" Except I'm not sure how well it pays. And what if I don't get along with other dogs the way I get along with this one? One step at a time. I'll cross that bridge, and all that.

I'm in the middle of making a mental financial plan when I hear a honk. "Claire! Is that you?"

Groan. Darcy. My ex-husband's perfect, beautiful (even after having a baby three months ago), and annoying wife. I stop. How am I ever going to explain this dog?

She actually puts her SUV in park and gets out, bringing baby Lydia with her. Darcy is adorable in a pair of brown slacks, a ribbed off-white turtleneck, and a fall sweater the colors of turning leaves. I'm wearing ripped Levi's, a Kansas City Chiefs sweatshirt, and a pair of hiker boots.

Darcy gives Ollie an uneasy glance, then turns to me. "Did you get a new dog?"

"Not exactly."

Baby Lydia grins when she sees me, and I go to mush inside. "Hi, little sweetheart," I coo to my children's half-sister. "She just gets prettier every time I see her, Darce."

Darcy flushes with pleasure and plants a kiss on her baby's downy head. "So, the dog? Where'd that monster come from?"

"I'm walking him for an elderly lady." Knowing I'm not going to get by without a full explanation, I replay the wrong-number conversation and Miss Lou's desperate plea for help.

"I think that's the sweetest thing." Darcy's eyes go all misty. For some reason, she has a tendency to put everything I do into sainthood category. She always attributes too much goodness to me, despite my best efforts to set her straight.

"Yeah, well, I'm getting paid for it. I think I might start my own dog-walking service."

A frown mars that perfect brow. "Are you hurting financially, Claire? I know your writing career is in a bit of a slump . . ."

I glare and consider siccing Cujo on her. Like I really need the "career slump" reminder from the woman who is married to my doctor ex-husband and living in an antebellum-style home in the ritzy section of town. Still, her eyes shine with sincerity and concern, so I stuff my irritation. "I have plenty saved to cover my expenses, but I'm thinking about making some extra cash for the wedding."

She casts a dubious glance at Ollie, who has sniffed the

ground and found a satisfactory place to relieve himself for the third time. What is Miss Lou feeding this dog? Darcy's cheeks bloom as she looks away. "You know we'd be happy to loan you the money. Or even pay for the wedding as a wedding gift. You don't have to do . . . this," she says with a wave of her hand.

I lift my head with dignity and make ready my pooper-scooper. "It just so happens I enjoy walking dogs. It's good for my glutes."

"Wouldn't you rather just do squats or the elliptical?"

"As a matter of fact, I have a knack for bonding with dogs. Isn't that right, Ollie?" He huffs out a great heaving sigh and drops to the ground.

"Oh, Claire. You're just being stubborn. I know you are."

I shrug and give Ollie's leash a bit of a pull. "Believe what you want. As you can see, he's ready for his nap, so I'd best get him back home." I smile at the baby. "Bye-bye, sweetums. Auntie Claire loves you." Lydia rewards me with a smile and a coo. I give Darcy the barest of nods. "Talk to you later, Darce."

Darcy's not always the most astute of individuals, but I can see by the hurt in her eyes that she recognizes my snub concerning her offer. Guilt is a familiar edge to my emotional psyche any time she's around. I have this love her/hate her thing going on in my head, and I wish I could just settle on one feeling or the other, because it drives me crazy.

I give her a sideways smile. "It's really okay, Darce. I appreciate the generous offer, but you know as well as I do that I can't let my ex-husband and his wife pay for my wedding." *Think, girl, think!*

Her expression falls. By George, I think she's got it. "I guess you're right. I just wanted to help. I didn't look at it that way."

I know she didn't. To Darcy, she's the one and only for Rick, even though she knows somewhere in her innocent mind that I had to come first. Otherwise, who are those four kids sitting at her table every weekend and half the summer? She truly sees us all as one big family. I humor her for the most part because I've learned it's just easier to do so, but sometimes she really does have to get a reality check. And now is one of those times.

"It's okay, Darce."

"I just hate to see you picking up—" she glances at her daughter and lowers her voice to a whisper "—poop."

I can't help but laugh at her discomfort. "Listen, Darcy, after four kids, I've cleaned up my fair share. Besides, using a pooper-scooper is easy compared to changing diapers."

A tentative grin tips her perfectly shaped pink lips, and I see the wheels rolling in her head. As a new mom, she's done her fair share of diaper changing over the past three months.

"Are you sure this is what you want to do to make money? I'm sure Rick could use an extra receptionist at the clinic." All it would take is one word from me, and I know she'd see to it that I have a job, whether he needs an extra receptionist or not.

"Thanks anyway. I like the fresh air and exercise." I grin. "I'm trying to lose another fifteen pounds before the wedding. Here's my chance."

"You know Greg couldn't care less if you have a few extra pounds." Hmm. Just when we're getting along so well, she has to spell it out about the extra pounds.

I raise my chin. "Well, I care enough for both of us." Ollie gets fed up with waiting for me and flops down again. This is the laziest creature I've ever met. And with teenagers at home doing nothing, that is saying a lot. "Oops. I better get going now, Darcy. I'll talk to you later. Let's go, dog."

Miss Lou is waiting in the living room when I get back. Ollie stands patiently while I unclick his leash and set it on the table. Dutifully he goes to her and rests his chin on the armrest of her wheelchair, just like earlier. I can tell he missed her. I have a feeling these two spend a lot of time like this.

"How did he do?" Miss Lou asks, rubbing his head and scratching his ears.

"Just great. Not a bit of a problem." I hope she doesn't want details. I might be willing to do a little cleanup, but I'm not discussing it with anyone. Besides, I'm still feeling a bit queasy from my first adventure in poop-scooping with Ollie.

"Oh, good." Her voice holds relief. She buzzes over to the coffee table and snatches up her purse. She digs inside and pulls out a bill. I feel guilty, and all of a sudden I hear myself saying, "That's not necessary."

"Don't be silly." She grins. "If it makes you feel any better, my son, Jerry, pays for my housekeeper, nurse, and dog walker. Guilt for never coming to see me."

I can't help smiling, but somewhere in her words I hear a hint of regret, and I wonder about Jerry. Does he completely ignore this sweet little old lady? I resolve to spend the next hour having chai latté with my own mother.

Miss Lou gives me a hopeful raise of her gray eyebrows. "I don't suppose I should count on seeing you in the morning? I know this was just a case of you having a good heart and wanting to help out an old woman."

"Actually, ma'am, I'm sort of looking for part-time work to

help pay for my wedding. If you need me, I'll be happy to walk Ollie twice a day."

"Isn't God good?" Her face glows and she gives me that toothless smile. "I prayed. I really did."

"That's good. You were an answer to my prayers, too."

We settle on price and time, and I leave feeling like I'm in the palm of God's hand. Like He's directing my path, guiding my way. Looking out for me. And most of all, I take this as a sign: that Vera Wang wedding gown is mine.

4

It's hard to believe my oldest child is seventeen years old today. I rush Ollie's second walk of the day and promise Miss Lou a nice long chat tomorrow morning so we can get to know each other.

I'm nearly bursting with excitement over Ari's party. I even caved and agreed to let Rick and Darcy hold it at their house. We've made a decision, my ex and I. Our daughter has grown up so much this past summer and fall, we feel she deserves her own wheels. Rick found a five-year-old red Jeep Cherokee for her. Not much wear and tear. Only sixty-thousand miles on the odometer. He's had it checked out by three separate mechanics, and we went half-and-half on the cost—which means I have to add a couple more clients to my dog-walking list in order to buy my share of the Jeep and still afford my gown. And I'm still not convinced it's all going to come together. For all the work and mess involved, dog walking pays appallingly little. At least Rick's covering Ari's car insurance. It's a miracle that we've reached a point in our relationship, as the divorced parents of four kids, that we can share this gift for our daughter.

I watch Ari stand with Patrick Devine, the pastor's son, who is in college this year and comes home only on weekends. He made the midweek exception tonight and drove the hour from Missouri State University in Springfield to attend her party. Ari dated him off and on for almost a year, but her antics over the summer, before she got it together, sort of soured Paddy on having a relationship with her. By the looks on both of their faces, I'd say it won't be long before Paddy realizes how much she's grown spiritually and in her character, if he doesn't already know. I'm almost sure they'll be back together by Christmas break.

"Look at those two." I turn at the sound of Tina Devine's voice. Patrick's mom is lovely, and she smiles fondly as her gaze rests on the same scene. "I wonder how long before they get back together."

"By Christmas?"

"For sure." She smiles. "Your Ari sure has grown up in the past couple of months, hasn't she?"

I nod, glancing about the room. I have to marvel. There are at least ten girls in various trimesters of pregnancy. Ari's passion for volunteering at the home for pregnant teens has led the church to purchase a fifteen-passenger van, just to haul them all to church on Sunday mornings, and more than one of the girls has made a decision for Christ.

My heart nearly bursts with pride for my girl, a feeling that was completely missing from our relationship over the past couple of years. I mean, any decent mother loves her kid around the faults. But loving and being proud are two very, very different things. Believe me, last year when Ari started sneaking out of the house and even got drunk at a party, I was definitely not a happy mother. Thankfully, that phase didn't last long, thanks to a great youth pastor and a ramped-up youth program at church. Shane exudes an excitement and fervor for God that spills over to the kids.

I watch Ari and Paddy a second longer, offer a hasty prayer

of gratitude to God for His goodness in my life, and turn my attention back to the pastor's wife. "Did Jenny make the cast for *The Lion, the Witch, and the Wardrobe?*" I ask Tina. The Devines' youngest child is about Shawn's age, and they played Peter Pan and Wendy over the summer. If you ask me, I think Shawn has a bit of a crush, but he insists they're "just friends."

"She's playing Susan." Tina's proud smile matches how I feel about Shawn playing Peter.

"Think John's going to catch flack for casting them both in lead roles again after *Peter Pan?*"

"Maybe." Her laughter is infectious. "I bet he doesn't care, though."

She's right about that. John Wells, our token atheist and town acting coach/children's theater director, isn't a bit worried about what people think. He knows talent when he sees it. I'm about to brag a little when Tina nudges me with her elbow and nods toward the doorway. A little smiles plays at the corners of her lips.

I follow her gaze just in time to see Patrick leading Ari from the room. I catch a glimpse of the unsuppressed joy on my daughter's face. Tina and I both breathe out a sigh and then glance at each other and laugh.

"Looks like my estimate was off by a couple of months," I say dryly.

Tina gives a little snort. "That kid of mine is a pretty fast mover when something—or someone—he wants is at stake. I don't think he wants to take a chance that anyone else will see what a catch Ari's become." Tina nods toward Kyle Tanner, a friend of Ari's since sixth grade. Buds to the end. Or is there more on Kyle's mind? His scowling gaze is watching the door.

"Oh." Surprise lifts my brow as I watch him turn slowly, releasing a hard breath and jamming his thumbs in the front pocket of ripped-out jeans that he probably paid eighty bucks for. I swore I'd never pay good money for deliberately torn clothes, but I'd say those are exactly like the ones Tommy got right before school started. "Kyle's got a crush on my daughter?"

"Looks like it."

I can't help but shake my head. "I never even saw that one coming."

Tina gives me a wink. "I did. He's been feeling me out about Patrick and Ari for a while now."

"Really? What did you tell him?"

She colors slightly. "That he'd better hurry if he wants a chance."

"Looks like he didn't hurry fast enough." I can't help but be amused by the whole thing. Not that I don't think Ari's worth having two great Christian guys fall over themselves to win her. Of course, as her mother, I've always known Ari had potential. But as her mother, I also know what a pain she can be. This is her senior year of high school. She's always been cheerleader-and-track-star popular. But since last year, when she became an advocate for pregnant teens, she's blossomed into a lovely Christian girl whom I've come to admire.

Pastor Devine motions for Tina. Her face brightens like Christmas lights at his attention. I don't know why this is so significant to me. She gives me a little wave. "I've been summoned." Tina flourishes as a ministry wife. Never seems resentful. Not that she'd call me and spill her guts to me, anyway. Still, I wonder if I'll ease into it with Greg or if the really content pastors' wives are born with whatever it takes to be good in the role.

I glance once more at the closed door, remembering the look on Ari's face as Patrick led her from the house. As much as I like Paddy, I worry a little that Ari's attention might be diverted from the teen pregnancy center to him, and that she'll lose her focus.

"Did you see Patrick and Ari?"

Darcy's voice is full of excitement as she approaches me from the side before Tina is even fully out of earshot.

"Yeah. I saw."

Her perky nose scrunches with a frown. "You don't sound very happy. I thought you liked him."

"I do."

"Oh, I see." Darcy gives me a knowing nod. "You don't want her to lose focus on the things she's accomplished in the past few months."

I heave a sigh because Darcy has my number this time. "I guess you're right."

"Don't worry, Claire. Ari is sincere in her commitment to these girls." Her gaze sweeps the room. "She isn't going to let a relationship distract her much. Besides, Paddy's gone all week long, every week. They'll only see each other on the weekends."

Now that's a thought that boosts my confidence a little. "That's true."

"Anyway, I just wanted to tell you that I think Greg's looking for you."

My heart skips a beat. "Where?"

"He's in the solarium."

Yes, my ex-husband has built his new wife a home with a solarium. Oh, well. I get my *Father of the Bride* house in just a few months. Who needs this antebellum monstrosity?

"Thanks, Darcy. I'll go find him."

A smile tips her full, glossed lips. "Don't do anything I wouldn't do."

Oh, there's that irritation again. Darcy just doesn't often know when to leave well enough alone.

The solarium door is open when I arrive at the back of the house. I spot Greg in the darkened room, standing next to the glass, looking out into the starry night sky. A gorgeous moon shines down, illuminating his face and giving him an almost surreal glow. His lips move silently. He's praying. Careful not to make a sound, I move inside and lower myself to the step. I watch him, this man I've promised to marry, and I feel that all-too-familiar ache in the pit of my stomach. The ache that says, "You'll never be good enough for this guy. Once he knows who you really are, he won't want you anymore."

Tears prick my eyes, and my nose starts to burn. I sniff—I can't help it—and Greg turns.

In the moonlit room, I see his eyes light up at the sight of me. With three or four long strides, he comes to me, holding out his hand. "Why didn't you speak up?"

"I didn't want to interrupt."

He brushes my mouth with his: soft, quick, warm. "But I was waiting for you."

That pretty much says it all. Greg loves me. Wants me. If only he had stuck to the original plan. I'd make such a great elementary teacher's wife. But a pastor's wife?

Standing with Greg, the moonlight shining through the solarium, the scent of lilies and daffodils fragrancing the air, I can almost forget my troublesome thoughts.

Behind me, Greg wraps me in his arms and rests his chin on

the top of my head. "How are the wedding plans coming along?"

Gulp. "Okay. Linda is matron of honor; Ari is a bridesmaid. Of course, Sadie is the flower girl."

"Have you found your dress?"

Oy.

"We can't talk about the dress. Bad luck." Good, Claire. Way to divert the situation. I haven't found a way to admit that I've become a pooper-scooper-carrying member of the dog walkers' club. I'm not sure why. Partly because I don't want him worrying about my finances. But also because I don't want him to think of me cleaning up dog poop. Not real sexy, if you know what I mean.

Greg lets out a chuckle. I can feel the rumble of his chest against my shoulders. "I'm almost sure we can talk about it. It's only bad luck if I see you in it before you walk down the aisle to me." His tone is wry, so I know he's accepted my explanation. But just to be sure . . .

"I don't want to take any chances."

"All right." He presses a kiss to my head. "Have it your way. I want to ask you a favor."

Slowly I turn in his arms. I grin up into his face and clasp my hands behind his neck. "What can I do for you, babe?"

His eyes flicker dark, then he seems to think better of whatever he was about to say—I can only guess he was about to take the bait and offer a little sexual innuendo. It's probably just as well that Greg lives several hundred miles away during these last few months before the wedding.

I tilt my head to the side and look him in those gorgeous brown eyes.

"The church in Shepherd Falls wants me to come preach for them."

The words pierce my heart like an arrow.

"We've already discussed this. I agreed to no honeymoon."

I see remorse spread across his face and I feel terrible. "I'm sorry, Greg. That was out of line."

He presses a kiss to my forehead and tightens his grip at my waist. "It's okay."

"What's the favor?"

"They actually would like for me to come next weekend and preach the Sunday service."

"Like an audition?" Hope rises. Maybe they won't like him. No. Stop it! They'll love him. And I want them to. What's not to love?

"Sort of like that, I suppose."

"So what favor do you need? Want me to type up your notes?"

His mouth curves upward in a tender smile. "No. I just want you by my side. You'll be my wife when I serve there this summer. I think it's important that the people get to know you, too."

Dread beats a drum in my temples, a loud throbbing beat that fills my ears. I'm staring at Greg's mouth as it moves, but trying to make sense of what he's saying escapes me.

Don't let me make a fool of myself and shame Greg. Please, Lord, please!

Two hours later, I lie in bed, waiting for Ari to get home from "talking" with Patrick. Apparently they have issues to discuss. Important life decisions that only a seventeen-year-old and a nineteen-year-old, both of whom are still supported by their parents, can possibly have to make. I'm trying to keep my focus on my daughter, and the clock, but Greg's expression of joy when I promised to go with him to Shepherd Falls won't leave my mind. I've tried everything—movies, books, squeezing my eyes shut and counting to a hundred, two hundred, three hundred. It's just no use. I can't stop worrying about it. I hate that I have to face this so soon. I thought I'd have a few more months to adjust to the whole Shepherd Falls scenario.

Don't misunderstand. In my heart, I want Greg to succeed. True, I have my doubts about being a pastor's wife. But that's not his fault. It's my own personal angst. And this is only for a few months. I need to trust him. Trust God. Love is not so self-absorbed. Mentally, I know this. But knowing it and feeling it don't always go hand in hand.

Only when the door downstairs opens and closes do I pull myself from the worry, stress, and utter dread of next weekend. I hear the kitchen faucet running as, presumably, Ari gets herself a glass of water. Will she come upstairs, tap on my door, and tell me all about her "talk" with Paddy?

I wait. Wait . . . still waiting . . . okay, I distinctly hear the fourth stair from the top creak. And then her door opens and closes. Darn.

Now I'm faced with a dilemma. Get up, go into the hallway, walk to her door, knock, and start the process of prying information out of her. But if a teenager doesn't want to give info, she's not going to give it. In my mind's eye, I see myself humiliated, slinking back to my room, frustrated by only minor details and no real news.

Moment of decision. Do I risk it? I throw off the covers. Yep. I'm willing to risk it. After all, minor details are better than nothing.

I reach for the door just as it opens.

I scream, Ari screams. We both stand, palms to chests, staring at each other.

"What are you doing?" she asks.

"Uh."

Then understanding lights in her eyes and she gets a look of smug amusement on her face. "Oh, my gosh. You were coming down to my room to milk information about my date, weren't you?"

"Don't be silly." I'm such a liar, and as previously mentioned, not a very good one.

"Yeah, right. Then where were you going? And don't say the—"

"The bathroom." I give a sheepish grin and shrug. "Okay, big deal. So you caught me. Come sit on my bed and tell me about your evening."

She laughs and bounces to my bed. "First of all, thanks to you and Daddy for the Jeep!"

"You're welcome."

"Daddy said it was your idea."

Well, I wasn't going to mention it, but yeah . . . still, it seems unfair not to give her dad credit for being on board with it.

"Dad's paying all the insurance."

She clasps her hands together in front of her chest. "Thank you, Lord, for Mom's ideas and Daddy's loaded bank account." She shoots the prayer heavenward in a slightly disrespectful manner.

"Watch yourself."

"Okay, sorry." But I know she's not really.

"So . . . you, Paddy. Back on?"

A flush of pleasure colors her precious face. "Back on." She wraps her arms tightly around her knees. "I think he's the one, Mom. Paddy thinks so, too." She holds out her left hand.

My heart stops. She's sporting a ring. On her ring finger. A circle of tiny diamonds surrounds an opal stone. I swallow hard. I'm not going to make more of this than it is. "How nice of him to buy you a birthstone ring. Shouldn't you be wearing it on the other hand, though?" Good. Subtle. Non-overreactive.

"It's a promise ring, Mama." *Mama?* Oh, Lord. This is serious. She's pleading with me, softly, gently. I search her face and she meets my gaze, not like a little girl, but like a girl on the verge of becoming a woman. My Ari is in love.

"What exactly does this mean to you and Paddy, sweetheart?"

Her eyes shine with unshed tears. "We know we'll marry someday. But we're not ready to plan a wedding."

Relief spreads through me, weakening my extremities. "Okay, so why the promise then? What if you decide you want to date someone else?"

"Like who?"

Like Kyle maybe, the childhood friend who is smitten with you? But I'm not going to be the one to suggest it. No sense in putting ideas into anyone's head.

I shrug. "You never know whom you're going to meet next year when you go to college." The very thought of her leaving me squeezes my poor heart with a merciless fist.

"No one is like Patrick, Ma."

"I know he's a special guy." I take her face in my hands. By some miracle, she doesn't jerk away. "I just don't want you to make such an important life decision this early. You have your entire senior year ahead of you. Then college. And if you think about it, you're a young senior at that." Ari was such an advanced four-year-old that we couldn't see keeping her out of school another full year just because her birthday fell in October instead of August. Now I wish I'd just let her wait the extra year to start kindergarten instead of testing her into early public school. She's growing up way too fast for my comfort.

"What are you thinking, Mom?"

"Just how grown up you are."

"Everything's changing."

I see sad nostalgia in her eyes. The same kind I feel in my own heart. I nod. "It is."

And that's the way life is. Isn't it?

5

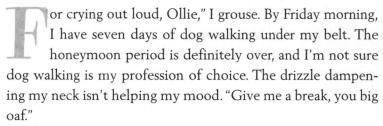

For crying out loud, Ollie," I grouse. By Friday morning, I have seven days of dog walking under my belt. The honeymoon period is definitely over, and I'm not sure dog walking is my profession of choice. The drizzle dampening my neck isn't helping my mood. "Give me a break, you big oaf."

My arms are about to yank out of their sockets. Ollie might do whatever Miss Lou tells him, but he completely ignores me unless it's time for a treat. Two hundred pounds of dog on the other end of the leash can pretty much take me wherever it wants. Every time he gets distracted by a new smell, I pay the price. And it's not that he hates me and is doing it on purpose just to make my life miserable. As a matter of fact, much to my chagrin, he adores me. Miss Lou says he whines by the door when I leave. If I were her, I'd feel a little insulted. She's fed him and cared for him for three years. Now she gets a little broken hip and has to stay in the wheelchair, and he defects to the first pretty face (or whatever) to come along and follow him around with a pooper-scooper. Just like a wayward husband. Okay, I'm projecting again. Darn that toad-sucking ex-husband of mine.

Will I ever get over it? It's not *him*. Honest, it's not. It's the rejection, the "you're not good enough to hold on to a man" that still rankles me. Still causes me to wonder, *Will I be enough for Greg?* Or . . . no. I will not go there. I won't think about what could happen. Greg loves me. He shows me in so many ways.

I let out a heavy sigh, and Ollie stops in his tracks and sits on my feet. "Ollie, what are you doing?" He moans and nuzzles me. "Get off me." I give him a bit of a shove and he takes the hint. "Come on. Your hour is up and I have another client to walk."

Claire Everett. Entrepreneur. Business owner. Dog-walker extraordinaire. In just a few days I've added three new dogs to my client list. Most I walk just once a day, five days a week, while the owners are working. Only Ollie gets special treatment and two visits per day, seven days a week. But I'm afraid dog walking isn't going to be enough to get me that dress. I'm seriously thinking of looking into other part-time work.

Ollie's galumphing steps quicken as we turn the corner to Maple Street, where Miss Lou has lived for forty years. The dog is really pulling hard on the leash, and he's starting to whine. "What's up with you?" I glance ahead and notice an unfamiliar black Jaguar in the driveway. My heart starts to pound a little and I quicken my steps to match Ollie's. I drop his leash as we walk inside.

"No! No! No!" The sound of Miss Lou's frail voice filled with dismay and fear clutches my heart. Without much thought I snatch up the fireplace poker and grip it like a sword. I'm not naturally brave, but when someone I care about is being threatened, I can hold my own. Ollie's one step ahead of me. I follow the sound of Miss Lou's voice. "Leave me alone, Jerry."

But wait. Where have I heard that name before? It doesn't matter. She knows her attacker. That will make it easier to identify him when the police arrive. Miss Lou hasn't been feeling well the past couple of days and hasn't gotten out of bed, so we head down the hall. Before I can stop him, Ollie bursts through the door. I follow directly behind, wielding the poker. A man is bending over Miss Lou.

"Get away from her!" I hear myself yell as I sprint across the room. The man jerks around. Fear widens his eyes. Ollie woofs and jumps on the bed, placing himself between Miss Lou and danger. Lucky for Miss Lou, she takes up the middle of the bed, or he'd have flattened her for sure.

The intruder puts his hands up to block the blow I haven't fully committed to. The poker comes down on his forearms. "Ow! Stop. I'm her son!"

"Don't hurt him, Claire," Miss Lou calls out. "He wasn't attacking me."

My chest is heaving as I register the situation. "You're okay?"

"Of course, you dear girl." She turns to the man, who is wearing a business suit and an overcoat. His hair is slightly spiked, but in a stylish way, square jaw and—wow, Miss Lou's son is a hunk.

Suddenly I'm self-conscious. I look back to Miss Lou. "I—I heard you call out. I thought you were—"

"Does that car in the driveway look like it belongs to someone who has to break in and accost an old woman?" Jerry snaps.

"Old woman, my foot." I smile at Miss Lou's outburst. My gaze lands on her son, but he's not laughing.

All right. This Jerry guy is a scowler. And scowling isn't very attractive, I must say. Well, on second thought, maybe it is. On him.

My defenses shoot straight up, and I glare right back at him. "Super car notwithstanding, how was I supposed to know you're her son? I've been walking Ollie for a whole week and I've never even seen you."

"Yeah." Miss Lou decides to get in on the action. "Claire has a point, Jerry. And as you can very well see, I'm not alone. Claire wouldn't let anything happen to me. She's like the daughter I never had."

I suck in a cold breath. What's she talking about, and how come I'm an ally without my permission? And way to go, Miss L., laying on the manipulative guilt trip with that daughter comment.

Jerry looks on with amusement. I sense there is something deep under the surface of this conversation. Something that is distressing Miss Lou.

I look from one to the other and settle my gaze on the elderly woman. "What's going on?"

"My son wants to farm me out to a nursing home."

I'm incensed! "What?" I turn my accusing gaze on Mr. Jerry the Jerk. "What do you mean, you want Miss Lou to go into a nursing home? She takes great care of herself."

"See?" The elderly woman tosses her arm across Ollie's massive neck. Ollie has relaxed onto his belly but refuses to leave the bed, and he's resting his head on Miss Lou's pillow, next to her head.

Jerry's lips go down at the corners. "Yes, well. It really isn't the *dog walker's* decision, is it, Mom?"

The way he says *dog walker* raises my ire. A lot. Snob.

"Well, I'm sure you two have matters to discuss that are above a mere *dog walker's* level of comprehension." I admit it.

My pride has been violated. I put on a bit of Eliza Doolittle cockney to stress my point.

I bend down and peck Miss Lou on her weathered cheek. Her face crinkles even more as she smiles and pats my face. "You're a good girl, Claire. Thank you for coming in to save me."

"Even though it wasn't necessary," Jerry says with pointed disapproval.

I sniff and give him my best glare of disdain. "Lucky for you."

His eyebrows rise, and he sort of grins. But I turn my gaze to my four-legged client. "I'll be back later, Ollie."

Ollie's ears go up in farewell, but I can see there's not a snowball's chance in you-know-where that he's going to budge an inch from Miss Lou as long as Jerry's in the house. And that's fine by me. I give him a scratch behind the ears. "Take care of her, boy."

"I heard that."

I jerk my chin. "Good. Then you're not deaf."

Miss Lou cackles.

"Pretty, isn't she?" I hear Miss Lou ask her son as I walk down the hall. I stop dead in my tracks because, come on, who could pass up the chance to hear his answer?

"Yeah, Mom. A regular Meg Ryan."

Sheesh. What a charmer. And, for his information, I've been told I have cute Meg Ryan-ish mannerisms.

"Oh, well. She's not interested in you anyway."

Yeah! So there!

"My loss, I'm sure," he drawls.

My face burns all the way to my ears. Jerk! It's all I can do to keep myself from rushing in there and telling him he should be so lucky to get me.

"She's engaged to a very nice man. A *preacher.*" She says it like she's making a point. Comparing.

I hear the scowl in Jerry's voice. "Good thing. He'll need a lot of prayer to be married to that one."

No wonder Jerry's single. He got all looks and no personality. Wish I could say that to his face, but I'd have to reveal my eavesdropping self in order to pull it off.

Oh, who cares what he thinks of me? Greg loves me. That's all that matters. Greg likes the way I look. I leave Miss Lou's house behind, still trying to convince myself that it's okay if every man I meet doesn't salivate over me. It's okay. Really! All I need is one man who pants for me. And I don't mean Ollie.

I drive to my next client's home, troubled by the thought that this son of Lou's might force her into a home before she's ready to take that step. Whatever happened to grown-up kids taking care of their elderly folks instead of carting them off to some nursing home, where only God knows if they're being treated right? I'm sure there are those circumstances when it's better for some parents to go to nursing homes, but not Miss Lou. She's still young at heart. Still has her marbles about her. She'd shrivel up in a place like that. Sure, there's an issue with her broken hip, but gee whiz, that's a setback, not a permanent thing. Right? She'll mend and be good as new.

I hear frantic peals of high-pitched barking when I insert a key into the lock of the little apartment building where Mitzy, the little yippy part-Chihuahua, part-terrier, lives. Angela, her owner, is a single, thirtysomething woman who manages a bookstore and has promised to order some of my back titles for her shelves.

"Coming, Mitzy," I call out as I open the door a crack. Open it too far and Miss Antsy Pants will zoom out the door and take off for who-knows-where. "Oh, Mitzy," I scold the tiny dog. "Your mama's going to be so mad at you. Would you just look at this place?" A full basket of laundry is scattered all over the room. A loaf of bread lies smack in the middle of the floor, where Mitzy has bitten through the middle and munched on the ends. And worse, the dog had an accident. "All right, young lady," I scold, not that Mitzy notices. She continues her joyful jumping up on me. I walk into the kitchen, appalled by the pile of dirty dishes in the sink. Suddenly I'm not so sure the mess in the living room is Mitzy's fault. Still, I open the cabinet below the sink, where Angela mentioned I'd find gloves and paper towels. "Just in case of an accident," she said. Yeah, right. Like she didn't know this would happen.

Dread fills me at the very thought of cleaning up doggie doo this way. Why-oh-why did I ever think dog walking was such a good idea? Why?

I take a deep breath and hold it. No breathing in. Kneeling down, I drape the paper towels over the mess. Oh, gross! How did I ever change diapers?

And Mitzy thinks we're playing a game.

"Stop licking me."

Her little paws press against my arm as she jumps up and licks me again.

"I mean it, dog. So help me, if you want to live to see to-morrow . . ." She's about as far down on my happy list as one can be. I glare at her, but she's wagging her tail, she's so excited to see me. My heart finally softens a little. Poor thing is so affection-starved, I can't stand to be cruel.

"But I'm still not happy with you, young lady!" I keep my voice firm, hoping she'll catch my drift that cleaning up her poop doesn't help our relationship any.

After flushing and spraying Lysol and doing some scrubbing, I replace the gloves in the cabinet and we're ready to go.

"Be still!" I command the antsy creature. Her ears go down and she sits while I slip the leash onto her collar. Her excitement is palpable. "All right, let's go pick up Spike and Toto." Not real original names, but the two boxers are, at the very least, obedient. I just can't walk them with Ollie since the big galoot has gotten so territorial with me.

Mitzy joyfully prances along as we walk a few blocks and pick up the four-year-old twins. The boxers go crazy with barking when I slide the key into the door. "It's just me, guys."

Thankfully the barking stops as soon as they hear the sound of my voice through the door. Their owners—married, childless lawyers working in the same firm—have them well trained. Unlike Mitzy, they don't jump up. I can tell it wouldn't take much for me to undo their training, though. The naughty side of me thinks it would be funny to get them doing bad things, but I need the job. And these two pay especially well. So, as per instructions, I don't allow any misbehaving—with my luck lately, it would probably backfire on me, anyway.

The walk starts out okay. We head down to the dog park—a recent addition to the town that, to be honest, I voted against in the election two years ago. I didn't want my tax dollars going to a dog park. I preferred the proposed new art center (which lost by a mile).

My cell phone rings, and Mitzy starts barking like crazy. "It's okay, Mitzy," I say firmly. She's jumping toward the sound of the chiming ringtone, and the twins are getting antsy. They like their peace and quiet. "Hush!" The phone rings again, Mitzy barks with her whole being, and I think she might actually become airborne. "Sit!" I command. Mitzy, of course, ignores me. Spike and Toto obey. But Mitzy's leash is now looped around one of my ankles. In my mind's eye I see every so-called comical dog-walking scene in the movies or on TV, and I know what's coming if I don't get control of the situation. I unloop the leash as I answer the phone and grab Mitzy up in my other arm.

"Hello?" I yell into the mouthpiece.

"Claire? What's all that barking?"

My stomach turns over at the sound of Greg's voice. We've talked every night since he left Sunday to go back to Tulsa, but I still haven't told him about my little side business. Maybe I should have spilled it by now. Maybe a reasonable person would have. But I know Greg. He'll want to come to my rescue. As any man in love would.

Here's the thing: I have enough money saved to pay my bills until the wedding, as long as I'm careful and stick with the budget. I've always been thrifty, and since the house was paid off in my divorce settlement, it's just a matter of day-to-day stuff, monthly utilities, and the phone bill. It's okay. No problem. Between what Greg's pitching in and what I have designated for the wedding, we'll have a nice but modest ceremony and reception. But I can't admit to him that I have my heart set on a gown that costs almost as much as the rest of the ceremony put together. If I did admit it, he'd insist on buying the gown for me. And I don't want that.

So he'd have no logical reason to assume I am dog walking. Still, my hesitation brings a repeat of his question. "Claire? The barking?"

"Oh, that. It's a dog."

"No kidding," he says wryly. "Where are you? I just got into town and you're not home."

My stomach jumps at the thought of seeing him a few hours early. "I'm out for a walk." I hedge but don't exactly lie. "You're kind of early, aren't you? Did you ditch classes?"

"No. My professor had a family emergency, so he canceled my last class. When are you going to be back? I thought we could spend some time alone before the kids get home from school."

A little brown squirrel scampers up a nearby oak tree, and Mitzy goes ballistic. She wriggles like a slithering fish until I'm forced to let her jump out of my arms. In a flash, she takes off after the furry-tailed creature.

I yank on her leash, but she completely ignores me.

"Is that dog close by?"

"Uh, yeah. I can't seem to shake it. Some people don't train their animals very well."

"Are you okay? Do you have pepper spray with you?"

My heart melts at the concern in his voice. "It's not a mean dog. Just a tiny mutt with a big voice. Don't worry."

"Okay. I'm going to go say hello to your mom and kill some time. Call my cell when you get back, okay?"

"Will do." I click off. "Mitzy! Be quiet." At the irritation in my voice, her ears go down and she gives me a sheepish look (which is kind of funny on a dog) and walks slowly toward me, as if to ask if I still love her. I relent and give her little head a couple of pats. Spike and Toto have both taken the opportunity to do their business, so I loop the leashes around a fence and use the scooper. *I hate this, Lord.* But I love that dress. I can handle this for a few months to get my Vera Wang.

I hurry through the rest of our walk, and the boxers are both panting when I get them back to their house. I water them and discuss the importance of staying off the furniture before leaving to take Mitzy home.

Mitzy senses I'm about to leave her and goes into a tailspin of anxiety, jumping on me, yipping, dancing on her hind legs. I kneel and gather her in my arms for just a second. "I'm sorry, sweetie. I have to go. Really, I do."

Loneliness. Poor dog.

I put Mitzy out of my mind as I walk to my van. Greg is waiting for me.

Greg.

This is his first visit home since I became a dog walker. I guess I'll have to tell him about it. I begin to formulate exactly *how* to tell him. I can't let him know I want a five-thousand-dollar gown and I'm willing to suffer the indignity of cleaning up after other people's dogs to attain that goal. That's not something a man is likely to understand. If I tell him I need the extra money, he'll worry about me and try to help pay my bills. And I've already made a firm decision that I will make my own way until we're married and paying mutual bills.

It's not his fault that I failed as a writer. But I'm not giving up completely. As a matter of fact, last month I finished a manuscript about a young waitress in a café and her relationships with the customers who come in. *Brandi's World*. It's whimsical, yet poignant. I think it's my best work—and Mom agrees. I've sent it off to three agents. If only a mother's endorsement were enough to convince these literary agents that

I'm destined to be the next *New York Times* bestselling author. So far, I haven't heard from even one agent yet.

This manuscript will mean a departure from the Christian romance I typically write.

And therein lies the problem.

According to my former agent, Stu-the-Weasel Lindale, my fans don't want anything but romance from me, and publishers won't buy something outside of the genre my name is known for.

What I'm looking for and praying for in an agent is a real kindred spirit. Someone who will recognize that I have the ability to write something other than romance. Really, I do. There's nothing wrong with a Christian romance, where a man loves a woman and they face difficulties that keep them apart and then they get together at the end. But after getting several of those under my belt, I'm ready to write a book that doesn't revolve around boy-meets-girl.

When I get home, Greg is sitting on my front step. Doggone it. I know I smell like dog, and Mitzy's mixed-breed hair is all over my Chiefs sweatshirt from that last little cuddle.

I force a smile and a steady tone. "Hey, I thought you were going to Mom's."

"I did for a few minutes. But she had a lunch date with Eli."

Mom met her new main squeeze at one of Tommy's skateboarding competitions. Eli's grandson is also a skater, although decidedly less talented than my son. A curious frown crosses Greg's features. "What happened to you?"

I clear my throat. "One of my—um—friends has a dog. And I cuddled it for a second." I smile, trying to sound like I'm not fibbing. "Remind me never to do that again. She got hair all over me."

"Was that the barking dog from the phone call?"

"Huh? Oh. Yes, as a matter of fact." Okay, that wasn't a lie at all. This is getting easier.

"I thought you said it was a passerby and you were trying to get rid of it."

Shoot! I can't keep this up. I'm not good at lying. Telling the truth was bred (and spanked) into me as a kid. I'm feeling worse and worse, and my heart rate is picking up. My nerves are going to be shot if I don't just get it over with.

"Okay, fine. I'm a dog walker." I jam the key into the lock and fling the door open. "Happy?"

"You're a *what?*"

"Um. Dog walker." I slip out of my shoes and leave them at the door.

"You're walking dogs?" He has a bewildered look on his face that might be funny if I weren't the one causing his bewilderment. "What for?"

I could make something up like: Hey, I just woke up one day and thought I'd try dog walking on for size, but I figure it's time to come clean. "I needed the extra money."

"You mean you're broke?"

I gather a deep breath and pull the coffee decanter from the hot plate. "Not exactly," I say, walking over to the sink.

"Claire, honey—" Greg takes the pot from me and sets it in the sink. He grips me by the shoulders. "Why didn't you tell me you needed help financially?"

Okay, a girl has two choices when she finds herself in this situation. One: give in to the damsel-in-distress opportunity, shed the tears she's fighting hard to ignore, and sink into Prince Charming's arms, allowing him to smooth away all of her troubles. Or two: buck up, be the modern, self-sufficient woman she is, and refuse to admit she wants a dress that costs five grand. I only have to think about it for a second. I pick number two. "I don't need financial help, Greg. I started a dog-walking business. And in just one week I have four steady clients. It's a pretty great accomplishment, and I'm actually pretty good at it."

"But you don't like dogs."

Bless his heart. He's really trying to wrap his mind around my new venture. I'll give him that. "I wouldn't exactly say I don't like them."

"Uh, yes, you would. I've heard you. Many times. Dogs smell. Dogs drool and then want to lick your face and arms. Dogs bark, dogs shed, dogs cost money to feed, they can't use a toilet . . ."

"Okay, already. I get it. At one time or another I might have mentioned that I'm not overly fond of the species."

"Lots of times." His eyes squint with amusement.

What is he—the Claire-hates-dogs police? "Well, that was before I met Ollie and Mitzy and the twins." I slip away from his grasp and resume the process of making a fresh pot of coffee.

"The twins?"

"Toto and Spike. They're boxers."

"Good grief."

I know, I know. That's what I think too. But I can't show him my aversion.

I raise my chin. "You're only skeptical because you've never been introduced."

Greg leans back against the sink while I finish making coffee. "Are you sure you wouldn't just rather I help out with some bills?"

I switch on the pot and it immediately begins gurgling as it starts to brew. I smile at the shell-shocked look on Greg's face—like he's still trying to picture me walking the dogs. "I'm taking care of myself, sweetheart."

"No word from any of the agents you sent the manuscript to?"

"Not yet." The optimist's response.

"And you'd really and truly rather walk dogs than take money from me?" He puts his arms around me and I sink against him, laying my head against his chest.

"It's what I need to do." There, I answered his question without lying and without revealing the true reason I'm walking dogs.

"Okay, but Claire . . ."

"Yes," I say, snuggling close, eyes closed, relaxing in my fiancé's strong arms.

"You're getting dog hair all over my sweater."

6

The one thing I despise more than anything in the world is that feeling you get when you're sound asleep in the middle of the night and something goes BOOM! and yanks you from a perfectly good dream. After a great dinner with Greg and Sadie and my kids, we went back to my place and watched a movie. Then Greg and Sadie said good night, and my kids and I all went to bed. I checked on the kids. I know they are all in their beds, sound asleep.

Or so I thought. But while I'm lying here at 2:00 a.m., analyzing the loud boom, the sound of the phone nearly sends me through the roof. Something must be wrong with Darcy or the baby. I whip up the phone from reflex and don't bother to check caller ID.

"Mom."

I'd know that guilty, worried, I'm-going-to-die voice anywhere.

"Tommy? Where are you?"

"In the driveway."

"You called me from the driveway? How?"

"I have your cell phone."

"Toms, what's going on?"

"Can you come out here? And don't yell at me."

"I never yell."

My heart is pounding in my chest as I slip into my leopard-spotted slippers and hurry down the steps, curiosity nearly driving me crazy. "Now what is the—"

My van is kissing the garage door, and neither seems too perky. Dented van, dented garage door.

It takes a second to sink in. "Tell me you didn't steal my van and run it into my garage door."

"The most important thing is that I'm okay. Right?"

For about ten minutes. "Where were you?"

"Kevin's," he mumbles.

"You took a middle-of-the-night joyride all the way across town? And you didn't wreck until you got home?"

"Kind of ironic, huh?"

"I'd say more like God's mercy. If you'd hit someone, you'd have been in big trouble, son. And not just with me."

"I'm sorry, Mom."

I look at my van and my garage, and I'm truly grateful to God for keeping my son safe, but I know that this is going to add more bills to my dwindling account. And after filing with the insurance company last year because of the tornado, I can only imagine what this might do to my premium.

"Go in the house and go to bed, Tommy. We'll discuss your punishment tomorrow."

"I really am sorry."

"So am I, Tommy." I'm so disappointed in him, and maybe even more disappointed in myself. After the whole incident with the lip ring and smoking last year, I honestly thought I'd seen the worst of it with Tommy. Apparently, I don't know the half of it.

Miss Lou's face lights up when I drag in the next morning after a perfectly wretched night's sleep. The only consolation: Tommy is dragging in with me.

The scent of cinnamon and nutmeg wafts through the house, making my stomach growl. "Mmm. Something smells really good!"

"I made coffee cake to go with our tea."

Our tea? Then it hits me that I had promised her some tea and a nice long talk after the dog was taken care of.

"Miss Lou, this is my oldest son, Tommy. He's going to be walking Ollie for me today, since it's such a nasty day."

She beams at Tommy. "What a sweet boy. My Jerry was always thoughtful like that."

"Get your leash, Ollie, my boy. Tommy is all set. Aren't you, Toms?"

He's eyeing the massive dog with dread. "Is he going to bite me?"

"No. But he might rip your arm off if you don't keep a tight grip on his leash."

Upon hearing the word *leash*, Ollie grabs his, walks to the door, and casts a dubious glance at the pouring rain. I clip his leash to his collar and offer the other end to Tommy while I open the door. Ollie and Tommy seem to harbor the same reluctance. Ollie hangs back a little. With a whine of dread, he looks up at me as if to say, "Be a sport. Give me a newspaper and a little privacy."

I can't help but laugh. "You boys be good."

Out the door they go. Ollie, needy and ready to get it over with, yanks Tommy along behind him. I watch Tommy hurdle a bush in front of the porch as Ollie pulls him like a kite in the wind.

"I hope you don't mind, Miss Lou. Tommy got into some trouble, and I thought it would serve him right if I made him walk Ollie in the rain."

She chuckles. "I don't mind a bit. How about a slice of that cake?"

"No thanks. I'm not hungry." Suddenly the weariness of the night before catches up to me and I prop my chin in my palm.

"Did he do something really bad?"

"Yeah." I tell her about the van and the garage. "And I've been saving up for a beautiful wedding gown, but now I'm not sure I'll ever be able to afford it. You know how it is when you find the perfect gown?"

"It's been a long time, but I certainly do remember the feeling."

"I just can't imagine wearing another one."

Miss Lou offers silent sympathy. She doesn't try to give me advice or tell me how she would handle the situation. Instead, she wheels herself over to the whistling kettle and pours us some tea.

I decide to change the subject and start the small talk, telling Miss Lou all about Ari's party, and even confiding in her my worry about Ari getting too serious with Patrick.

"I suppose times were different when I was a girl," Miss Lou says around a swallow of her warm tea. "I was barely fifteen when I married my Alfred, and I've never once felt cheated out of life." Her eyes take on a faraway look. "We would have been married seventy years this Christmas."

"How is it that Jerry is so young?"

A cackle reaches her throat, and I'm happy to observe her wide grin. She must've found her dentures, for her smile flashes pearly white teeth instead of the gums she normally reveals with her laughter. "Alfred and I tried to have children the first ten years of our marriage and we finally gave up. Just figured the good Lord knew what He was doing. I was in my mid-forties when God surprised us with Jerry. Alfred was ecstatic to have a son."

And now that same son is trying to force her into a nursing home. I wonder what ol' Alfred would think of that.

"I hope I'm not being too nosy," I say hesitantly. "But what do you think you will do, Miss Lou? Will you move into assisted living?"

"I don't want to, but Jerry seems very worried about me. He can't check on me as much as he'd like."

I barely keep back a snort. If the man really cared about her, wouldn't he invite her to come live with him? Even my brother, Charley, built a nice place for our mom—even if it didn't work for her. His heart was in the right place.

I'm just finishing up my tea when the front door opens. Raising my eyebrows, I glance at Miss Lou. "That was quick. I can't believe Ollie let him come back before his hour was up."

"Well, you know how he hates the rain." Miss Lou sends an affectionate smile into the air, and I know she's picturing the wimpy horse of a dog.

"True."

"Mom?"

Okay, that's definitely not Tommy's voice. *Jerry.*

I brace myself for another fight. If Jerry thinks he can get by with bullying his eighty-five-year-old mother, he's sorely mistaken.

He stops short and scowls when he sees me. I scowl right back to show him I will not be intimidated and I'm not going anywhere.

"You remember Claire, Jerry." Miss Lou, bless her heart, tries to ease the tension.

"Oh, yes. The dog walker."

"That's right. The dog walker *and* friend of your mother's." There. I said it. And he should know in no uncertain terms that his mom has someone on her side.

He inclines his head toward me in a haughty "I'm a rich son of a gun" sort of way. "If you'll excuse us, Claire," he says. "My mother and I have some things to discuss."

"Well, I'm waiting for my son to get back from walking Ollie."

"Oh? I didn't realize you employed slave labor."

"Jerry!" Miss Lou interjects. "Claire has a perfectly good explanation for why her son is walking Ollie today. And it's not your affair."

I grab my slicker and slip it on. "I'll wait for my son in the van."

"You'll do nothing of the kind, Claire."

"It's all right," I reassure the elderly lady. "Toms will be back any time. I wouldn't want to interfere with the important things your son needs to discuss with you."

I bend and kiss Miss Lou on the cheek. "Call my house or my cell phone if you need me." I turn to Jerry with a glare. His expression has softened, but as soon as he captures my gaze again, the hardness returns.

"I'll be gone tomorrow," I say with attitude. "Will you come by and walk Ollie for your mother? Or should she just plan on hooking him up to her wheelchair and going for a ride?"

His eyes narrow as though he senses the challenge in my request. "I think I can manage."

"Good." I zip up my raincoat with flourish and slam my hat down on my head.

He scans me from head to toe and . . . is that amusement I see in his eyes? I can only imagine the picture I make in my non-Meg Ryan sort of way. Still, does the man have to be so blatantly obvious in his condescension?

I jerk my chin, and off I go through the rain to my van.

Maybe spending tomorrow with his mother will serve to change his mind about sending her off to an old folks' home.

I only have to wait about five minutes before the soaked pair make it back to the house. I watch Tommy as he knocks on the door and waits there with Ollie while Jerry brings him a towel to dry off the beast.

I lift my gaze, and when I do, I find Jerry is watching me.

Curiously, my heart skips a beat.

But there's no time to analyze the oddity, because Tommy opens the van door and slinks into the seat. "Can we just go to Dad's now?" He sulks all the way to Rick and Darcy's, and then refuses to tell me good-bye when I drop him off at his dad's for the weekend.

Greg picks me up at five thirty the next morning so we can drive the three hours it will take to get to the small town on the border of Missouri and Arkansas. The ride is beautiful. The winding, hilly roads are flanked on either side by golden and red leaves as the maples and oaks prepare for winter's inevitable arrival.

Greg's fingers lace with mine as he drives his Avalanche one-handed. I watch him; he watches the road. Strong jaw, a straight nose, cheekbones that are wide and not too high. He's so good-looking that sometimes I just can't believe he could be interested in someone like me.

As if he senses my perusal, he glances away from the road and gives me a second of his gaze. "What are you thinking?"

I shrug. "What a catch you are."

He smiles brightly—making me feel guilty that I don't tell him that kind of thing more often—and tightens his fingers around mine. "Even after all I'm putting you through? Forcing you to become a pastor's wife. Asking you to give up your honeymoon. It's a lot to ask, I know. You sure you want to marry a guy like me?"

"Well, now that you mention it . . ."

He laughs and brings my fingers to his lips for a brief kiss. "I wouldn't blame you."

"First of all, you aren't forcing me to become a pastor's wife. I'm choosing to marry you because I love you. And I've already warned you, I'm going to be lousy preacher's wife. So, really, you're the one who needs to rethink the decision." My lips slide into a smile so that he knows he'd better not. "Of course, if you try to get rid of me, I'll run after you until I wear you down."

"Fat chance I'd ever try to get rid of you," he says with the husky undertones of a man in love. "You're stuck with me."

My heart is aflutter as he winks and gives me that incredible smile. "Good. But remember, you've been warned. And by the way, my love," I say, keeping my tone light and my gaze fixed on his handsome profile, "you didn't cancel our honeymoon. You postponed it. And I'm going to hold you to a Hawaiian honeymoon even if we're in our sixties when it finally happens."

"That's right. We postponed it. And I promise, we'll go to Hawaii as soon as we can get away."

With Greg's schoolteaching, he won't get another vacation until a year after our wedding. So our honeymoon won't be happening for a good long time. But I have reconciled myself to that. As long as I get my Vera Wang gown. And it's not even about the designer label. It's that dress. The gorgeous, amazing gown that looks as if it were made with me in mind.

And suddenly there I am, seven months from now. A collective gasp arises from the congregation as they see me and stand to their feet. Greg, at the other end of the aisle, looks as though he might burst with pride that I, Claire Everett, am his bride.

"What are you thinking about?"

I snap out of my dream and come back to the truck. "My dress."

"Don't worry about it. You look great." He gives me a quick sweep, taking in my deep blue suit—and for the record, I'm not wearing a dress; I'm wearing dress pants with a long suit jacket.

"Thanks, Greg."

Now, when I say "my dress" to Linda or Darcy, they immediately know what I'm talking about. A woman's wedding is all-consuming, but Greg has other things on his mind. For the first time, I take note of the faraway look on his face during the long stretch of silence. "Are you nervous, Greg?"

Such a thought hasn't occurred to me until this very second. But when I think about all he has at stake, yes, it makes sense that his nerves might be on edge a bit.

"Nervous? No."

I give him a light backhand across his bicep. "I can't believe you're lying on the Lord's Day, especially when you're planning to preach in a few hours. What are they teaching you in that Bible school?"

A sheepish grin spreads across his lips. "All right, so I am nervous."

"You're an awesome preacher. You're going to knock 'em

dead." I lace my fingers through the hand he immediately holds out to me. "If it's any consolation, I'm a little nervous too." And by "a little" I mean *a lot*, but he doesn't need to worry about me. Not with the huge job he has ahead of him. If I had to stand up in front of a congregation of strangers, I'd probably faint dead away.

"You?" He grins and looks at me askance. "What do you have to be nervous about? All you have to do is sit on the front pew and look beautiful."

"An impossible task for someone who is merely passable in the looks department and by no means beautiful!"

"A matter of opinion."

"You know, in all seriousness, you truly aren't the only one who's going to be on trial today. A good preacher needs a proper preacher's wife. The congregation will be checking me out, too."

Greg shakes his head. "Speaking on behalf of the men, mostly they'll be looking at your legs—which are great, by the way."

"Greg!" Again, I'm wearing pants, so no one's going to be looking at my legs. Thank goodness!

"Sorry. And the women? What will they be judging you on?"

"Hair, makeup, clothes. They'll want to know if I can cook."

"Can you?"

"Very funny. And for the record, I've been trying new recipes."

"How are the kids taking it?"

Not well, to be honest. Tuna puffs with white sauce ended up in Ollie's food dish, and the kids threatened to go live with their dad if I ever dared fix spinach-stuffed chicken roll-ups again. But I'm not telling Greg about that.

"What? Now you're marrying me for my cooking?"

"Hardly," he drawls, then pretends to duck.

"Hey! Be nice. I'm working on it."

"Don't worry about it. I hear McDonald's has added healthy items to their menu."

"I'm not your average McDonald's kind of girl."

His voice deepens. "Then what kind of girl are you?"

I can't help but send him a wink. "More the Pizza Hut variety. But I often order a salad to healthy it up a bit."

He laughs. I adore the way his eyes crinkle every time his lips curve upwards in a smile. Contentment overcomes me, and my heart sings as the sun shoots rays across the sky, splashing magnificent fingers of red along the horizon. If only we could stay like this forever—alone on a winding country road, laughing, loving, holding hands. Planning the future.

My four-thirty wake-up call catches up with me before we're an hour down the road. The car's rhythm works like a rocking chair, lulling me, and before I know it, I'm unable to respond to Greg's conversation. I'm vaguely aware of mumbling a sleepy apology as my head falls against the window. And that's the last thing I remember until . . .

"Claire, it's time to wake up." Greg's voice is soft, and he gently shakes my shoulder.

"Okay, I'm up," I say without opening my eyes.

"Seriously, honey." His voice sounds a little weird. But my eyes refuse to open. "Claire!" He shakes me a little harder. "Wake up. I mean it. We're here. Literally. In the parking lot . . . and people are staring."

Okay, that sinks in. My eyes pop open. I squint against the blinding sunlight shining off the windshield of a silver Mercedes parked next to us. A Mercedes? Didn't expect that. It appears Greg's congregation has at least one swanky member.

I hope they're tithers. The door opens and I stare, speechless, as a pair of long, tanned legs slides out of the car.

Greg clears his throat, and I know he's forcing himself to look away, but that throat-clearing says it all. Miss Marilyn Monroe Wannabe grins past me, and I see her eying my man. Claws unsheathe. If she wants a fight, she'll get one.

Turning to Greg, I carefully scan his face, giving him the full force of my suspicious nature.

"What?" He shrugs and grins, and I want to slug him.

"What do you mean, what? Got a guilty conscience or something?"

"Nope. I looked away." He leans over and brushes a kiss to my lips while bringing his hand up to the visor. He flips it down, revealing the mirror. "Better fix up. We can't stay out here all day. I have a sermon to preach."

The thing about preachers is . . . they're still men. They can be distracted by pretty women with long shapely legs and too-short skirts. But guess what? This preacher is a good man. He looked away. He loves me. And he loves God. And I have every intention of doing my best to help him protect himself against women who need attention. Anyone's attention, but especially preachers'. You know what I mean.

Full of my pious intentions, I take in my reflection with the kind of confidence only a secure woman can have. Only . . . good grief. No wonder that woman looked at me with such smug victory. She saw the smeary mascara and absent lip gloss. And my short, spiked hair that looked so chic at five this morning is now plastered to the side of my head. I have one spiked side and one flat side. I look like something out of an eighties sci-fi flick. As much as I try to fix it, I know from wretched experience that only water and some finger combing is going to help.

"Can I please have your keys, Greg?" I beg as panic fireballs through me.

"Where are you going?"

"Look at my hair!" I could just die. "I have to find a bathroom with a faucet so I can fix it pronto."

"Claire, I'm pretty sure the church comes with a ladies' room."

I feel a gasp coming on. Why do men have to be from Mars? "I can't go in there looking like this."

He gives my hair a once-over and nods. "I have a hat in the glove box. I only use it on really cold days."

He wants me to go in there wearing a suit and a stocking cap? Oh, Lord, please take me now. "No, thanks. I'm not walking in with bad hair or a hat. Now please. Are you going to hand over those keys, or do I have to get hysterical and make a scene right here?"

"And that would be better than going inside to fix your hair?"

"I mean it, Greg. I can't get out of this truck with my hair and makeup looking like this." I drop my voice as a vanload of kids tumbles out and heads toward the church, glancing curiously in our direction. "It's too humiliating."

His eyes flash with worry. "Claire, church starts in thirty minutes."

"I know. I'll hurry. I promise."

"You're going to let me go in there alone when the Mercedes lady is standing at the door waiting for me to come in?"

Oh, that's a great tactic. As God is my witness, I can't stop myself. I swing my head around, and sure enough, there she is. . . .

So what's a woman to do? I turn back to my man, slip an arm around his neck, and draw his lips to mine.

When I pull back, I've forgotten about what's-her-name and care only about this man I'm going to marry. "I love you."

"Ditto." By the look of love and devotion in his eyes, I know I have nothing to worry about. Greg opens the door and slides out of the Avalanche. He reaches over me and slips the keys into the ignition. With his face an inch from mine, he searches my face. "Please don't be late."

His closeness makes my heart race. "I promise," I whisper. Who knows why I whispered? Seemed like the thing to do. "Thank you."

He pulls out of the door, careful not to crack his head on the doorframe. I feel a little guilty when he rakes his hair back as he shuts the door with his other hand.

"I'll make it quick." I slip the truck into reverse and back out.

Cars continue to pull in, and people are casting curious glances at the woman with bad hair in the big truck who is actually driving the wrong way through the parking lot. I avoid making eye contact with anyone. For such a teeny-tiny town, Shepherd Falls Worship Center has a lot of members.

I pull into the first gas station I find, sprinting out of the truck and rushing to the door. Locked! The sign says: CLOSED ON SUNDAY.

No! Please, God. Please don't let Shepherd Falls be a blue-law town. The blue law. Are there still towns that don't allow retail sales on Sunday? Is it wrong to pray that a town doesn't observe the fourth commandment? Remember the Sabbath to keep it holy. Okay, I know . . . semantics. Saturday is technically the Sabbath. But Sunday is the day Christians observe it. So let's don't argue semantics when my hair looks this scary. Besides, it just can't be a blue-law town. I won't let it be. Surely this is a fluke. But I drive to the next building and, sure enough, find a darkened store, and the next, and the next. The town is closed up. Sheesh, no wonder they all go to church. There's nothing else open! Oh, that doesn't sound good. But my hair! It looks bad. Really, really bad, and I can't go into that church and shame myself and my fiancé.

Tears threaten to spill over. What am I going to do? What? What? What? I saw one stinking café on the town square, but guess what? CLOSED.

Then it hits me. I brought along a bottle of water. I whip the truck into the parking lot of a closed mechanic shop and pull down the visor.

Oh, ouch. I forgot how bad it was. And to top it off, I've been gone for over twenty minutes. Don't panic. That's why I went with the short spiky do. Splash a little water, do a little scrunchy thing, and my hair is good to go. Oh sheesh. Not so much with my makeup. That's going to take a little more work. I pull out Kleenex and backup paint and go to work. By the time I'm even close to presentable, the clock reads 9:10. My heart sinks. Greg's going to be so disappointed in me. Oh Greg, I'm sorry!

I make it back to the church in another ten minutes. 9:20. Greg'll probably divorce me before he even marries me. I slip into the church and tiptoe through the empty foyer to the swinging, double doors. I push slightly and peek through the crack. Perfect—they're praying. I can slip in and . . . crud, where's Greg? And again, where did all these people come from, for crying out loud? I can't see through the sea of bodies. I'm betting there are at least two hundred and fifty people crammed into this church building. Not exactly fire-safe, I think grouchily.

Okay, there's nothing I can do but go through the doors and look down the pews.

But where the heck is Greg? My eyes scan from one side of the church to the other. Sheesh, did I come to the right place? And then I see him. On the very front row. Just as I'm about to race up the aisle, the pastor gives an "amen" and everyone raises their bowed heads. Shoot!

I spot an empty space on the back row, but it's in the middle of the row. There's a gentleman sitting on the end, so I give him a little tap on the shoulder. "Could you scoot?" I whisper, quite nicely, I might add.

He gives me a growly face and shakes his head. "The wife just took the twins to the bathroom. They'll be back in a minute." So much for him being a gentleman!

Humiliation burns my cheeks as I apologize and step back to the double doors. There's no choice. I must either make a spectacle of myself and walk to the front of the church while everyone forms their first opinion of me, or retreat like the blubbering coward I am and go wait in the truck.

I choose plan B, and back I go through the doors. Tears blur my vision as I look around for a ladies' room. Poor Greg. How am I going to explain that I didn't do it on purpose? A woman with tired eyes and a couple of twin toddlers exits a door at the end of the hall, and I can only conclude she's going to be sitting with the "gentleman."

I pass her in the hallway, and she gives me a shy smile. I smile back and nod a greeting as I slip past and proceed to the bathroom. There are soft speakers hanging along the hall. I can tell that the pastor is about to introduce Greg—the man of God who is going to kill his fiancée for not being reliable. Okay, I'm going back. I can't let him be all alone in there without the support of someone who loves him. I give myself a once-over, then leave the bathroom and head back down the hallway toward the sanctuary. Halfway there, a door opens and I'm assaulted by the sound of howling children.

"Lukey, stay in here," a frazzled voice calls. "Can you grab him?"

"I'm on it," I reply just as a redheaded, freckle-faced little Opie boy no more than two or three years old giggles and sprints past me. With catlike reflexes I reach out and snatch him up. "Oh, no you don't, Lukey, my boy."

He struggles against me as I return him to his jailer.

"Thank you so much." An elderly woman is sitting in a rocking chair surrounded by children, and she appears to be the only adult in the room.

"Are you doing the nursery all by yourself?" I ask incredulously.

She nods and I'm instantly drawn to the twinkle in her eyes. "You offering to help?"

Ah, and just like that, I've found my place for today. Plus now I have a great excuse to offer Greg. The poor woman needed some help handling all those little monsters. What kind of person would I be if I turned my back on this obvious cry for help?

The Lord works in mysterious ways.

7

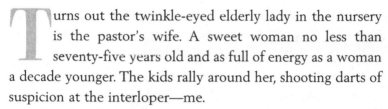

Turns out the twinkle-eyed elderly lady in the nursery is the pastor's wife. A sweet woman no less than seventy-five years old and as full of energy as a woman a decade younger. The kids rally around her, shooting darts of suspicion at the interloper—me.

Kids. Even frowning ones are cute at this age. Still, when Mrs. Miller deposits a small, sleeping creature in my arms, I'm taken aback by my feelings of nostalgia and—Oh. My. Gosh.—is that a little bit of longing I'm detecting deep within my breast?

The tiny cherub can't be older than a month or two. Tops. He coos in his sleep, and I see a baby Greg lying in my arms. Where did that thought come from? I grab myself by my mental bootstraps and give them a firm upward yank.

Okay, this was never supposed to be part of the deal. We decided no children. When Greg brought it up, I explained that we already have five between us, and after all, I'm not exactly a spring chicken anymore, and neither are my eggs. True, he never exactly said, "Yes, darling Claire. You've shown me the foolishness of my instinctive caveman desire to extend my family line by bringing a man-child into the world." But I definitely took his, "We don't have to talk about it for now," as compliance.

"Alex is a cute little guy, isn't he?"

I force myself to swallow the boulder lodged between the vertebrae of my neck and nod without sound. Mrs. Miller's arms are filled with a bottle-smacking pre-toddler, a fat-cheeked little girl dressed in pink ruffles with white tights stretched over the rolls on her legs. I smile despite my suddenly renewed fear of babies.

"He's our newest member."

"Mmm?" I say forcing my gaze away from the little girl's beautiful long lashes, brushed against her rosily healthy cheeks. I should have another daughter.

"Alex. The baby you're holding. He's the newest baby in the church." She winks and giggles. "Must have been something in the water during that time. We have six babies between the ages of one and six months. And two more mothers will be delivering within a couple of months."

Something in the water? I took a sip from the water fountain, didn't I?

Note to self: Once married to Greg, boil water before drinking, bathing, or cooking—oh—well, you know what I mean. I'm taking no chances. I just can't even imagine starting over again. Breast-feeding, diapers, sleepless nights. Sure, I'm being practical. But a new baby . . . one with Greg's dark eyes and my lighter hair . . .

I lower my gaze once more to the bundle in my arms. He shudders a sigh and sucks at the air, no doubt dreaming of glorious warm milk. My heart turns to mush.

"I hear you and Greg are planning to marry this summer?" Mrs. Miller turns the baby upright, patting her back.

"Yes. In June."

Clearing my throat, I purposely look away, hoping she won't proceed to ask about wedding plans.

But she doesn't get the hint.

I look up and catch a confused frown squeezing her thin, gray eyebrows together. "But isn't Greg taking the church in June?"

"Yes, ma'am." And for some reason, I feel like a tattletale.

"But he's coming the first Sunday of the month. When are you getting married?"

"The—um—first Saturday."

She gasps and her eyes go wide. "Are you telling me *this* place is your honeymoon? Greg will take over for Hank and me the *day after* you get married?"

I have to bite my tongue to keep from saying, "I'm afraid so." Instead I give a nod and smile as falsely bright as possible.

"Well, that just won't do." She scowls and shakes her head as Little Miss Pink blows a loud burp in her ear then settles into an adorable sleep across Mrs. Miller's thin shoulder. The older woman walks across to a crib and gently lays the baby down, covering her with a soft pink blanket.

She whips around and comes straight back to me. "Now, what are we going to do about getting you a decent honeymoon?"

I've always been the type of person to take pride in my self-reliance. I'm a roll-with-the-punches, can-do, twenty-first-century woman. So this morning's mushiness about the babies is disconcerting, to say the least. But even more than my biological clock resetting itself is the fact that I actually opened up to Mrs. Miller and shared my disappointment over not having my honeymoon. I'm a little ashamed of myself for caving in.

But the pastor's wife has one of those faces that just invites you to spill your guts. And when she does it over bottles of milk and adorable babies, how am I supposed to resist the urge to drop my head on a sympathetic shoulder (metaphorically speaking) and list my woes one by one—starting with the tropical beach and a grass-covered hut?

The babies are quietly entertaining themselves or sleeping. So Mrs. Miller's attention isn't too divided. And between the occasional "Let's not put that in your mouth, honey," and "Do you need a diapey change, precious?" I unload the whole wretched tale. I end with a completely unconvincing, "But I really do support Greg's ministry, and if I need to give up my honeymoon in order for him to do God's will, then it's the least I can do. Reasonable service, right? After all, I'm a living sacrifice."

She looks at me askance, totally not buying it. "Reasonable service is one thing. Starting a marriage out on the wrong foot is another. Even the apostle Paul would most likely agree with me." Her short grandma perm bounces as she gives an emphatic nod as if to say, *that settles it!* "Of course, church lore says he was divorced."

"Well, the important thing is the marriage, not the honeymoon," I chant my mantra. It's second nature now to tout the importance of marriage as compared to fulfilling my fantasy of two weeks of sun-splashed beaches and passionate nights with Greg inside a grass hut.

But again, Mrs. Miller doesn't buy it. She laughs melodiously. "Trust me. Greg doesn't want to deny you this honeymoon. It'll be your best argument ammo for the first ten years of your marriage. It's going to cost him a fortune in roses and possibly jewelry. Perfume for sure. This one little mistake could cost thousands of dollars."

I shake off the enticing sparkle of dazzling blue diamonds. "I wouldn't hold it against him like that."

"Then you must be Mother Teresa."

Well, Mother Teresa I'm not.

"So basically, you are saying that for the sake of my marriage, Hawaii is almost a necessity?"

She winks and nods. "I'd think so."

When the first parent arrives to claim her child, I haul myself up from my chair and head toward the door. "Thanks for the talk, Mrs. Miller."

"My pleasure." She smiles and hands Alex over to his mother as I slip out in search of Greg. "Thank you for the help and the company."

I find him in the sanctuary, surrounded by church members anxious to shake his hand. I stand in the back by the door and watch him greet each one with the same smile and polite deference. He looks pastoral. Pride mingles with regret at the realization that he was fabulous, as I knew he would be, but I missed his first sermon in Shepherd Falls. Why didn't I push aside my own intimidation and just walk right up to the front and perch myself on the pew?

As if sensing my perusal, Greg looks up, and just for a split-second his eyes flash anger before he carefully replaces the stormy gaze with a smile for—oh man!—Mercedes woman.

Okay, he might be mad at me right now, but he's still mine. And I'm not going to stand by and watch another woman attempt to sink her claws into my Greg. I hotfoot it down the aisle—now why didn't I do this earlier?—and stop at Greg's side. Despite the fact that he's ticked off, he turns to me with a tight smile and encircles me in the crook of one arm. "This is my fiancée, Claire Everett," he says to Legs.

She extends a graceful hand to me, but I can sense the tension beneath her polite veneer. "So nice to meet you, Claire," she says semi-warmly.

"Nice to meet you, too." I give her an expectant raise of the eyebrow and turn to Greg.

His cheeks color a bit. "I'm sorry. I don't remember your name, ma'am."

Her expression drops a bit, but she recovers faster than a grasshopper moves across a field. "Benita Kramer." She has the audacity to wink. "Better get used to it. I never miss a service, so you'll be seeing a lot of me. And it's 'Miss,' not 'Ma'am.'"

She doesn't even bother to include me in that little announcement. Her contact-enhanced baby blues are focused squarely on Greg.

Mr. Clueless smiles and takes her outstretched hand. "It's nice to meet a pillar of the church."

Pillar—my eye. Jezebel is more like it.

"I'll be looking forward to your next visit, Pastor Greg." She sashays past him and gives me a cursory glance while I practically choke on her perfume. "And, of course, you too, Claire."

"Of course."

When the last of the hand-shakers leaves the sanctuary, I turn my frozen smile on Greg. My insides are quaking at the thought of having to explain myself.

"So, it—um—went well, huh?"

He scowls and grabs his Bible from the front row. "You'd know that firsthand if you'd been here." He casts a scathing glance at my head. "Nice hair."

"I'm sorry, Greg. Really. But it was unavoidable—my being late anyway. I drove from business to business like a maniac, and nothing was open. I could have gotten into an accident, I was driving so fast. Except there was no one else on the road. But that's beside the point. The point is that, while trying to get back here for the service, I had to use a bottle of drinking water and the mirror on your visor to fix my hair." I give a nervous laugh. I mean, that's kind of a funny picture, right? Me trying to wet my hair down with a bottle of water? Maybe we can share a humorous moment and get over the fact that he needed me and I wasn't there for him.

Except Greg's not laughing. Yikes. Tough crowd. He's obviously waiting for the rest of the story. I lose the grin and sigh.

"So, I got back here, but the pastor was praying and I didn't want to take a chance on interrupting the service by walking all the way to the front."

"You didn't have to walk all the way to the front. You could have sat anywhere. Somewhere! As long as you were here. I was humiliated when Pastor Miller asked me to introduce you and you weren't anywhere in the sanctuary."

Remorse tightens my gut. "I'm sorry."

"Where were you?" he asks, and hope rises in me at the softening of his tone.

"I tried to get a seat in back. But some man wouldn't let me in. Like I said, I didn't want to make a spectacle of myself and embarrass you, so I left the sanctuary. I was going to sit in the truck, but the nursery was packed with kids and only Pastor Miller's wife was back there working. She sort of asked me to help. I actually enjoyed it a lot."

"There you two are." Before we can say anything else, the Millers sweep into the sanctuary. "Claire and I have been getting to know each other," Mrs. Miller says to no one in particular.

"So I've just been informed." Greg's response is accompanied by a smile, so I'm hoping Mrs. Miller's warmth will soften him up and make him more willing to forgive me.

"I have a roast and potatoes in the oven waiting for us back at the house," she says as though we've already accepted an invitation to lunch.

Pastor Miller slides his arm around her waist. "My wife makes the best roast beef in the whole United States. You two best join us for lunch or I'll eat every bit of it." He pats his paunchy gut.

Greg looks at me, and I give a nod.

For the next hour we call an unsteady truce, but I'm aware of the underlying disappointment in Greg. I let him down. I really do deserve his anger.

As we get ready to leave, Mrs. Miller gives me a tight squeeze. "Now you remember what I said about that honeymoon," she says loud enough for Greg to hear.

"What was that about?" he asks once we pull away from the curb.

A couple of hours ago, Mrs. Miller's reasoning made sense and gave rise to hope, lift to the wings of my swooping dreams of a tropical tan. But now as I share her thoughts, Greg is staring at me from the driver's seat like I might be absent a few marbles.

"That doesn't really make much sense."

I give him a casual shrug. "Don't blame me. Mrs. Miller is the one who said it."

"Mrs. Miller said if we don't go on our honeymoon to Hawaii our marriage is doomed to unhappiness and possibly failure?"

"Well, she didn't say Hawaii necessarily, but since we already made the plans . . ."

Greg's frustration manifests in his drumming fingers on the steering wheel. I can tell he's trying to keep his cool. "Claire, we've been through this. You agreed. I was willing to turn the professor down. But it's too late now. I've already committed to it."

Disappointment knots my stomach as if this is the first time I've heard about the loss of my honeymoon. I should have known better than to get my hopes up.

"You're right, of course," I say with the best smile I can muster, which isn't much. "I got carried away. You can't just back out." Even if there are seven months for your professor to find a replacement. But hey, don't mind me. And just like that, my bubble bursts once again.

We finish the drive in virtual silence. I know I've disappointed him terribly today, first by missing his first sermon in Shepherd Falls, and now by asking him to give up his first significant preaching assignment. There won't be time to smooth things over. As soon as Greg drops me off at home, he will have to drive back to Tulsa for tomorrow's classes. I'm not really in much of a mood for smoothing anyway. I'm still trying to untangle my knot of disappointment. Only problem is, for the first time I've allowed myself a thought that I'd purposely rejected in the month since Greg dropped the bomb on my plans: Greg is putting his need to step into the ministry, even if only for a few months, ahead of my need to go away to be alone with my husband. I mean, even Jacob gave Leah a bridal week. And he didn't like her much. Chains of discontent form around my heart.

Greg pulls up at my house around four o'clock and puts the pickup into park. He doesn't kill the motor. I turn to him.

"Do you want to come in and have something to eat before you leave?"

His eyes scan my face. The tense lines around his mouth ease up some, but not a lot. He reaches out and cups my neck, drawing me to him. Silently, his mouth covers mine. I cling to him and return his kiss with equal fervor. Disagreements are difficult for us. Especially major, course-altering disagreements. The last time we had a big one, we broke up for months. We almost didn't get back together. But I gave in. Agreed to be a pastor's wife.

Why is it that I'm the one who always has to back down in this relationship? Anger builds, and I break off the kiss. As irritated as I am, I don't want Greg to leave town on a negative note, so I give him a quick hug and turn away before he can see the tears building in me, threatening to cloud my vision and spill over any second. "See you next week."

I slip out of the Avalanche and quickly shut the door. I feel like our relationship is getting out of control again. Like something is not right. Is it just about a honeymoon? If so, what does that say about us? Here we are, just a few months away from the wedding, and we can't agree on keeping the honeymoon plans. As differently as we see things, is Greg the right man for me? Maybe I should turn him loose so he can find the right pastor's wife who doesn't care about Hawaii. Something I'm going to have to think about this week. How can I bear to let him go? On the other hand, is love really enough to keep us together?

I just don't know.

8

Monday morning, I don sweat pants, sweatshirt, baseball cap, and gloves and climb into my beat-up van—which will stayed crunched-in until I get the garage repaired out-of-pocket, thanks to Tommy.

I head to Miss Lou's. I'm surprised to find that I honest-to-goodness missed the old lady and her dog during my Sunday away.

I open the door to find Miss Lou juggling Ollie's leash from hand to hand as she slips her arms into her coat.

"What are you doing?" I walk inside, stuffing her key into my pocket, and glance at my watch. "I'm on time, Miss Lou. Is Ollie sick or something?"

She answers me with a hacking cough that leaves her gasping as she starts to speak. "Good morning, hon. I meant to call you. I'm afraid I won't be using your services with Ollie anymore."

Stung, I glance at the animal, who hasn't stopped licking my hand and pressing against my thigh since I got close enough to pet him. "But why, Miss Lou? What have I done? Is this about Tommy? I was going to make him walk the dogs on Saturdays, but I don't have to."

"Oh, no. You haven't done anything. Nothing at all. You have been so sweet, and Ollie just adores you." Her voice cracks, and I see tears well up in her faded eyes. "Jerry won't pay for dog-walking services anymore."

Red-hot indignation burns my chest. "Is this his way of trying to force you into a home?"

"Yes." Her sigh is deep, and I hear a bit of a rasp.

"Miss Lou, I'd consider it an honor if you'd allow me to continue on as Ollie's dog walker."

"Nothing would please me more, but I can't pay you. And I know you need the job to buy your wedding gown."

I drop down in front of her wheelchair and take one gnarled hand between mine. I'm taken aback by how warm her skin feels, and I suspect she's running a temperature. "I want to walk Ollie. With or without payment."

I mean, what's Jerry thinking? Forcing his eighty-five-year-old mother out into the street to walk her dog!

Without allowing for any more argument, I pat her hand, take Ollie's collar, and head toward the door. I pause and turn around as Miss Lou breaks into a fit of coughing. "Miss Lou, will you please go get into bed?"

"I suppose I'd better," she says in weary compliance.

Ollie and I see her to bed before making our way outside. Ollie is enjoying himself immensely. It's hard to tell sometimes with the monster of a dog because his size prevents the usual spring dogs get in their step, that lightness that speaks of contentment. But I've learned to recognize it in Ollie. Sometimes I think he actually smiles.

After our walk, I take him back to Miss Lou with a promise that I will be there this afternoon, pay or no pay. She's practically crying when I leave to go walk Mitzy and the twins.

I walk the other dogs with flourish, excitement building in

me with each step. Today is the day I go to Tammy's Bridal and put down my first deposit on my five-thousand-dollar dress. Ten percent—five hundred dollars. That will allow me some breathing room at least.

After I drop off the dogs, I hurry home, lighthearted and ready to shower and put on something that reveals a woman more than classy enough for a Vera Wang gown. The phone rings as I am putting the finishing touches on my makeup.

"Claire?" The man's haughty tone arrests my attention. Especially since I don't recognize the voice.

"Who is this?"

"Jerry Calloway. You walk my mother's dog."

Oh, yeah. Now I recognize the voice. What does he want? I decide to come right out and ask him. "What can I do for you?"

"You can stop walking my mother's dog."

"Sorry, Jerry. No can do. Poor Ollie has needs."

He growls through the phone. "I *know* the dog has needs."

"What do you expect her to do—wheel him around outside, or let him do his business on the floor?"

"Neither."

"Well, if you can teach Ollie to use the toilet, you might become a rich man." Oh, good one. This guy is starting to tick me off. Does he honestly expect me to abandon her?

"Very funny," he says in a tone devoid of humor. "I want you to mind your own business and let me deal with my mother."

"Gee, Jerry. Until you start treating her right, I'm afraid I'm going to have to make this my business."

"I do treat my mother right."

"Okay, maybe we have a different idea of what *right* means."

"I went to her house to walk Ollie right after you left today. All right? I wouldn't have let her wheel herself out."

"Then why all of this?"

"My company is transferring me to Japan, and I don't know what to do about her while I'm gone."

My heart softens a little. Very little.

"So you thought you could force her to give up her house and her independence and move into an old folks' home? I have to tell you, Jerry, that sounds a little like elder abuse to me."

"Abuse? Don't you think you're overreacting just a little?"

"No, I don't. At the very least, it's coercion." I decide to give him a really good guilt trip. He deserves it. "Do you know what I saw when I got to your mom's today?"

"I give up."

"Your mother struggling into her jacket with Ollie's leash in her hand. She had every intention of going outside—I don't know how she thought she'd get down the steps—and walking Ollie herself."

"I got tied up, or I would have been there on time," Jerry says, heavy on the defense.

"The point is that she has a cold and a broken hip and shouldn't be bluffed or bullied into taking matters into her own hands."

A heavy sigh escapes him. "I just don't see why she's being so stubborn about entering Countryside."

"Well, who would want to be tucked away in a home without loved ones around?"

"I would take her myself if I wasn't going to be in Japan for the next two years. Can you imagine what it will be like for her to be here without family to help her?"

Okay, this is the point where I should keep my mouth shut. But I tend to not be great at that, so here I go: "I hadn't really noticed you taking very good care of her anyway."

"Then you don't have very sharp perception, Claire."

"Tell me, then. How will your being in Japan be any different from your being here, other than the occasional visit?"

"I pay for housekeeping, dog walking," he says, emphasizing *dog*, "and someone to buy her groceries or take her to the store when she feels like getting out herself. What more can I do?"

"I think that's pretty obvious, Jerry. Do I really need to spell it out?" Uh, how about giving her some of your precious time, bucko?

"I don't live the high social life and neglect my mom, if that's what you're implying. I work twelve hours a day. I do my best to see her every couple of weeks."

He sounds sincere. Still, I picture the loneliness in her eyes, hear her wistful sighs, and remember the way she reminisces about the old days when Jerry was a little boy.

"I am frantic to get her taken care of before I move."

"Yes, but a nursing home? She'll hate it, Jerry. Surely you know that."

He hesitates. "You've grown close to my mom, haven't you?"

"I think so. For a dog walker."

"Okay, fine. I'm sorry. Listen—could I have an hour or two of your time?"

My heart jumps into my throat. Have I somehow given off the wrong vibe? "Uh, Jerry. I—"

"This isn't a date. Trust me."

I'm a little put off by the amusement in his tone—what, now I'm not even date material?

"I'm not going somewhere with a stranger."

"We're not exactly strangers," he drawls. "The way my mom talks, we're practically family. Seriously, I want to show you something."

"What could you possibly want to show me?"

"Are you always this suspicious?"

"I prefer to call it cautious."

"Come on. Mom says you need another job."

Miss Lou!

I can hear the smug assurance in his voice as he continues, "Well, I know a place that needs to hire a housekeeper, pronto. I mentioned that you might be interested. It would be daytime with no weekends."

"What kind of housekeeping job keeps banker hours?"

"The kind where the night lady and weekend help don't want the day shift."

Okay, I have to pause a minute. The thought of anyone hiring me as a housekeeper is laughable. I need my own housekeeper, and had one back when I could afford it. Still, this sounds like something that might work.

"All right. For the price of an interview, I suppose I could spare an hour." My mind floats back to my five-thousand-dollar dress, my vision of perfection. In that dress I will become Mrs. Greg Lewis. I have no business jaunting off with Jerry-maybe-he's-not-such-a-jerk-after-all. But then, he did say it's not a date.

Thirty minutes later, his black Jag pulls up in front of my house.

"Nice car," I say as he holds open the door. "Now I see why you have to work so much."

"Ouch. You know how to drive the sword in deep, don't

you?" He leans in close, and the smell of his cologne and closeness of his face cause an involuntary pickup of heart
rhythm—for which I am not responsible. And the fact that
Jerry is a hunkarama in no way excuses his lack of nurturing
toward his mom.

"This is a company car. A perk for my expertise."

Okay, now I'm impressed. "Some perk. What is it you do
again?"

"I work for a software company, developing business software. When a company restructures its program, I travel to
wherever they are and train their staff."

"That explains why you're gone so much."

"Apology accepted."

I give him a sideways smile. "I still think it was wrong to
make her walk her own dog."

"I already told you, I wasn't going to make her walk her
own dog."

"She didn't know that, though. So essentially, you abused
her mentally."

"What are you, a psychologist?"

He maneuvers the Jag across the intersection and through
town until we're outside the city limits. "Hey, where are we
going?"

"You'll see." He smiles pearly white. A lesser woman might
be swept off her feet by such a magnificent Brad Pitt smile.
But I'm committed to the man I love.

"So you didn't answer my question. Are you a dog-walker-
slash-psychologist?"

"No. I'm a dog-walker-slash-slightly-out-of-work-writer."

"Slightly out of work?"

"I still have royalties coming in, but no new contracts. And no agent. Not to mention I just took on a pro bono dog-walking client because my boss fired me." I give him a pointed look.

"Sorry, but no one forced you to stay on for free." He doesn't look sorry enough to change his mind, unfortunately.

We turn off the highway onto a long country lane. A gold and red blanket of leaves covers the road, and a lane of thinning trees lines our way. At the end of the lane sits an enormous old home, a three-story Victorian that looks like it was lifted from the pages of a decorating magazine.

Jerry pulls into a semicircular drive.

"And we're here because . . . ?"

He winks his baby blues and slips the gearshift into park. "You'll see."

I step out of the car, immediately taken in by the acres and acres of rolling fields behind the house. A family of deer are grazing in the distance. Close enough for me to enjoy their beauty. Far enough away not to be startled by the attention.

"Nice, isn't it?" Jerry asks, pulling me from the beauty of the autumn leaves shimmering in the oak trees at the edges of the field. I give him a nod.

"Let's go in," he suggests, pressing his palm to the middle of my back to guide me.

Unbidden, a shiver takes hold of my body. I refuse to look at Jerry in case he's noticed my reaction to the feel of his warm hand through my shirt. I clear my throat in order to gain my composure. "You going to tell me why we're here?"

"Not the patient sort, are you?"

"Nope." I toss him a cheeky grin.

"You'll have to wait a few more minutes."

The front door opens, and three elderly women exit onto

the porch. They smile and continue on their way to a circle of cushioned outdoor furniture awaiting them.

I'm starting to get the picture. Especially when I notice a carved-out wooden shingle above the doorway: COUNTRYSIDE RETIREMENT COMMUNITY.

"I see what you're up to," I say abruptly. "You want me for an ally against your mother."

I wheel around to leave the way I came, but he grabs my elbow, once again jolting me with his touch. What is going on here?

"Just take a look over there." He nods toward the three women, who appear deep in conversation. "Do they look lonely, neglected, or as though they might shrivel up and die in this place?"

I have to admit, they look pretty robust. Probably healthier than Miss Lou. He takes my silence for what it is—grudging acknowledgment that this place isn't so bad. But that doesn't mean I think Miss Lou should have to leave her home of fifty years and take up residence among strangers.

We step inside and are immediately greeted by a fortyish woman with high rosy cheekbones and soft blond hair. "Mr. Calloway," she says with a smile, "how nice to see you again." She looks at me. "And you must be Mrs. Calloway. I'm so glad you've decided to come look around. I know your mother-in-law would be very happy here."

Jerry's grinning at me, a merry-eyed grin that I can't help returning. "Thank you," I say, returning the woman's hand-shake. "I'm just a good friend of the family."

"Sandy, I'd like to introduce Claire Everett. Miss Everett is engaged to be married soon." He winks at me. "To a preacher." My cheeks warm at the memory of Miss Lou warning him I'd be off the market soon if he didn't try to woo me away from Greg.

Like that's ever gonna happen. I mean, really. He can wink all he wants, but that doesn't change the fact that he's trying to stash her away in a facility for the elderly.

"Actually, it's *Ms.* Everett," I say with a tight smile.

"Ms. Everett would like to inquire about the daytime housekeeping position."

Her brow lifts and a wide smile cracks her made-up face. "Mr. Calloway speaks very highly of you."

"If my mother decides to move into this beautiful home," Jerry says, playing her like a fiddle, "I would feel so much better knowing she has a friend here to help ease her adjustment."

"Oh, most definitely." She turns her eyes to me. "Can you start next week?"

"We'll have to discuss that a little later, won't we?" I say with a condescending smile. "For now, Sandy, let me ask you something."

"Yes?" She turns wide eyes to me, and even Jerry leans in a bit closer.

"What are your policies regarding large animals?"

"Oh, we don't allow pets. Some of the residents are allergic."

"I see." I send Jerry a "that's that" look. No way Miss Lou's giving up Ollie, and there's no sense in even broaching the topic.

Jerry's voice slices the air. "Can residents receive pets as guests if a family member or good friend of the family—" he looks at me pointedly "—brings them to the house?"

She gives a bright nod. "Of course. We encourage family

members to bring beloved pets to visit. It keeps the residents' spirits up."

"So just to be clear," Jerry says, "if a good friend of the family were to take in the resident's dog, they would be welcome to bring it to visit."

"As long as the dog has had all its shots and is well behaved. Of course, the visitor must obtain approval ahead of time. And the animal must stay outside."

"Of course," Jerry says, flashing her that million-dollar smile. "Well, then. Could we bother you for a tour, Sandy?"

Her cheeks blossom. "It's no bother at all. I'd be delighted."

The tour lasts for half an hour. I have to admit, it's a charming place. The rooms are large, with lots of windows. There are ten suites in the house, and there are another fifteen apartment-like rooms with kitchenettes behind the main house. One registered nurse and three nurse's aides are on call at all times. Meals are eaten together in the large dining hall.

I can't help but turn and stare at the place as we drive away. I wouldn't mind living there myself.

"Well?" Jerry says, without even waiting for me to bring it up. "Don't you think my mother would be happy there?"

I shrug. "It's definitely the best money can buy. I assume you'll be bearing the financial burden?"

"Mother's retirement money will be kept safely in her account and won't be touched by anyone but her. We've set it up this way so that she can maintain her freedom. I'll be paying her monthly bills."

"I thought residents of places like this have to sign everything away."

"Mother will just have to sign consent that they be named

custodian of her affairs in the event that I die or stop paying her bills—which I won't."

I study his face as he stares out the window. "Why aren't you married?" I blurt out without even taking a second to consider how it might sound. "Not that I care, personally." Oh sheesh. That didn't help.

He gives me a sideways grin. "Interested in the position?"

"I'm afraid not. I have a position of my own."

"And there's my reason for still being single." He peruses my face for a second before turning back to the road. "When I was younger, I was too busy building a career to try to build a relationship. By the time I realized I wanted someone to share my life with, all the good ones were taken."

I give a flippant shrug. I have to. It's my only defense against the attraction I'm feeling for Jerry. "Look on the bright side. In another ten years, the men your age will be starting to have their first heart attacks. Just take care of yourself in the meantime and maybe you can nab yourself a widow."

He laughs. "Now there's something I hadn't thought of."

"Well, now you know there's hope."

"Sort of like reading the obituaries looking for an apartment."

"You're such a romantic."

"So what did you think of the house, honestly?"

"I thought it was very nice. I just don't know why my opinion matters."

"Mother's formed a close attachment to you, and I think if you encourage her, she might be more willing to consider the move."

"I appreciate your position, Jerry. Really, I do. I admit that

I've snapped to conclusions about you, and you're probably not as bad as I first assumed."

The corners of his lips twitch. "Probably?"

I give him a nod because the jury is still out. "Even if you are doing all this for her sake, I don't feel right about trying to talk your mom into doing anything she doesn't want to do. And she's been pretty clear that she wants to stay in her home for as long as she can."

"That's just it, Claire. She *has* stayed in her home as long as she can. She has a broken hip, a weak heart. Borderline diabetes. I need to get her into a place where she can be taken care of. What more do you expect me to do?"

"Let her stay in her home."

"And who is going to take care of her?"

"It can't be any more expensive to hire a full-time nurse than it would be to move her into Countryside."

He sighs. "The turnover rate for home health-care workers is very high. And you never know who you're getting. We're currently between nurses, and we've had three already."

My heart goes out to him as I see the worry lines etching his face. "Okay. I'm not making any promises that I'll do it, but if the subject comes up naturally, I might be inclined to bend my responses your way. For a price, of course."

Suspicion hardens his eyes and they turn from soft pools of blue to sapphire-blue stones. "There's always a price."

Heat rushes to my cheeks.

I was going to bargain to get my pay back for Ollie. But Jerry can just forget it. I wouldn't take his money if it was the last thing standing between me and wearing a gunnysack as I walk down the aisle.

9

Can this day get any worse? There I was, this morning, all ready for the beginning of a good week, only to find out that I've lost out on twenty dollars a day for walking Ollie. Then I got practically kidnapped by a man wanting me to talk his mother into going to an old folks' home. I'm about to blow my top like a lava-spewing volcano. I get this way every time my plans go awry. And to top it off, Greg didn't call me last night when he got back to Tulsa. So quite frankly, I don't know if he even made it back alive.

The ride back to my place with Jerry was about as quiet as the one I had with Greg yesterday on the way home from Arkansas. I'm just a ray of sunshine for men, aren't I? When he let me off, I slammed his door, headed straight to my van, and drove to Tammy's Bridal.

The one good thing about today is that I put down a five-hundred-dollar deposit on the Vera Wang.

I have no idea how I'm going to come up with another $4,500, and according to the little salesgirl, I only have three months or I lose the dress.

Tonight is Monday movie night. We implemented it last year during my attempt to change our family dynamic from totally ignoring one another to interacting on a regular basis. It worked pretty well. That and the fact that I'm out of contracts at the moment so I'm spending all my time with them anyway.

At five o'clock, I grab the keys. "I'm headed to the video store. What's for supper? Pizza, hamburgers, or tacos?"

After a well-rounded debate, I settle things by choosing pizza. Naturally.

"Whose turn is it to pick the movie?"

"Mine!" Tommy's voice squeaks, a telltale sign that manhood is just around the corner. The kids never seem to tire of teasing him. Luckily, it doesn't happen nearly as often as it did last year.

"You picked last week, Tommy," Shawny pipes in. "I get to pick."

"Wrong, munchkins," Ari says, rolling her eyes. "It's her turn."

By "her" she means me. I was all set to sit through a teen flick or a cartoon. This is a pleasant surprise. To me, anyway. Ari's expression is anything but pleasant, and by the disdain in her tone, I know she fully expects me to pick an eighties brat-pack flick like *St. Elmo's Fire* or *The Breakfast Club* (scratch that—rated R).

"How about *Father of the Bride?*" I say brightly, expecting at least some support.

Instead I get a roomful of groans. Except from my mom. She's joined our little family for movie night since she moved back from Texas. I am feeling especially affectionate toward her this evening. I guess going to Countryside with Jerry made me see my mom in a new light. She's only ten years younger than Miss Lou. How did she ever get to be so old? It's just so hard for me to fathom my mom ever being at that stage where I'm taking care of her instead of the other way around. "How about we let Gram choose tonight?"

Mom's eyebrows go up. "You're asking me?"

Okay, it's probably a mistake. I feel all four sets of my children's eyes glaring through me. Apparently they'd rather watch Molly Ringwald than one of mom's black-and-whites.

"I get to pick?" she says. "Well, let's see . . . anything with John Wayne is good."

"How about *Hondo*?" I look around at my children in silent appeal, and each nods. I can usually get by with old movies as long as they're westerns.

So we're settled on a movie. That was easy.

"Okay, I'll be back in a sec. Call for pizza while I'm gone. And order me a salad, please."

I can't stop thinking about Mom all the way to the video store. Mom with her white hair and varicose veins and the arthritis beginning to give her finger pain, especially when the weather sets in. But at least Mom has me and the kids here. And if push came to shove, she could always go back to living with my brother Charley. I mean, that downstairs apartment he built for her is just sitting there empty. Right?

But the point is, my mother will never be faced with having to sell her home and move into a care facility.

Somehow I find myself turning onto Miss Lou's street. I suddenly have a brilliant idea: I'll invite Miss Lou over for family night.

I pull into the drive and knock on the door. Ollie lets out a woof. "It's just me, boy," I call through the door. I have a key, but I don't want to startle Miss Lou by walking in on her if she's watching TV a little too loud or dozing off. I definitely don't want to take a chance on causing her weak heart to give out altogether.

I wait for a minute, but grow concerned when I don't hear the sound of Miss Lou's "Come in, hon."

At the memory of her hacking and coughing this morning,

my mind starts running rampant with visions of the poor old lady on the floor, calling for me with a voice too frail to be heard. I wait no more than three minutes and pull out my house key. Ollie is still woofing inside, and I know he knows it's me, so there must be something wrong.

I open the door. "Miss Lou? It's Claire. You okay?"

Ollie comes to me and opens his massive jaw. He grabs my hand gently but firmly and slathers me with drool.

"Okay, buddy, take me to Miss Lou."

He drops my hand and trots ahead of me down the hall.

"Miss Lou?" I call. "It's Claire. I'm coming down the hall toward your bedroom. Don't be afraid."

I enter the dark room, all at once alarmed by the raspy breathing coming from the dark lump of covers on the bed.

"Miss Lou?" I reach out and touch her shoulder. She moans and shivers, but doesn't wake up. On instinct, I press the back of my hand to her forehead, then pull back quickly. She's hot enough to fry an egg.

Ollie gives a little whine and edges his monster head between me and Miss Lou. He sniffs her, then looks up at me as if to say, "Well, what are you going to do about this?"

I slip my cell phone from the case attached to my jeans and call 9-1-1, then place a call to my family.

"Now, don't you worry about a thing," Mom says graciously. "Eli and I have everything under control."

"Eli?" What's Mom's boyfriend doing there?

"Yes. I invited him over. He seemed so lonely tonight."

I squash my irritation. Okay, there's nothing really wrong with Eli. But this whole Mom's-got-a-boyfriend thing is uncomfortable. Especially when they're holding hands or something. I just keep picturing Dad's face. It's not fair. I know that. So like I said, I squash my irritation.

"Okay, Mom. I'm not sure what time I'll be home. Miss Lou isn't conscious, and I'm going to the hospital."

"Yes, that's the right thing to do. I'll take care of the kids until you get back."

I hang up with the relief that comes from knowing someone is available to step in and cover your back.

I hear the ambulance arrive and go to the door to let the EMTs into the house. I already had the forethought to lock Ollie in the bathroom. Poor dog is barking his head off. I only hope he'll forgive me for keeping him locked up. But it can't be helped.

I wait for the EMTs to gently load Miss Lou into the ambulance, then I let Ollie out. He bounds past me to the door and lets out a howl in response to the sirens moving away from the house.

"I'm sorry, boy. I know it's tough. But I'm going to be right there with her."

It's not easy, let me tell you, to move a two-hundred-pound dog away from a door he wants to block. And after I used the dog-biscuit toss to get him into the bathroom, he's not falling for it again.

"Ollie, move it!" I finally say in my firmest voice. His ears go back and he slinks out of the way. I mean, really, this dog is ridiculously huge. If he wanted to eat me for lunch, he could. Instead, he makes like a wiener dog and gets out of the way. Which is a good thing, because I don't want to take any chances that Miss Lou will wake up without someone familiar at the hospital with her.

My mind goes to Jerry as I drive a bit above the speed limit.

He should know about his mom. I grab my cell from my purse and dial 4-1-1.

"Directory assistance."

After giving the recorded voice the name of our city and state, I discover Jerry's phone number isn't listed. Why am I not surprised? I suppose Miss Lou has his number somewhere. I resolve to look for it as soon as I know she's out of the woods and I'm comfortable leaving her alone.

The ER is abuzz, as one might imagine—everyone filled with their own worries. I head straight for the counter, where only one person seems to be on duty. "Excuse me." She looks up, glares, and points to the phone receiver pressed to her ear.

Well, excuuuse me! Not to be deterred, I whisper, "I'm sorry. I have to find out about an elderly woman just brought in a few minutes ago."

With a nod, she presses her hand to the mouthpiece. "I'll be right with you. I need some paperwork filled out on the woman. We were about to call her a Jane Doe."

She finishes her call and turns her attention to me.

"Are you next of kin?"

"No."

"Any relation?"

"I'm her dog walker."

I see the startled look in her eyes and decide I'd better elaborate. "I started out as just a dog walker. Now she's a dear friend. As a matter of fact, I went to her house tonight to invite her over to my house for family movie night. We were going to watch *Hondo*, and I thought she might like it since it's an old movie."

I'm rambling. Nervous habit.

She's not paying attention anyway. "I need some information

on her. Can you fill out these papers with as much as you know? And do you have any idea how to get in touch with her family?"

I shake my head, feeling helpless. "I'm sorry. She has a son, but his number isn't listed, so I'm not sure how to get in touch with him."

Then I get an idea. "Her name is Lou Calloway. And she has a broken hip, so she was here just a few months ago for surgery. You might be able to find some contact information about her next of kin by looking up her records." One good thing about a small town is that there is only one hospital. I don't have to guess where Miss Lou had her previous surgery.

The receptionist hesitates a second and then gives a nod. "Good idea. If you can go ahead and fill those out to the best of your ability, I'll see what I can find out from her records."

My best isn't much. I know her name and age, but not her birthday. I know her address and phone number, but nothing else. I give the nurse behind the counter a helpless shrug when I turn the clipboard back in. "I'm sorry. I just don't know much. Did you get in touch with her son?"

"I have a number for a son named Jerry. But I can't get through."

A doc in scrubs comes down the hall. "Any family for the elderly woman brought in a while ago?"

The nurse shakes her head. "We're still working on it. But this is the woman who dialed 9-1-1. She's a friend of the family."

"How is she?" I ask, without waiting for the doc to acknowledge me.

He turns to me now. "It's not good. She has pneumonia brought on by influenza."

"The flu?"

"In the elderly and the very young, the flu is serious, sometimes deadly." He looks down at a chart in his hand. "What's your friend's name?"

"Lou Calloway. Is she going to be okay?"

"We have her on IV fluids to rehydrate her and antibiotics to fight the pneumonia. She's still unconscious."

"Can I see her?"

"Sorry. We've transferred her to ICU, and only family is allowed. But we'll update you if there is any change in her condition."

"Thanks." For nothing, bub.

The doctor strolls away and slips into the next curtained room. I wander around until I find the ICU, where I tell the nurses at the counter that I'm with Miss Lou and ask them to keep me informed of her progress. Then I step into the empty waiting room. A fuzzy TV plays a sitcom I don't recognize. I settle onto a teal vinyl loveseat and slouch, resting more on my spine than my behind.

The thing about watching fuzzy TV is that the eyes and mind begin to play tricks, and even if you're perfectly wide awake, you suddenly find your lids drooping. At least I do. I'm so sleepy. . . .

"Claire?" From the foggy recesses of a sleep-darkened forest, I slowly ascend toward the light. Okay, not so slowly now. Someone is shaking my shoulder . . . roughly.

"All right, already! I'm awake." I grab my shoulder and rub, glaring up at . . . Jerry? I sit up fully, still rubbing my shoulder. "Oh, good, they finally got in touch with you."

"What is wrong with Mother?"

"They haven't told you yet?"

"Not until they verify that I'm her son."

"What about your ID?"

"I ran out of the house without my wallet."

That admission of concern speaks to my heart. "They won't let me go see her, either. So how about I fill you in, confirm your parentage, and then you can keep me updated?"

"Deal."

I give him the *Reader's Digest* version. How I found her, called 9-1-1, etc., etc.

His expression softens. "You went over there just to ask her to join your family for a movie?"

"And pizza."

"That's very kind."

"I wasn't only doing it for kindness. I also enjoy her company. And I felt she needed to get out of the house."

"Did you notice any flu-like symptoms today?"

My heart drops because I've asked myself over and over why I didn't pay closer attention to her cough earlier. "I had to hurry in and out today. And yes, I heard her coughing and sent her to bed. But she didn't mention not feeling well, so I assumed it was a simple cold. I'm really sorry, Jerry."

Jerry runs his hand through his thick hair. He smiles. "It's not your fault, Claire." The sound of my name on his lips sounds disturbingly sweet.

"I knew something like this would happen." He gives me a pointed look. "Now do you see why she should be in a care facility?"

"I don't know, Jerry. It's really not my call." What does he want me to say?

"I'm going to check on her. You're free to go."

For some reason the way he says "You're free to go" really bugs me. Like I'm his humble servant.

"Actually," I say, chin up, "we had a deal. I fill you in and you update me, remember?"

His face flushes. "Sorry. Let's go."

I guess he figures I'll follow him. Which I do, of course. I'm prepared to forgive his lack of gentlemanly courtesy considering the situation. I watch his shoulders slump a bit as he leaves the waiting room and heads down the hallway to speak with anyone who might give him information about his mother. It strikes me that I don't really know anything about Jerry. Is he a Christian? Does he like football? The slump in his shoulders, the swipe of his hair, all body signals that attest to his concern for Miss Lou. Guilt edges through me. Perhaps I've misjudged the man. When I sink back into my teal vinyl chair, I send a quick prayer upward. For Miss Lou, for wisdom to guide her son during this time. For an eighty-five-year-old woman, she gets around pretty well, but she *is* eighty-five. How would I feel if I were leaving the country and my mother were staying with no family to keep an eye out for her? I have to admit, I can see his point.

10

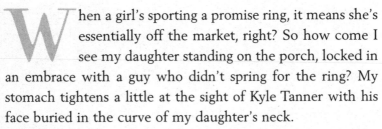

When a girl's sporting a promise ring, it means she's essentially off the market, right? So how come I see my daughter standing on the porch, locked in an embrace with a guy who didn't spring for the ring? My stomach tightens a little at the sight of Kyle Tanner with his face buried in the curve of my daughter's neck.

I glance at the glowing clock on my dash. After midnight. Not only is it a school night, but Ari knows she's not supposed to have guys over when I'm not home.

She pulls away lickety-split as soon as my headlights beam across the porch.

I try not to let anger rule my tongue. But to be honest, I'm so disappointed in her.

Kyle passes me on the steps without making eye contact. "'Night, Ms. Everett."

"'Night, Kyle."

Ari lets out a slow breath as though she was holding it against the very real possibility that I might open up on her right there and cause her no end of humiliation. I lift my eyebrows. "Were you expecting me to make a scene?"

"Yes." A flat answer. Unrattleable, this kid. Any other kid would trip over herself to explain, but not my Ari. Stubborn little twerp. She'll wait for my interrogation, and no doubt I'll feel stupid before all is said and done.

So, hey, I'm going to change tactics. Catch her off guard. "Is Gram still here?"

"Of course. She's asleep on the couch, which, by the way, is why Kyle and I were talking on the porch."

I breeze past her and open the door.

"Considerate."

Okay, you know how Popeye ate spinach and he got this huge burst of power? That's me at this moment.

"That's it?" Ari's tone is all at once suspicious and nervous. "What's it, hon?"

You know how Tinker Bell gets strength when you clap? I'm getting a standing ovation, baby!

"It wasn't what it looked like."

Oh, the power. I slip my jacket from my shoulders and hang it in the foyer closet. "Do you think we should leave Gram on the couch?" I ask, feeling Ari's frustration.

"It's pretty late to be waking her up."

"I agree." I head toward the stairs. "It's late. I'm going to bed."

"Mom!"

I figure I've played the power card long enough. I've won this battle of the wills. I gather a deep breath and turn back to her. "Go ahead. Explain."

"Kyle is dealing with a certain problem, and he needed someone to talk to."

I don't even bother to hide my smirk. Not that I could have if I tried. "He doesn't have any male friends to—" I do air quotes with my fingers "—talk to?"

"Mother, I assure you it's not what you think."

"Oh? And what do I think?"

She scowls and folds her arms across her chest. "That he

has a crush on me and is using the—" she does some air quotes of her own "—I-have-a-problem-and-need-to-talk excuse."

I concede the point with a nod. Maybe she's more astute than I give her credit for.

"Well, that's not what he was doing."

I can't help the shrug lifting my shoulders. "I hope not." I give a pointed look to the bling on her finger.

"I'm not cheating on Patrick, if that's what you're implying."

I give another nonchalant shrug, while relief tidal-waves over my heart. A deep breath pulls through my lungs, and I capture my daughter's full gaze. "Ari, just be careful. I watched Kyle at the birthday party, and if that wasn't a look of love in his eyes, then I've never seen one."

She returns my gaze, a frown playing between her eyes. "What do you mean? We've known each other forever."

"I know. Tina and I were watching when you and Paddy left together, but we weren't the only ones."

Understanding lights her eyes, and sort of adds to my confusion. "I see. Well, don't worry, Ma." She steps around me and brushes my cheek with a kiss. "Everything's going to work out fine with Paddy. We love each other."

I watch her climb the steps, looking more grown up than she has any right to look when I still think of her as my little girl. As she disappears at the top of the stairs, it strikes me that I'm not sure if I'm more upset about her openness about her love for Paddy or her attitude about Kyle. It just proves her inability to see past what a guy tells her to the truth of the matter. I mean, there was no mistaking the look of pain in Kyle's eyes when he watched Patrick and Ari leave the house that night.

Ari's bedroom door closes with a click, and I continue my ascent. After checking on the boys, each of whom are tucked in safely and snoring away, I make a detour to my office before going to bed. After all, it's been more than eight hours since I checked my e-mail, and I know *someone* must have sent me a message in that amount of time.

Turns out, I'm right. A very important someone has sent a message: Bonnie Wright, my first-choice potential agent.

> Dear Ms. Everett,
> Thank you for your submission to the Bonnie Wright Agency. It is quite easy to see why you have such a passion for *Brandi's World*. The heroine, Brandi, is a young woman many will identify with. The premise is solid, and I would love the chance to shop it for you.
> If you're still interested in the possibility of partnering with our agency, please advise as to when might be a good time to speak on the phone.
> Sincerely,
> Bonnie Wright
> The Bonnie Wright Agency

One, two, three. I'm counting. You should never get excited about anything until you count to three (at least) and reread the e-mail. So that's what I do.

Okay, *now* I'm excited. My heart is beating so fast in my ears, I think I'm going to burst an eardrum from the inside out.

Is this my second chance, Lord?

I honestly thought it was all over. That I might as well kiss my writing career good-bye and be prepared to stand by

Greg's side and raise the kids, do the bake sales, head up the ladies meetings, and that's that.

Compared to my former agent, Stu, Bonnie is the difference between a Starbucks mocha latte and Sanka (Stu's the Sanka). On a one-to-ten scale of likability, respect in the industry, and an eye for a good story, Stu is a four to Bonnie's ten. So if she's serious about representing me, and I'm not reading more than I should into her e-mail, I have a great reason to be optimistic.

I draw in a deep breath and position my shaking fingers on the keyboard.

Dear Ms. Wright,
Thank you for your response to my proposal, and for your interest in the possibility of representing me. I'd be happy to speak to you whenever it is convenient. Below are my home and cell numbers.

I look forward to hearing from you.
Sincerely,
Claire Everett
www.claireeverett.com

Gotta throw in that Web site. Bragging rights, you know.

I let the computer fall asleep as I read and reread the e-mail ten times. You really don't have too many chances to make a first impression in this business. Okay, Claire, just suck it up and click send.

And just like that, I've entered what I hope is the next phase in my career. In any case, I've done all I can for tonight. I'm beat. This evening's events have left me feeling like I've been run over by a truck.

When I left the hospital, Miss Lou was in a state of what the doctor called a "light coma." He believed she'd come out of it, but the extent of her loss of brain function was unknown.

My heart is heavy for the precious older lady. I know I haven't been acquainted with her all that long, but some people just shoot straight into the heart and it's like you were created to have a relationship. That's Miss Lou. I adore her.

I pull on my freshly washed SpongeBobs and nestle down beneath my cozy comforter. My head makes a nice dent in the pillow, and my eyes shut of their own accord. For about three seconds.

"Ollie!" I forgot about Ollie. The big baby will be making all kinds of noise. We can't just leave him there without human companionship. He needs to be around people.

I sit up, throw off the covers, slip my feet into my slippers, and head down the steps.

"Claire?" Mom's voice nearly sends me through the roof.

"Sheesh, Ma, I forgot you were still here."

"Well, I can certainly leave!" she huffs.

"That's not what I meant. I'm sorry. I was just startled for a sec."

Mom pulls herself from her offended state and nods. "Where are you going at this time of night?" A frown mars her brow and I feel a little bit like I did as a teen when I came in after curfew. "What time is it, anyway?"

"Around one." I lace up my second Nike and stand, grabbing my hoodie from the coat closet and slipping it over my head. "Miss Lou is still in a coma, and I just remembered Ollie. He's probably going crazy."

She scowls and shakes her head. "That dog. What are you going to do with him?"

Hmm. I hadn't actually gotten that far. "I don't know. I guess I better bring him here for the time being."

Mom's jaw drops, and I'm afraid she might lose her dentures. "Are you serious?"

"He's not a loner breed, Mom. Mastiffs need their family."

I get a deep "Harrumph!" from her. "Well, lock your van door when you leave. You never know what crazies are waiting at a stoplight to jump unsuspecting women."

Rolling my eyes. "Okay, Ma. I'll be sure to lock the door."

November in Missouri is such a great time of year. The air is crisp and cool, but not too cold usually. I love the clear, moonlit nights where I can see my breath. As I walk into such a night, suddenly my fatigue is gone and my chest expands with well-being. In my south-central Missouri town, everything shuts down about ten, so by one in the morning the only people still on the street are nightshift workers and a handful of harmless drunks staggering home from the bar.

It takes me five minutes to drive the couple of miles to Miss Lou's.

I pull into the drive, and my stomach takes a dive. Jerry's Jag is parked there, like he owns the place. Which means Miss Lou is all alone. What if she wakes up and is afraid? I make a split-second decision to go back to the hospital. Jerry generously put my name on the list of people who can visit her in ICU.

I'm just about to back out when I see Jerry in the driveway, waving his arms at me. "Claire! Wait."

Alarm bursts through me. Please, God—not Miss Lou.

I slam the van back into park and fly out the door. "What is it? How is she?"

He gives a huff and jerks his hand toward the house. "What are you doing here in the middle of the night?"

"I came to check on Ollie."

"Same here, but that ignorant dog won't let me in. Will you please do something?"

I stare, letting his words sink in. Letting my heart rate slow back to something medically acceptable. "Your mom's not worse?"

"No. She woke up."

"And you just left her at the hospital all alone?"

"Believe me, I wanted to stay. She insisted I check on that horse in there. But he won't let me."

It must be a combination of relief at hearing Miss Lou is better and the mental image of Ollie blocking the door, but I can't hold back the laughter.

He purses his lips together. "Okay, yeah. It's hilarious. When you're finished having your fun, will you please convey to that dog that I'm okay?"

Who could resist such a moment? I fold my arms across my chest. "Well, I'm not convinced that you're all that *okay*." I level my gaze at him. "As a matter of fact, from what I've seen so far, I don't think you're all that nice."

He takes a step closer, undeniable anger flashing in his eyes. "Where do you get off judging me? You don't know me. You don't know how much I love my mother. I'm only trying to do what I think is best for her."

I'm about to respond with righteous indignation about how his mother is a human being with all of her faculties and she should have the right to decide whether she stays in her own home or not, and just because he's moving across the ocean doesn't mean she should have to give up her freedom. But Jerry isn't done. As a matter of fact, his voice and expression soften. "I appreciate that you've helped her with Ollie and provided some companionship, but you're not her child. Responsibility for her care falls to me, and I'm doing what I think will be best for her."

I find myself drawn to the sincerity in his voice and the surprising lack of haughtiness.

"All right. I'll help you get inside."

"I'd appreciate it."

"For the record, I was just kidding around."

His brow goes up. But he doesn't respond.

Silence spans the length between us as he follows me onto the porch and to the door. I reach for the handle, and Ollie's low growl warns me off. "It's just me, Ollie," I say, keeping my tone even. "It's okay, boy." He whines long and low and my heart goes out to him. He pushes hard against me when I step inside. I scratch behind his ears, amazed at the extent of my compassion. "Miss Lou will be back before you know it."

"Actually, Claire—" Ollie's head snaps up at the sound of Jerry's voice.

"It's all right, boy. Jerry isn't going to hurt anyone."

The hair on Ollie's back relaxes a bit, and he allows Jerry into the house, but I can tell the dog isn't a bit happy about it.

"Actually, Claire, what?" I ask, patting Ollie on the head and heading toward the kitchen to find his food bowl.

"The doctor doesn't think she'll be able to live alone after this."

I give a sarcastic snort. "How much did you have to pay him to get him to say that?"

His eyes narrow, and I know I shouldn't have said it.

"Sorry," I mumble. "Kidding again. Still, I don't see how he can predict how she's going to heal."

"Most women her age just go downhill at this stage once they start getting ill. She broke her hip and developed pneumonia all within a couple months. He also found some infected sores on the backs of her legs from all of her time in that wheelchair. She's being treated for them, but with her diabetes, she's having trouble healing. They're pretty bad."

My eyes grow wide, and I'm filled with a sense of remorse. "I'm sorry, Jerry. I had no idea." I stop pouring dog food and face him. I'm taken aback by the depth of sorrow in his eyes. This man loves his mother.

"There's no need for you to be sorry," he says. "But maybe you can stop helping her fight me on this."

Tears burn my eyes. "I see your point."

"I'm glad. Because I don't intend for her to come back to the house. I need to hire someone to pack up her things and clean the house. I was hoping you might be interested. I know Mom would feel better about having you here than a stranger going through her things."

I swallow past a lump in my throat and nod. "I'd be happy to do it for her."

He reaches out to touch my arm, and Ollie shoots between us. He doesn't growl, but he definitely conveys "lookie no touchie" to Jerry.

Jerry gives the dog a quirky grin, the first sign of boyishness I've seen from him. It sort of makes my heart trip. "Okay, boy," he says to Ollie. "I don't blame you for wanting her all to yourself."

What?

Is this guy seriously flirting with me?

"Now, about Ollie," Jerry says, and then I get why he's being so nice all of a sudden. "We need to find him a home, and I was wondering if you could take him until we find someplace for him."

I'm such a sucker.

11

I feel like a five-year-old trying to sneak a kitten into my room. Only my kitten happens to weigh two hundred pounds. But I know I can't leave him downstairs or Mom will wake up in the night and have a heart attack. Truly.

When Tommy's door opens, I nearly jump a mile out of my skin. "Sheesh, Tommy, what are you doing?"

"I need to use the john."

"Fine."

"What's that dog doing here?"

Tommy's still holding Ollie responsible for the walk in the rain on Saturday. Ollie recognizes my sleepy boy. His tail starts thumping and drool gathers at the sides of his mouth.

"Aren't you going to say hello, Tommy?"

"Hi, dog." He reaches out and gives Ollie a scratch behind the ears as he passes us on his way to the bathroom.

I step into my bedroom. "Ollie," I say, doing the Nestea plunge onto my fluffy comforter. "Find a spot to sleep." My eyes close before the words are even out. "'Night, Ollie."

My ringing phone snaps me from a lovely wedding dream. I reach for the receiver and give a groggy, "Hello?"

"May I speak with Claire Everett, please?" The tone is abrupt and sounds a bit New Yorkish.

"Mmm. This is Claire. Who's this?"

"Shall I call back later? You sound . . . ill."

"No, I'm fine." Lucidity slowly begins to creep through the fog. "What can I do for you?"

"This is Bonnie Wright, from the Bonnie Wright Agency."

At that moment, a giant bear rises from the floor beside my bed. He stands up, and from the corner of my eye, all I see is brown fur moving across my room. I gasp.

"Is everything okay?" my dream agent asks.

I try to get it together while Ollie walks around to my side of the bed and rests his chin on my covers.

"I'm sorry. My dog scared me." I pat his head to let him know I forgive him. I glance at the clock. Nine o'clock. *Nine!* What about the kids? Are they all sleeping? Not to mention it's Ollie's usual walking time. But we slept in after not getting home until after three in the morning.

Okay, settle down, Claire. If the kids are already late for school, thirty more minutes aren't going to matter much. And Ollie can hold it for a little while. If I can, he can. Right now I need to concentrate on landing this agent, who might very well be the answer to my career problems.

So I push back the image of the kids sleeping in like it's summer vacation, and I ignore Ollie's soulful eyes telling me he has to go.

"Thank you for calling, Ms. Wright. I'm sorry for being so scattered this morning. A good friend is in the hospital and I didn't get home until late." Never hurts to play the sympathy card.

It works, and her voice warms. "No problem, and please call me Bonnie. Should I call back later?"

"No. Not at all." No way am I going to take a chance that

she'll decide the crazy author on the other end of the line isn't worth the effort.

"Good, then I'll get right to the point."

I hold my breath and tune out Ollie's soft whining.

"I love the premise of *Brandi's World*. I think you have a strong idea, and I'd like to shop it as a series."

"D-does this mean you're willing to represent me?"

"Without question."

Yippee! Yahoo! And hallelujah!

"Thank you," I say breathlessly, knowing full well I sound desperate. But I am. Why hide it?

"I'll e-mail you an agency agreement later and you can print it out, sign it, and send it back to me."

"Sounds great." Okay, I'm starting to get my cool back.

But Bonnie's next words give me pause. "I have a few questions about the story, and I'd like you to work to strengthen the concept before we send it out. Maybe add a little hint of romance to Brandi's life."

Immediately my hackles rise. I have a strict hands-off policy. At least I did with Stu. Of course, on second thought, since he didn't know the first thing about what works and what doesn't, maybe it's time to let someone stretch me. The names of no less than half a dozen well-known, best-selling authors scroll across my mind, each of whom I know is a client of Bonnie's.

"All right, tell me what you have in mind."

When I hang up the phone an hour later, Ollie is starting to get desperate, and quite frankly, so am I. But we make it. There are no signs of life in the house other than Ollie and myself, so I assume Mom has gotten the kids off to school for me. Good ol' Mom.

I stomp up to the attic and find the gate I used when the kids were babies. I lock Ollie in the kitchen so I can go out and walk the other dogs. Of course, if he figures out how flimsy the gate is, he'll knock it down, but I highly doubt that's going to happen. He's such a mild-mannered dog, and he doesn't like to upset me. Even now he looks at me with pleading in his eyes, but I'm firm.

"Go lie down and be a good boy. I'll be back after I walk Mitzy and the twins."

He seems to get it, and drops to the floor right in front of the gate.

I hurry to the van. I don't want to be late for poor Mitzy. She had another accident yesterday. Several. The apartment reeked almost as though Angela hasn't been there in a few days. As a matter of fact, yesterday the poor dog seemed so distressed when I took her home that I hated to leave her. I'm definitely going to have to charge more if I'm to be expected to clean up after Mitzy's accidents.

I arrive, as usual, to the sound of Mitzy's incessant barking. The poor thing sounds miserable. I slip my key into the door, but it doesn't work. Hmm. Maybe I have the wrong one. I check it against the key for the twins' house. I know this is the right one. "I'm working on it, Mitzy. Hang tight."

"You can work on it until the cows come home, but that key ain't never going to work in the new lock."

I spin around at the gruff male voice.

"You a friend of Angela's?"

"Actually, I'm her dog walker."

He gives a deep scowl, pulls a cigarette from his shirt

pocket, and places it between his teeth. "Figures, she can hire a dog walker but can't pay her rent. She's been dodging me for two weeks. Comes in just long enough to get clothes, but hasn't spent even one night here."

Uh oh, sounds like a situation I don't want to be involved with.

"Can you let me in long enough to get the dog?"

His fat face is shaking side to side just like Ollie's before I get the words out. "No can do. Her place stays locked up until animal control can come get the mutt."

Okay, Mitzy is so not a mutt!

"When are they due to arrive? Because if Angela hasn't been here for awhile, that means Mitzy is only getting to go out once a day. She always knocks her water dish over too, so she's probably really thirsty."

He takes a long drag on his cigarette, and smoke curls into the air as he exhales. "Not my problem."

"It might be if you knew she was here and didn't give the poor thing food or water. That's called animal neglect, buster. Do you want to be responsible for a dead dog?"

He sizes me up, squinting against the smoke wafting up toward his eyes as he takes another drag. "How well do you know Angela? Any idea where I can find her? She owes me rent for two months."

"Did you try the bookstore? She's the manager."

"Yep. No one's heard a word from her in two weeks."

Poor Mitzy!

"Look, I'm sorry she stiffed you. But guess what? If we can't find her, I'm not getting paid either. So what's it going to hurt for you to let me get the dog?"

He gives his cigarette a flick, sending a long line of ash to the ground. He grabs a ring of keys from his belt and jangles until he finds the right one.

"Thank you." I step inside and—good grief! The smell nearly knocks me over. The super gives a grunt of disgust. "Look at this." A growl rattles his throat. "It's what I get for renting to a meth head. This is going to cost through the nose to get a cleaning company to come clean this up."

Through the nose, huh? Fitting. The sooner I'm out of here, the better. But then again . . .

"How much is through the nose?"

"What do you mean, little lady?"

Nails on a chalkboard, this guy. Still, he can annoy me all he wants as long as he hires me to do the cleanup. As gross as that sounds, I can't count on my new agent to get me a new contract and therefore an advance check anytime soon. The Vera Wang is worth a little bit of gross.

"So how much do you usually pay for this sort of thing?"

His gaze shifts. The last of the great negotiators. I know I can get more than he's about to offer. "Usually a couple of hundred, but for this place, I'd pay three."

"I'll do it for five, and you know anyone else would charge you seven for this pigsty." I have no idea what I'm talking about, but I hold my breath, hoping against hope that he doesn't know I'm bluffing.

"Five hundred, eh?" He strokes his chubby, stubbly chin. "Okay, you got yourself a deal. But I expect it to be done by the end of the week."

"Deal. But you provide the packing boxes."

"I'll get the boxes," he says, like he thinks he's driving a hard bargain. "You bring the cleaning supplies."

"Fine, but I don't haul anything out of here. I'll get everything boxed and ready to go, and after you get the apartment cleared, I'll come back and give it a thorough cleaning."

"Fine, fine, but it seems like a person oughtta haul the boxes to storage for five hundred dollars."

"Well, I'm not going to. Do we have a deal?"

"Yeah, we got a deal."

"Great. I'll start working on it tomorrow."

"Come by apartment number one and I'll have a key ready for you."

Mitzy is on cloud nine when I clip her leash to her collar and we start our walk to pick up Toto and Spike.

The gray sky opens up, cutting our walk short, so I drop the twins off a few minutes early. Then I head for the apartment building when it hits me . . . what am I going to do with Mitzy? Then brilliance strikes, like a bolt of lightning. I know exactly where she belongs.

"Get that dog out of here. You know I don't allow animals in my house." Mom stares at me like I've lost my marbles as Mitzy prances into the living room like she owns the joint. She flies into Mom's lap, and from the fury in Mom's eyes, I see the error of my ways.

"Mitzy!" I say in the gentle but firm way I have developed when speaking to her. "Get down."

Her ears drop dejectedly, and she hops down and sits dutifully at mom's feet. It's as though she knows she's auditioning.

"I thought you might like a companion, Mom."

"I have one." Mom shoots a pointed look to the new five-by-seven photograph of her and Eli on their recent trip to Branson.

"I know, but I mean a companion when Eli isn't around."

Mitzy sighs and flops down, leaving us to hash it out while she sleeps, her funny little head pillowed on Mom's house shoe.

Mom gives her a cursory glance, but doesn't shove her away with a toe. I see this as a positive sign. "Where did you get this mongrel?"

I give her the *Reader's Digest* version of poor Mitzy's plight. "And with Ollie at my house, I can't keep her." One dog is more than enough. And Ollie is more like four regular-sized dogs. Ten of Mitzy.

Mom scowls, but I'm not convinced that she really is set in her "no." Mitzy snuggles in a little closer, playing her part like she's vying for an Oscar. I wish I'd have had the forethought to take her to a groomer and get her all gussied up complete with a pink bow. Darn. That would have closed the deal. No way even my mother could have resisted that.

"Well, I don't see why I should have to keep a dog just because you've started this ridiculous business for yourself."

"You're right, Mom. I'm sorry. I'll just take her to the Humane Society. As cute as Mitzy is, I'm sure she'll find a home."

"Don't try that reverse psychology stuff on me."

I can't help but smile. "Come on, Mitzy. You're not wanted here."

Mitzy opens one eye like she's been faking sleep, then puts a paw over her nose, closing her eye again. But she isn't inclined to budge.

"Mitzy," I say, a little more firmly. "Come here."

"No need to yell at the poor dog. She's been neglected and abused enough as it is," Mom says. "Clearly, she doesn't want to go with you."

Then my mother does something I never thought I would see in my lifetime. She bends forward, lifts the dog into her lap, gets a Mitzy kiss for her trouble, and looks up at me. "I'll keep her."

I'm sure my jaw drops to the floor. "You will?"

"Is she housebroken?"

"For the most part."

"I suppose I'll have to hire you to walk her for me."

Watching her with that dog sends a surge of love through me. For Mom, not the dog. "Got any of that chai latte mix left, Mom?"

Now it's Mom's turn for surprise, and I feel a prick of guilt. I guess it has been awhile since I spent a casual hour drinking tea and chatting with her.

"It's in the cabinet with the coffee. But you'll have to fix it. I have a dog on my lap."

An hour later, I've returned home and trudged up to my office to start working on the changes my new agent suggested. I edit and write new scenes for the next four hours until I hear the slam of the front door.

Kids are home.

We have a deal. After my surgery last year, I promised I'd only work until five o'clock each night, and usually that's no big deal. But since I had to miss out on family movie night last night and then slept through the alarm today, I feel like I need to greet them.

Ari's blood-curdling scream pierces the air. "Mom!!! Help!"

My heart leaps to my throat. Ollie. I forgot they don't know he's staying with us. And Ollie doesn't know they belong here.

I get downstairs in three seconds flat only to find all four kids shaking and huddled together in an uncommon show of solidarity.

Tommy, self-appointed man of the house, is slightly forward, wielding his . . . skateboard.

"Tommy, what are you doing? You know Ollie's not going to hurt you."

Bursting into belly laughs, Tommy turns and mocks his cowardly siblings. "You're so gullible."

"What's it doing here, Mom?" Ari asks, the fear in her voice replaced with irritation.

"Miss Lou is in the hospital, so we're keeping him for awhile."

"Mo-ther!"

"Cool!"

"We got a dog?"

Only Shawn seems unfazed. He steps forward, pats Ollie on the head, and walks into the kitchen. Ollie must feel a bond, because he tags along after my boy.

"I can't believe you brought that bear into the house, Mother."

At times like this, I remember Ari is still a teenager and not the adult she likes to pretend to be. "Believe it, hon."

"Can I ride him?" I guess Ollie would look a bit like a pony to a child Jake's size.

"He's as big as a horse, isn't he, bud?"

He grins and nods. "So can I?"

I ruffle his hair and grin at him. "What do you think?"

"Aw, Mom!" His expression drops. Then he brightens. "Can I at least tie him to my wagon?"

"Jake! He's a dog, not a pack mule."

"So what about you?" I turn to Tommy. "Do you have an opinion about the dog staying with us?"

He shrugs. "I don't care. Be easier to walk him on Saturday—if you're sticking with that."

"I'm sticking with it. Until you pay for the garage door."

"I'm going to be working that off for the rest of my life."

"Not quite. Do you need a ride to The Board? You haven't been to practice since Thursday."

"I'm not going today. I'm tired."

There's a shock. I can't remember the last time my son was home before six on a weekday. "Are you feeling sick?"

"No. I just have a lot of homework."

Homework . . . right. I can see something is bothering him, but I know better than to pry. "Do you want an after-school snack?"

He shakes his head and walks past me.

Okay, the kid wants to do his homework *and* doesn't want to eat? He knows I provide the world's best mind-numbing junk food for snacks. Cheetos, Oreos, the occasional Go-GURT when I'm in a particularly healthy mood. So anytime one of my kids turns down a snack, there's cause for concern. That being said, the homework thing is even more disconcerting. Tommy hasn't voluntarily done his homework since third grade, when it was fun to do little worksheets with Mom.

I'm about to follow him up the steps and demand an answer when the doorbell chimes.

I open to the sight of an enormous vase of roses. If I'm eyeballing it right, I'm guessing two dozen.

"Claire Everett?" The delivery man peeks around the spray and gives me a once-over, like he can't figure out why anyone would want to shell out the kind of money it costs to send me two dozen red roses. And I'm ashamed to say, the first face that comes to mind is Jerry Calloway. I hate that my heart lifts at the thought that he might have sent me flowers to thank me for taking Ollie.

I reach for my purse, but the delivery guy shakes his head. "The tip's taken care of."

I thank him again and close the door just as Ari comes back into the living room. "Whoa, are those for me?"

Yeah, it's all about her. Like her college-guy boyfriend can afford something like this. "Nope. They're all mine." I grin, reaching for the card.

"Go, Greg!" Ari says, leaning close to take in the fragrance of the roses. "You guys fighting or something?"

"No!"

"Then he must really miss you." Ari sends me a cheeky grin and heads to the stairs. "I'm going to do my homework." Now, Ari doing homework isn't such a stretch of the imagination. So there's no cause for alarm here.

"Okay. If you need any help, call me."

"Yeah, right, Ma. Like *you* could help *me*." She's right. Her coursework exceeded my comprehension last year. But she doesn't have to be a brat about it.

I slide the card from the envelope.

I love you.
Greg

A smile tips the corners of my lips, and I press the card to my heart. After the last couple of days I've had, this is like pouring soothing aloe vera on a sunburn. Even though I completely disappointed him at his debut in Shepherd Falls, he's sending *me* flowers.

I snatch my phone from the clip at my waistband and start to punch in his number.

Something presses hard against my leg. I glance down at Ollie. He's holding his leash between enormous jaws.

Sigh. Calling Greg will have to wait. Jake bebops into the living room, sucking on a banana Popsicle, and plops down in front of the TV. His chunky face scrunches as he smiles at *The Fairly OddParents* on Nickelodeon.

"Come on, Jakey. Let's go walk Ollie."

He jerks his head at me and frowns in confusion, like I'm speaking Swahili or something. "Can't I watch TV?"

"Ollie really likes you. He'd probably really be glad if you came along."

Quandary passes over his angelic features. And then Jake does something I've never seen him do without being forced . . . he shuts off the TV.

The walk starts off great. Jake's walking next to Ollie's head, one arm slung casually over the massive neck while the other hand is occupied with the banana Popsicle. He tells me all about his day at school, including the episode where he was forced to stand against the wall all during recess just because Tyler Ames took the ball away from him and Jake knocked him down. We discuss boundaries, and all is going well when Ollie suddenly does something unspeakable. He stops in his tracks, lifts his head, and snatches the Popsicle right out of Jake's pudgy hand. "Hey!" the sound of Jake's outrage has no effect on Ollie. He drops the treat on the ground and laps it up.

My son turns a gaze of disbelief on me, his eyes blazing

with accusation. If I hadn't forced him away from after-school cartoons, he wouldn't be in this predicament.

"Shame on you, Ollie." Poor Ollie is used to getting all the leftovers. The smell of that Popsicle must have been (excuse the pun) dogging him since we left home a couple of blocks ago.

Ollie doesn't seem to mind the scolding. He polishes off the frozen treat and looks at Jake. Jake is absolutely fuming, his face red with fury. "Dumb dog!"

Ollie's ears drop, and I think he gets it as we resume our walk. "Come on, Jake. He just wanted to share with his new friend."

"I'm not his friend anymore." Wow. Tough guy.

"Come on, Jakey."

He walks ahead. Ollie picks up the pace to follow his new buddy.

"Okay, fine. Poor Ollie is lonely, missing Miss Lou, but don't let that stop you. Go ahead and be mad about a little Popsicle."

Jake glances over his shoulder and focuses on the animal. "Okay. I forgive you," he says. "But don't ever take my snacks again. If I want to share, I will."

Ollie gives him a slobbery lick that turns my stomach. But Jake giggles with delight. He slings his arm across Ollie's neck and we resume our walk.

And that's that.

12

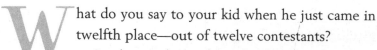

What do you say to your kid when he just came in twelfth place—out of twelve contestants?

On the way home from the skateboard competition, total silence thickens the air in the van, and I'm almost afraid to breathe. If I open up discussion, I risk humiliating Tommy when he's not ready to discuss it. If I talk about something else, he might think I don't care.

I turn to Greg for support, but he's driving, and his mouth is moving, so I figure he's praying about his sermon tomorrow, when we'll head back to Shepherd Falls. It's been two weeks since the last fiasco, and I'm determined not to blow it this time.

He seems to sense I'm watching and turns to me. He grabs my hand without a word and presses it to his lips. "It'll be okay," he says, for my ears only. But I'm not too sure.

"Loser!" Oh, Lord. It's begun. From the backseat, Shawn begins to mock Tommy. And being the bigger of the two, by quite a lot, Tommy is definitely not about to take any garbage from his younger brother. I hold my breath and wait. Nothing. Nada. Not a word. I raise my eyebrows and catch Greg's eye again. He sends me a wink.

"Shawn, apologize to your brother," I say. I mean, if the kid's not going to speak up for himself, I'll have to do the proper parenting thing and get on the one who actually tried to start a fight.

"I don't care if he apologizes or not." Tommy's belligerent bravado cuts through me like a dozen knives.

"Well, I do." I fix my gaze on Shawn. "Now, bud."

"Sor-ry," he says in a tone that tells me how unsorry he really is.

Without bothering to turn away from the window, Tommy shrugs. "Whatever."

Usually the whole family shows up for things like this, but Rick had to work this weekend and Darcy didn't want to bring Lydia around all the noise. Greg's daughter, Sadie, and my Jake are tight friends, and we decided to let them stay with Darcy for the day. Ari had her own plans with Paddy, and Mom and Eli had already made plans to see the Festival of Lights at Silver Dollar City this weekend before she knew about the competition. So it's just the four of us. And considering Tommy's dismal showing at the competition, I'm sort of glad.

Today's loss is disconcerting, mainly because Tommy has placed in the top three in every competition he's been in. Not that I think he should always be the best, but for him to do this badly compared to how he's done in the past surprises me.

"So what do you think happened, Toms?" I can't help asking.

He just shrugs. "I suck, that's all."

"Oh, you do not! And don't use that word."

"Whatever."

"And don't say *whatever*."

So much for letting my inner nurturer come out. But

sheesh, the kid's attitude stinks these days. And we were doing so much better. I think I'm going to have to ask Rick to have a talk with him.

But for now, I really want to cheer him up. "How about we stop off at Incredible Pizza?"

"Yeah!" At least Shawn has the decency to show a little enthusiasm.

"Can't we just go home?" Tommy asks.

"I guess we can take you straight to your dad's."

He nods. Shawn groans. "Man, how come he always gets his way?"

Because he's the one who crashed and burned! But of course I can't say that. "Hush, Shawny," I correct gently. "We'll go to Incredible Pizza another time."

"Man." He kicks the back of the seat, which just happens to be the one Tommy occupies.

Tommy whips around. "Cut it out, stupid!"

"At least I'm not a loser!"

"At least I'm not a sissy actor in tights."

"I don't have to wear tights in *The Lion, the Witch, and the Wardrobe.*"

"You probably wish you could—wimp."

"That's enough, you two." Greg's deep voice boasts authority that commands respect. Still, I can't believe the boys actually obey.

I flash him a grateful smile. He smiles back, and we share one of those parenting moments designed, I think, to bring couples closer. Relief washes over me like a nice warm summer rain.

The drive home takes almost an hour, and by the time we get there, the sky is spitting out drizzle—enough to turn the windshield wipers to medium. Temps are dipping, and I can't help but wonder if we're going to have a bit of freezing rain or snow tonight.

We stop by the house to check on Ollie and pick up the boys' things for the rest of the weekend. I switch on the light and call after the boys, who have dashed up the steps. "Ten minutes! The weather is getting nasty, and I don't want to get stuck in it."

"Want me to take them?" Greg asks. "I know you have to walk Ollie."

Technically, Tommy should be walking him, but since he's feeling so bad about his performance, I guess I'll give him a break. I give Greg a grateful nod. "That would help. I could get his walk in now before it gets any nastier out."

"No problem." Greg opens the coat closet and grabs my hoodie and my raincoat and hat. "You don't want to get sick."

Love bursts through my chest. Instead of taking the proffered outerwear, I slide my arms around him, clasping them behind his back. He doesn't hesitate, but draws me closer. The thumping of his heart is like music to my soul and his warmth lulls me. I have no desire to be anywhere but in these strong arms, listening to his even breathing, and feeling his cheek against my hair. "I love you, Claire," he murmurs. "I'm tired of leaving you every week."

Well, whose big idea was it for you to move away, buster? "Yeah, me too." I sigh.

"Marry me." His arms tighten with the intensity of the words.

"I am marrying you. Or did you forget?"

"I know. But what if we go ahead and get married—soon? Really soon?"

"We talked about this last year, remember? When you thought it might be easier all around if I could just move in with you after the tornado totaled my roof?"

"That was different, though. That was for convenience, and you were right to turn me down." He pulls back a little and I take my cue to raise my chin and look him in the eye. Those dark eyes, that at this moment are way sexier than Andy Garcia's.

My stomach trips up a bit, but I keep my wits about me. "Greg . . ."

But apparently he's thought this through. He won't let me reason with him. "Listen, if we get married now, it's not just about convenience, like last year, but about our need to be together."

Okay, what exactly does he mean by "be together"? I recognize that look in his eyes, and the way he stressed the word *need*. And believe me, I'm flattered. Not to mention the fact that there are times I wish the wedding were closer too, for the exact same reason, but we're talking about joining our lives here. It's important. Too important to hurry up just for . . . you know. "Is this about sex?"

Red creeps over his face. "It's better to marry than to burn." Oh, now he's quoting the apostle Paul.

Be that as it may.

I pull out of his arms. "You'll just have to keep simmering for a few more months, Pastor. Because—trust me—it's better to burn than to deny a woman her chance for a dream wedding."

By the time I get back to the house, my arms feel like they're about to release from their sockets. I had no idea Ollie could move so fast. I wonder how Miss Lou ever walked him, even before her surgery.

Speaking of poor Miss Lou—she sounded plenty depressed earlier when I told her I couldn't see her today. The way she said, "I understand, honey. You have your own life," nearly broke my heart. Her voice sounded more frail than ever. And for the first time, I think Jerry is right—she can't go back to living on her own.

I spent the week cleaning up Angela's filthy apartment, and the five hundred dollars went directly into my private savings. So far I've only saved about four hundred dollars, plus the five hundred, so I'm inching along toward the price of the Vera Wang, but nowhere near ready to pay it off. I start working at Countryside care facility on Monday—two days from now. Miss Lou seems more ready to move in now that she knows she'll be seeing a familiar face every day. I haven't held regular job hours in years—not since I finally started making more money writing than I made waiting tables.

The house is in dire need of a little pick up. It never fails—when we're rushed like we were this morning, the house is trashed from last-minute chaos. I glance at the clock. Greg should have been back by now, unless traffic was unforgiving. Even in a town our size, Saturday night traffic can get pretty congested.

I utter a sigh as I step across the threshold. I mean, gee whiz, why can't they pick up their own shoes? I snatch up Tommy's skateboarding shoes that he callously discarded when we got home, and a pair of Jake's, and toss them in a basket at the bottom of the stairs for easy access when I lug them upstairs.

Minutes later, I'm standing outside Tommy's room—where

a distinct odor wafts to my sensitive nose. Normally, I'd just leave his room alone when he's gone. But I have this sick little feeling. And as much as I hate to admit this: the room has the distinct odor of marijuana. I'm going to kill that kid! He was up here for ten minutes gathering his stuff for his dad's overnight. That must have been some quick smoke sucking. I wish there were any possibility of mistaking the smell. I'd love to give my kid the benefit of the doubt.

Just for the record, here is my privacy policy: I believe my children have the right to privacy when they're (a) getting dressed, or (b) using the bathroom. Otherwise, they can assume I will eventually barge in uninvited and that I will check from time to time to see whom they're e-mailing. And if they are careless enough to leave a journal open . . . well, that's just asking for it, isn't it?

I begin a frenzied search. Sniff out and detect. I'm the marijuana-nator. That boy is going to wish he'd never touched the stuff when I'm through with him. Oh, yes. His life is about to change.

13

Greg finds me sitting on the couch, staring, chin in palm, at my son's stash on the coffee table in front of me. The sight of tobacco and papers, plastic bag, all of it, just makes me sick to my stomach. I've progressed through anger and on to grief. I'm sure I'll go back to anger eventually, and quite frankly, I'll need to by the time Tommy gets home. But for now I'm allowing my thoughts to focus on memories of his childhood. Those gap-tooth grins and enormous Dumbo ears. A red hat with a drawstring at his chin, and cowboy underwear. Oh, my boy. Never once did I see any signs he would grow up to be a skateboard-riding, long-hair wearing, lip-piercing wannabe, pot-smoking hood. Okay, there's the anger coming back.

"Good grief. Is that what I think it is?"

"Yep."

"Is there, uh, something we need to talk about here?"

Okay, if it weren't such a stinking situation, that would be funny. "Are you nuts? This isn't mine."

"Oh, good." Why does he sound so relieved? Sheesh. I haven't smoked a joint since college—pre-salvation.

"Greg!"

"I mean, whose is it?" He drops down next to me, and we stare at the stuff together.

"Tommy's. I smelled it, went looking, found it, and now I'm going to have to hurt him for bringing drugs into my house."

A wave of grief washes over me at the thought of my boy going down this heartbreaking path. I bury my face in my hands and allow the tears to fall. Greg's arms encircle me.

I've been heartsick only a couple of times in my life. Once when I miscarried a baby, between Ari and Tommy. And again when Rick left me. And now. But those times were before I knew Jesus. I never expected to feel this way again after giving my life to Christ. Newness of life. New mercies every day. That's what I was promised. Joy unspeakable, full of glory.

"Let's pray about this." Greg kneels in front of me. He takes my trembling hands and begins to pray.

I can't say the words of my heart, but God knows. He feels my pain. He understands because as much as I want Tommy protected and whole, God does even more.

I can't even concentrate on Greg's prayer, so loud are my own inward pleas. *Cleanse him, Lord. Heal him. Create in Tommy a clean heart, O God, and renew a right spirit within my boy.*

But guilt nips on the heels of supplication. *You're to blame for this, Claire. You didn't watch him closely enough. You've let him hang out with skater freaks and spend the night with kids whose parents you don't know.*

On and on, the accuser of the brethren screams in my mind. *Your fault, your fault, your fault.*

"Oh, Greg! It's all my fault."

"No, Claire. It isn't."

I repeat the inner accusations, but Greg won't agree with me. "Those are lies from the devil. Tommy knows he is to blame."

My bruised heart tries to take comfort in his words, but it's no use.

The phone rings, and Greg's low undertones reach me from the kitchen. Then he appears. "Honey, it's Jerry Calloway."

"Jerry can suck an egg."

When I called Miss Lou earlier, Jerry hadn't been to the hospital to see her in two days. So I'm more than mildly ticked off at him. Combine that with my current situation, and let's just say I'm in no mood to be polite.

"He says it's important, about his mom. You might want to take it."

I snatch up the cordless next to the couch. "Hello?"

"Your voice sounds strange."

"Well, we can't all sound like Meg Ryan, can we?"

"Meg Ryan? Okay, obviously you're in a bad mood. Must be a woman thing."

Figures he'd say that. He's probably the type to dismiss any woman's bad mood as PMS. The thought just annoys me. So for that reason alone, I don't give him a chance to move on with his train of thought. Instead I sit up, my anger finally strong enough to spur me to action. "Yes, I'm in a bad mood. And it's not a woman thing."

His chuckle boils my blood. "Dare I ask?"

Honestly, I don't even know why, but I open my mouth and out pops, "My son has been smoking pot." My voice cracks with fresh tears.

I hear the hesitation in his voice, and I think maybe he's about to offer me a little sympathy. He sucks in a breath. "Oh, well. Boys will be boys." So much for sympathy.

"Thanks, Mr. Sensitive. Just wait until it's one of your stupid kids."

"Take it easy," Jerry says, and I can hear in his voice that he's distressed by this new crazy Claire.

"Don't tell me to take it easy, Jerry. Boys can be boys when it comes to playing football and competing for girls' attention. Boys can be boys when it comes to pulling each other's fingers. Boys can be boys when they wrestle each other black and blue. But I will not sit by and allow my son to do drugs, for crying out loud!"

"Personally, I think pot is one of the drugs they should legalize," he mutters.

"You would."

"Okay, so we have a difference of opinion," Jerry says with that lazy indifference that drives me crazy. "I just called to let you know my mom is going to be moving into Countryside sometime this week. She has a list of things she'd like to have boxed up to bring with her. Do you mind?"

Still shaking from my wild burst of indignation, I gulp down a couple breaths of air and force my mind to switch gears. "I'll stop by the hospital on Monday around ten thirty and see her. I can get her list then."

"Sounds good. I'll tell her to be watching for you."

"Thanks."

We hang up without any more mention of my outburst. I figure Jerry doesn't want to start the tirade all over again. And, really, my adrenaline is still pumping a little too hard anyway.

Greg comes into the room and sets a cup of freshly brewed coffee on the table next to me. I think for a second that I hear the "Hallelujah Chorus." He's a good man, a godly man. A man I can count on to sit next to me and hold my hand during the hard times.

Sitting down on the couch, he draws me to him. "We're going to get him through this."

"Why didn't I know he was doing stuff? I had my eyes completely closed. I mean, he goes to The Board every day—a place owned and run by the church. Other than the occasional lip, he's no trouble. I thought after we caught him smoking last year, that was the end of it. Now I see it's just the beginning." I give a shuddering sigh. "I'm so afraid of what else he's been exposed to."

"All of your questions will be answered in due time, Claire. Don't drive yourself crazy."

I nod and reach for the phone.

"What are you going to do?"

"I need to call Rick and Darcy."

Darcy picks up and answers with her cheery voice. "Hello?"

"Hey, Darce, it's me."

"Claire, hi! Did you know we're supposed to get an ice storm tonight?"

"I thought it looked like we might."

"I just hope Rick's careful driving home."

"Oh, he isn't home yet?"

"No. He wanted to stop by the hospital to see a patient. She's a young mother, and she's had so much trouble. Rick isn't sure they can keep the baby in utero long enough for a successful delivery."

"What are the kids doing?"

"Jakey is still playing with Sadie. We talked Greg into letting her spend the night. Shawn had an extra rehearsal tonight. And Tommy and Ari went to the youth party."

The party. Something I'd forgotten about, but it gives me a

chance to put my plan into action while Tommy isn't in the house.

"Do you want to talk to Jakey?"

Impatience shifts through me. "Is he right there?" In other words, did he hear her ask me if I want to talk to him?

"No. They're in the family room."

"Then no. I need to talk to you about something."

"Sounds serious."

"It is." I fight tears as I give her the 4-1-1.

"Oh, Claire. Poor Tommy. I want to smack him."

The same emotions as mine. I want to give him pity and pain. How's that for consistency?

"Darce, while he's gone, can you go look around his room?"

"You bet I will. He'd better not have brought that garbage into my house."

I know how she feels.

"Darce, I need to ask you not to say anything to him. This is a situation that Rick and I will need to discuss and then decide how to go about talking to Tommy."

"All right, Claire. I understand. I'll go check his room before he gets back."

"Thanks. If you mention it to Rick, ask him not to confront Tommy until I can be there. Okay?"

"Of course." Her tone is clipped in a very un-Darcyish manner. She's usually Little Miss Ray of Sunshine.

"Is something wrong?"

"Yes, Claire. It's just that . . . well, sometimes I think I'm never going to be considered in the discipline of the kids. I mean, if I find something in my house like pot, why shouldn't I be allowed to confront the person who brought it in?"

I close my eyes against the migraine threatening to split my head. Still, I keep the irritation at bay as I try to explain some-thing that should be common sense. "If Tommy cusses or you catch him lying or he breaks one of your household rules, by all means, Darcy, you have every right to call him on it. But something like drugs is a big deal and something his parents need to confront him about. Would it be right for me to start bottle-breaking Lydia without your input?"

"Of course, you're right. I've just been going through some emotional issues since Lyddie was born."

The nickname comes as a surprise. "We're calling her Lyd-die now?"

"Isn't it cute?"

As a bug in a rug. "Yeah, real cute." Although I like *Lydia*. Why change it? "Have you talked to Rick? It might be hor-mones."

"I just hate it when he acts like a doctor with me!" she spits out.

"Uh, FYI, Darce. He is a doctor."

"I know that. Don't you think I know that my own hus-band is a doctor?"

Wow, Darcy acting *mean*. I've never seen this before.

"Okay, don't talk to him about it, then. But you should def-initely go see someone."

The sooner the better.

Greg is waiting patiently when I hang up the phone.

"Everything okay with Darcy?"

"I guess she has a little postpartum craziness going on." But I can't think about Darcy right now. My mind won't wrap around anything but Tommy.

"Is she going to see a doctor? I heard you suggest it."

"I hope so," I murmur, hoping he'll let it drop.

I consider yanking Tommy out of his party and confronting him tonight, but I quickly dismiss the idea. Rick and I have finally come to the kind of parenting relationship where we share things equally where discipline is concerned. I wouldn't want him to disregard my feelings and go after one of the kids for something this big on his own.

Greg and I sit in silence for a little while, and my eyes are growing heavy. Finally, with a sigh, I give in to my body's demand.

I'm just dozing off when Greg shifts and presses a kiss to my forehead. "I have to go. We have an early morning tomorrow."

My mind is fuzzy from sleep, I guess. Because I can't seem to figure out what he's referring to. Why do we have an early morning? "What do you mean?" I remember even as he voices the answer.

"I'm preaching in Shepherd Falls."

I pull back and stare him full in the eyes. "Do you mind if I don't go?"

His eyes cloud with disappointment and I'm conflicted. But my son has to come first. "I'm sorry, Greg. I just want to stay close to home right now."

He nods and brushes his knuckles against my cheek. "I understand, sweetheart."

I spend the next few hours trying to calm my raging emotions. Prayer, music, Bible reading. But the image of Tommy smoking that junk won't leave my mind. Relief floods through me when Rick finally calls after he returns home from the hospital around midnight.

"What's going on, Claire?"

"Didn't Darcy tell you?"

"Yes, and by the way—" he drops his tone—"she didn't find anything in his room here."

His voice sounds a little weary.

"You okay?"

"Yeah. We were put on alert this weekend."

"Alert for what? Is there a hurricane I don't know about?" Lord knows, we've had our share of them across the southeast and the Gulf states in the last couple of years.

"For the Middle East."

Air leaves my body in a whoosh. "Oh, wow. You're going to Iraq?"

"Kuwait, probably."

Well, that's safer than Iraq, but still. "How's Darcy taking it?"

"Do you even have to ask?"

Darcy's emotions have always been a little on the sensitive side, but given her hyper-emotional state lately with postpartum depression (if my hunch is right), she's probably a wreck, which also explains her tension earlier. "When do you leave?"

"We may not. We've just been put on alert to make sure all of our gear is ready and accounted for. If we get called up to active duty, we'll be deployed as early as January."

"Sounds to me like it could happen, Rick."

"Yeah. I'd be surprised if it doesn't." He clears his throat— a sign I recognize well. He's ready to change the subject, which is just as well, because we have a pressing situation with Tommy.

"So what punishment are we looking at for Tommy?" he asks.

"I thought I'd take his TV and computer."

"Good. We'll take the TV and computer out of his room here, too."

That was easy.

Next topic. "What do you think about getting Toms into counseling with Dr. Goldberg? He helped Shawn last year during his whole issue." That would be the nasty-poetry-due-to-lack-of-attention issue.

"Might not be a bad idea."

I hear Darcy's voice in the background, and it sounds anxious. Not like Darcy. Rick answers her, but I can't make it out.

"Listen, Claire, I need to go. We'll talk to Toms after church tomorrow. I have other things to deal with right now."

I get the uncomfortable feeling he's blowing off our son's problems. "Hey, look, Rick. If it's too much trouble for you, then don't worry about it. You were the one who insisted on helping with Shawn's discipline last year after the illustrated-poetry incident. And you did everything but heap coals on Ari's head after she started sneaking out last spring and summer, after the tornado."

"And I was right in those instances."

"Maybe so, but if you think that the-best-two-out-of-three parenting is okay, you're wrong. And right now, your son needs your guidance."

"Claire!" Rick hasn't raised his voice like this in a long time. Not to me. I'm taken aback. Angry. Indignant. But his next words stifle my reply. "Not now, okay?"

"What is wrong with you tonight? Sheesh!" My exasperation with him finally shoots over the dam and splashes downward.

"Let's just drop it, okay? I'll come over after church in the morning, and we can hash this out with Toms then."

"Fine. Consider it dropped." If I'm testy, it's because I have a right to be, considering the *marijuana* and all! "I'll see you tomorrow."

We hang up and I feel more alone than I've felt in a very long time.

14

The house is freezing when I wake up in the morning. I shiver and hop all the way down the steps, wishing desperately I could stay under my nice warm comforter. Ugh, whose big idea was it to turn the heat down to sixty-six degrees to conserve electricity? Oh, yeah. Me. Sigh. Well, whose idea was it to get a dog? Once again, I have only myself to blame. Well, myself and Jerry.

Ollie rolls out the red carpet when he sees me shuffle toward the kitchen wearing my slicker and hikers. A quick glance outside reveals a thick layer of ice. Yuck. Will they cancel church?

"Let's get this over with, Ollie."

I don't have to tell him twice. He makes a run for it as soon as I open the screen door, and takes me along for the ride. In a split second my hikers stamp down on an icy patch of step and heaven suddenly seems a lot closer than it was thirty seconds ago. I lose my grip on the leash. Dazed, I lay there, staring up at a gray sky that looks suspiciously like it just might release more icy pellets. Before Thanksgiving. I can count on one hand how many times in the last ten years we've had ice before the end of November.

Ollie lopes over me and lands on the porch. He sits and whines as if to say, "Will you stop goofing off and let me back in, already?"

"You big oaf! I think you've injured me."

A warning growl deep in Ollie's throat alerts me to some-one's approach just before I hear the crunch of boots on ice. I turn my head to the side. My neighbor from a couple doors down stops, stands over me, and raises his Sean Connery brows.

Ollie's growl escalates to a bark.

"A little cold for snow angels, isn't it, Ms. Everett?"

"Talk to my dog about that."

"I would if he'd stop that appalling noise."

"It's okay, Ollie."

I reach out to John Wells, and he pulls me up with surpris-ing strength, considering he's in his seventies and I'm not ex-actly a twig.

"What are you doing out here, anyway?"

"A gentleman always knows when he's needed."

The old softy. He must have seen my spill. "I'm touched." I smile.

His lips twitch in amusement. "Actually, I was coming out to get my Sunday paper and couldn't help but notice your un-fortunate predicament."

So much for being looked after. Oh, well, who needs him?

John is an aging actor who has played almost every rep-utable or nearly reputable stage in the world. He settled into my neighborhood last year, when he moved to town to be close to his adult daughter, with whom he's never had a rela-tionship.

I pray for John a lot, atheist that he claims to be.

"Well, that just shows how little you actually know of me, then, doesn't it?" I smile at him. I like John; I really do. He's suave. But beneath all that high-falutin' speech and attitude, he's really got a heart of gold. Last year he started coaching Shawn in acting, free of charge.

"How is the play coming along?"

"As well as can be expected, with a group of amateur children whose parents don't want to spring for private acting lessons. Your son and Miss Devine are the only two in the entire group who can act even reasonably well."

I roll my eyes because I know he's taking all the credit for both Shawn's and Jenny's talent. "And that, no doubt, is due to your excellent coaching."

His gray mustache twitches with mirth. "Most assuredly."

"What will you be doing on Thanksgiving Day?" I ask, because the holiday is this Thursday and it's just the kind of thing you ask people this time of year.

"I hear Shoney's has a delicious turkey buffet."

"Brandi didn't break down and invite you, huh?"

"I'm afraid I haven't made my daughter's holiday list quite yet. And you know her grandmother would disown her if she invited me to taint the purity of her house."

That much is true. John wasn't just an absentee father; he simply didn't love Brandi's mother nor, according to him, did he ever pretend their relationship was anything other than what it was. When he was through with her, he sent her home to her family. In due time she discovered her pregnancy, but John wasn't interested in being domesticated. The rejection destroyed Brandi's mother, and Brandi (the inspiration for my novel *Brandi's World*) was raised by her maternal grandmother, which is why John has every right to assume he wouldn't be welcomed for Thanksgiving.

"How about joining my family?" I have been planning to

ask him anyway, but the opportunity never really presented itself. So now is as good a time as any.

"I really couldn't impose." I see the pleasure on his face. John Wells rarely gives in to emotion, but if I had to guess, I'd say he was dreading that turkey buffet at Shoney's.

"I insist."

"Thank you kindly, then. It would be my honor to join your lovely family for a day of thanks."

He turns to go, and I have a thought. "Hey, John."

Angling his body, he returns my gaze. "Yes?"

"I was just wondering." I toss him a cheeky grin. "When a man doesn't believe in God, who exactly is he giving thanks to?"

"Why, to you, of course, my dear. For sparing a poor man the choice of second-rate buffet food or canned soup. I relish the thought of a home-cooked Thanksgiving dinner. So thank you, from the bottom of my heart."

He tips his hat and walks away, shoulders erect like he has just gotten the final word.

The weather is too dangerous for driving, and according to my portable radio, all but a couple of churches in town have cancelled services. I'm disappointed. I had hoped for fellowship, the chance to pour out my heart to God. But I suppose I can do that with or without a ten-member band and just the right lighting.

When Ollie and I get back to the house, I replenish Ollie's food and water, then pour a cup of coffee to thaw myself out. Ollie walks to the refrigerator and camps out on the rug in front of the freezer section. "No, you can't have a Popsicle, you big pig. Go eat your dog food."

I swear, he adores those things. I happen to know Jake has been sneaking them to him ever since the fateful day of the popsicle snatching.

Ollie gives a depressed sigh and lays his head between his paws. He closes his eyes in compliance, but I know he's thinking, *When is my boy getting home?*

If only that were the biggest problem I had to worry about. But there's Tommy. Last night's discovery comes rushing back to me. Rick would have come over after church, but since church was cancelled, I imagine he'll wait until the roads are salted and bring the boy home later. I don't mind. That gives me more time to prepare emotionally, spiritually.

The weather breaks by midmorning, and road crews have made it to the main streets by noon, but it's three o'clock before our roads are clear enough for Rick to venture out with Tommy. They've already called off school for tomorrow, as I knew they would. With so many rural kids who ride the buses, it doesn't take a lot of inclement weather to cause a snow day. So Darcy is keeping the other kids with her while Rick and I talk to our son.

I've just settled back into the house with a mug of fresh coffee when Rick and Tommy show up.

I give Tommy a hug, and I want to smile, but all I can picture is the sight of my boy, his lips pursed around a joint, sucking in that garbage, befuddling his brain—like it needs any more befuddling than it already has. "Okay, let's get started."

Rick gives a nod.

I've been praying for wisdom, words, peace, compassion, firmness. But now my palms are sweaty, and I'm not sure how to begin. "Sit down, Toms."

"Am I in trouble?"

"Yeah, son. You are in trouble." I sit next to him on the couch.

His face is red from nerves, and he lets out a short laugh as he looks from me to Rick. "Dad. She's freaking me out. What's going on?"

I gather a deep breath to steady myself. "I found your stash of marijuana."

The red deepens, but he sits up a bit straighter as though he's being unjustly accused. "I don't know what you're talking about. What marijuana?"

"Don't play dumb, son," Rick says.

"No, seriously."

Innocence plays across his face. A lesser mother might not catch the swift swallow as his throat succumbs to the drying effect of nerves. But I know better.

"Tommy," I say, leveling a gaze as him. "Let's pretend you don't think we're total morons."

"Mom! I don't know what you're talking about. How could you think I'd be dumb enough to mess with drugs?"

How indeed?

When he sees we're not budging, he loses the look of utter innocence. "Fine." He flings himself against the back of the couch, rebellion etched into his face. "I knew it was there. But it isn't mine. I was just holding it for someone."

Yeah, right. Do I look like I just fell off a "stupid" truck?

Rick gets to him before I do. "I think you'd better level with us, son."

"I am!"

That's it. I've had it! "Tommy!"

His face is mottled with red. "Tank!" He jumps to his feet and glares at me. "Tank! Tank! Tank!"

Who is this kid?

"Tommy, apologize to your mother." Rick's commanding tone takes me by complete surprise. Apparently it does Tommy, too. The boy's eyebrows go up, and his mouth clamps shut. But that's not good enough for his father. "Do it! And sit down. I've had enough of this."

"Sorry," Tommy mutters, dropping back down on the couch.

Go Rick!

Rick levels his gaze at our son, who is suddenly looking a bit green. "I want you to look me in the eye and tell me the truth, Tommy. Be man enough to own up to your mistakes."

Part of me is happy that Rick's taking the lead. The other half wants to cry, "How can he be man enough to own up to anything when he's still nothing but a baby?"

"Okay, it's mine. Whatever."

Yes! Step one accomplished. Admission of guilt. Okay, we can do this.

"Better watch that tone, Toms," I say, trying not to lose it. "You're in enough trouble as it is."

He glares at me. "How many times do I have to tell you it's Tank?!"

"And how many times do I have to tell you that's about the dumbest name in the world?"

Get a grip. Deep breath. I will not lose it.

"So here's the deal, *Tommy*." I lean closer so that there's no mistaking my point here, which is that I'm royally ticked and I have the power to make his life a living hell. "You've lost your TV and your computer for an indefinite period of time."

His eyes get as large as I've ever seen them. But he recovers like a trooper and shrugs. "I don't care."

"That's good. Then your three-month grounding on top of losing your TV and computer shouldn't be too much of a burden. I figure you'll, what, read a lot of books?"

"So I don't have a TV or a computer and I'm grounded for three months. What else? Shock therapy?"

"Don't tempt me." Good comeback! "And I'm going to have to know where you got the stuff, Toms."

"What? No way."

"No way?"

I look at Rick. Rick looks at me. I shrug. "Okay, Toms. Your choice."

"Good. Then I choose not to tell."

I take a breath like I haven't finished my previous thought. "Just like it's my choice, mine and your dad's, whether we let you get your learner's permit in February or make you wait until after you take driver's ed this summer."

His mouth drops open with the force of his shock. "You can't do that."

Oh, don't you just love it when a kid says "You can't do that"?

"See, that's where you're wrong. I can do anything I want."

"Fine. Then I won't get my learner's permit."

Oh, he's so cute when he's calling my bluff.

"Well, that's your decision."

A scowl. A folding of his arms. His expression changes. Softens. Surrenders.

"All right. There's a guy who hangs around in the alley behind The Board."

"The alley I caught you smoking in last year?"

"Yeah."

"I thought Shane was supposed to hire bouncers to patrol that alley."

"Only on the weekends."

"Okay, you know we have to go to Shane about this."

"Mom! No! He'll kill me."

"Who? Shane?"

"No," he says, impatience edging his voice. "The guy who sold me the stuff."

Rick puts his foot up on my coffee table (my coffee table!) and leans his elbow across his knee. "Enough. Who is he?"

I see the indecision on Tommy's face. And, yeah, there's quite a lot of fear. "Toms, I know this has to be scary. But this guy is preying on young boys. He needs to be stopped before he does any more damage. Plain and simple—" Rick's still being John Wayne "—no name, no learner's permit."

"I'll tell Shane. Okay?"

I can see the kid's nervous. Stalling for time. But I'm willing to go along with him for now. I glance at Rick. He looks like he's about to blow a gasket. "Rick, I think we can let it go for now and let Toms tell Shane. Don't you?"

He gives a grudging grunt. "All right." He turns to Tommy. "But you'd better tell him."

Relief slides across Tommy's face. I'm not sure if he's relieved to be buying more time, or if he honestly thinks Shane can protect him from the big bad drug dealer better than his parents can. Either way, it looks like he's going to be getting his learner's permit after all.

15

Rick leaves a few minutes later, after promising to set up Tommy's appointment with Dr. Goldberg. I'm going to schedule an appointment with Shane and hope for the best.

He decides to keep the other kids for another night since there's no school in the morning. Tommy stomps upstairs to his room.

Before Rick has been gone even ten minutes, the phone rings. "Hello?"

"Claire?" Miss Lou's sweet, frail voice seems weaker than before. My heart lurches with concern.

"Hi, Miss Lou!" I keep my voice bright to mask my worry. "How are you feeling today?"

"Oh, not too bad." She gives a breathy sigh. "Just lonesome."

Smile. "I'd love to come visit you."

"That would be so nice." Her voice catches in her throat. "I haven't seen my Jerry in days."

Irritation hurdles through me. "I'll be there in half an hour."

I hang up the phone and call upstairs. "Toms. Come on down here. We're going to visit Miss Lou in the hospital."

He grumbles, but apparently decides this is not a battle to fight. When we get in the car, he turns toward me, his face darkened with belligerence. "I want to go to Dad's."

"Really?"

"Yeah."

"Then you'll have to ask me nicely."

Silence. He's not giving an inch.

"Or you could sit with me, watching Miss Lou eat apple-sauce without her teeth in."

"Will you please take me to Dad's?"

Amazing how quickly they change their tune.

I stop off at the gift shop and find a stuffed dog. Not exactly a mastiff, but close enough. She's napping when I arrive, so I sit quietly and think about what to do with Tommy. My mind goes back to Dr. Goldberg, the psychologist who did some family counseling for us last year. He's a messianic Jew with a sweet, sweet spirit and a way with the kids.

Miss Lou gives a little moan. My head jerks up at the sound, and I'm hopeful she's waking up. I've been here for twenty minutes, waiting to visit, but she seems to have fallen into a deeper sleep. Her mouth drops open and she snorts.

Okay, so there's not really any point in hanging out here, is there? I set the little stuffed dog at the foot of her bed, along with pictures of Ollie I took before coming over today. At least she'll know I was here.

I tiptoe out of the room, and run smack into a rock-hard chest. "Jerry!"

His arms are around me, steadying me. "Claire! What are you doing here? I thought you were coming tomorrow."

"I was—am, but your mom called me this morning and asked me to come."

"That was sweet of you."

I give him a shrug. "Not really. I did it to comfort myself. She makes me feel better."

His mouth dips in amusement. "Well, I'm glad we could help."

"We? You don't make me feel better. Only she does. And what are *you* doing here?"

"She's my mother. Do I need a reason?"

Don't say it, Claire. Don't say it!

"Nice of you to remember that."

Shoot, I said it.

Irritation drips from him, but I can tell he's trying not to show it. Instead, he resorts to mockery. "I'm glad I could measure up to your lofty expectations, for once."

You know, I'm in just a bad enough mood today that I really don't give a rip if Jerry is offended or not. "Is it lofty to expect a man to treat his elderly mother well?"

His eyes narrow. I take a bit of satisfaction in the fact that I got to him. "You mean, because I want to make sure she's taken care of before I leave for Japan?"

"No. I mean, because she told me you haven't been here to see her in the hospital."

"Is that so? And what do you think I'm doing here now? Dating a nurse?"

"I wouldn't doubt it."

"Have I failed to mention that my mother's short-term memory was affected by the coma?"

"What?"

"Yes, it was. I have been here every day since she came to the hospital. And I have the nurses to vouch for me."

"Really? I had no idea."

"Well, now you know."

He says it like I owe him an apology, which in all honesty I know I do. But doggone him, he makes me so mad.

He waits. I wait. He wins.

"Fine. I apologize. But considering your record before your mom was hospitalized, I don't think anyone would blame me for assuming."

"Anyone ever tell you you're really bad at apologizing?"

That pulls a smile from me. "Most people just take what they can get."

"I suppose I should feel honored, then."

"Will your mom be spending Thanksgiving in the hospital?"

He inclines his head in a nod. "'Fraid so. The doctors are willing to release her Wednesday, if she is still responding well and doesn't relapse. But apparently the staff at Countryside doesn't admit new residents on holidays because there are too many visitors to corral."

"Makes sense, I guess. Still, don't you hate to think of her being in the hospital on a holiday?"

"I'll be right here with her," he drawls. "If you're implying that I'd celebrate with turkey and the works while my mother wastes away on hospital food, you're just wrong."

I feel the blush creep to my cheeks. "Actually, I wasn't thinking of that at all. I just meant that her last holiday before going into a care facility shouldn't be spent in the hospital. Why don't you take her to your house for the day?"

"Mainly because I live on the third floor of an old Victorian-mansion-turned-apartment-building. And there are no elevators."

"At least you have a good excuse." Truly, I know it's not his fault, but the thought of Miss Lou hooked to tubes and gadgets when she doesn't absolutely have to be just doesn't sit right with me at all!

"Hey, Jerry. What about asking the doctor to release your mom to come have Thanksgiving dinner at my house?" At the very least, she could visit for a few hours and then come back to the hospital.

He's developed a crease between his eyebrows, so I hurry on before he can act upon the refusal that is most likely forming on his lips.

"I mean, doctors let long-term patients out lots of times for special events. I've seen it. As a matter of fact, I have a cousin whose daughter was on IV antibiotics awaiting brain surgery, and they blocked the IV one day and let my cousin and her husband take the little girl to the zoo."

"Claire . . ."

"If your mom is only going to be here on Thanksgiving because Countryside won't admit her until Friday, then there should be no problem."

His warm hand covers my mouth. "Claire, shhhh."

Oh wow, what's my heart doing in there? Racing, that's what. Traitor. What would Greg think?

"I'm not saying no." He gives me a beautiful white smile, and his eyes are actually . . . tender.

"Yo . . . noft?" I say through his fingers.

He moves his hand. "No. I was going to say, we accept."

We? Oh, good Lord. Panic shoots through me at the thought of Greg and Jerry in the same room.

Jerry-the-Astute cocks an eyebrow. "What, you weren't inviting me, too? That's kind of rude, considering I just told you the only plans I had were to spend the day here with Mom."

"Oh, don't be stupid," I snap—and I can only attribute my outburst to my crazy reaction to his touch. "Of course you're invited, too. Dinner's at three. Don't bother to dress up. I'll be wearing jeans."

"Thank you, Claire." Oh, man. There's that look again. "This means a lot to us. Can I bring anything?"

Yeah, a big fat stick to hit me upside the head with. Maybe that'll knock some sense into me.

16

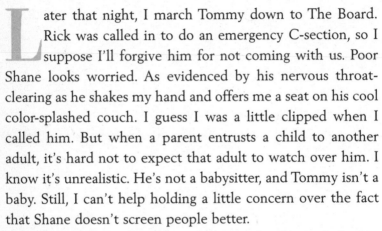

Later that night, I march Tommy down to The Board. Rick was called in to do an emergency C-section, so I suppose I'll forgive him for not coming with us. Poor Shane looks worried. As evidenced by his nervous throat-clearing as he shakes my hand and offers me a seat on his cool color-splashed couch. I guess I was a little clipped when I called him. But when a parent entrusts a child to another adult, it's hard not to expect that adult to watch over him. I know it's unrealistic. He's not a babysitter, and Tommy isn't a baby. Still, I can't help holding a little concern over the fact that Shane doesn't screen people better.

I didn't tell him what was wrong over the phone. Only that I wanted a meeting with him. He flashes a tentative grin that turns to dread as I begin to recount Tommy's confession.

The disappointment in Shane's eyes is something akin to shell shock. I swear he's this close to crying. His face reflects incredible sadness. Remorse. He obviously feels responsible. He walks around to the front of his desk, leans toward Tommy, and commands his gaze. "I'm not going to ask you who sold you the drugs. But I am going to say a name and I expect you to be honest."

"I'm not a narc."

"Come on, Tommy," Shane says. "We both know who it was."

"I said, I'm not a narc."

"Thomas Frank. If I say you're a narc, then that's exactly what you are." Then, "Scott Cannon."

Tommy shifts his gaze. Oh, yeah. That's admission.

"Well, I guess that's all we came to tell you, Shane. And to let you know that Tommy won't be back to The Board for three months."

"I understand."

"What? What do you mean?" Tommy shoots to his feet. "If I don't practice for the winter competition, I'll come in last again."

Unbelievable! "Maybe you don't know what being grounded means, son. But your skateboarding days are effectively over for three months."

Shane shakes his head. "Tommy, you know we have strict policies about drug use. I'm afraid you're out of the sponsorship program for the rest of this year. We might reinstate you next year if you can prove you're ready to be a sportsman. You boys are role models. I can't endorse someone who takes drugs."

I could hug this youth minister. Who says wisdom is reserved for the aged?

"I can't believe this!" Tommy slams out of the room, and I return my attention to Shane.

"If it makes you feel any better," I say. "You're doing a great thing here. Just get those druggies away from my boy and his friends."

"I will. Even if I have to hire a bouncer to stand guard during every hour we're open."

My work here is done.

A few hours later, we're in the middle of watching *Hondo*, the family movie we had to forgo last week when Miss Lou ended up in the hospital. About the time John Wayne throws the kid in the river and lets him sink or swim, Greg calls. Finally.

"Greg, thank goodness. I've been so worried."

"I'm sorry, honey. The roads were horrific. I had to drive really slow all the way to Arkansas. I was two hours late for the service, but they'd cancelled anyway. I stayed at Pastor Miller's house until the ice melted enough for me to drive home around noon. And there were still some of the lesser-traveled highways that I had to take it easy on."

My heart swells with relief that he's okay. Still . . . "I tried to call a hundred times." Pout. Pout.

"I left without my cell yesterday. I'm sorry. My charger isn't working, so I had it plugged into my mom's charger downstairs. I just forgot to grab it on the way out."

"All right. I'm glad you're back okay."

"Know what the best part is?"

"That you're not dead at the side of some ice-laden highway?"

The sound of his laughter zings to my heart. "That too. But I was thinking, I have the entire week off and we can spend every day together."

"That sounds wonderful, Greg." For some stupid reason, tears form in my eyes.

"Are you watching the movie or not, Mom?" Tommy asks, his belligerence unmistakable.

Before I can fuss at him, though, Ari takes his side. "Family movie night. No phone calls. This is our time."

"Okay—all right. Greg?"

"I heard. I'll see you tomorrow?"

"Sure. Oh wait. I can't—I start at Countryside tomorrow."

"Oh, yeah." His glum reply melts my heart.

"Well, at least I negotiated to have Thanksgiving off since I made dinner plans before I started work." Not to mention that Sandy was so desperate to have me start, she agreed to do housekeeping herself that day. I'm not sure how much pull Jerry had in getting me the job. But Sandy's bending over backwards for me. Almost as though she's working for me instead of the other way around.

Greg says a reluctant good-bye. I attempt to concentrate on the movie, but my mind keeps going to the new job ahead of me.

I have to admit that I have never really been all that close to any elderly folks. At least not those of advanced years who require assisted living. So I'm not sure what to expect. My job is housekeeping only. Period. I'm a little nervous about working with the elderly, working in a housekeeping capacity, and working a regular job like this, period. It's been a long time since I've held a punch-a-time-clock sort of job, and my stomach is tied in knots.

Sleep eludes me for the most part, and I'm bleary-eyed when I arrive at Countryside the next morning. But I fall into my routine quickly. By noon I'm all scrubbed out, not to mention pooped. And speaking of poop . . . no, let's not. Let's just say, not all the residents are as independent as Miss Lou.

"Psst. Irene, let's go!"

I frown. I don't remember an Irene on the list Sandy gave me of residents and which room or apartment they're each in.

But the voice persists. "Irene! Get your buns over here."

I turn. Who knows? Maybe I can get Irene's attention.

A tiny white-haired doll peeks around the corner of the room I've just finished mopping. "Irene! Are you coming or not?"

Is she talking to me?

"Excuse me?"

She cackles, showing a mouthful of dentures. "Let's go before the boys see the movie without us."

"What boys?" Does she need help down to the television room?

"Why, Jimmy and Coot, silly. Who else? Stop trying to be funny and come on."

Ah, it's starting to dawn on me. This poor old woman doesn't have all of her marbles. I smile, and get a scowl for my trouble.

"Where's your lipstick, honey? You need some color."

"I don't like lipstick."

"Oh, stop being such a chicken."

Okay, I'm not a chicken. "I think you've mistaken me for someone else, ma'am."

"Mistaken . . . fine, just do whatever you want, but I'm going with Jimmy to see *Gone with the Wind*."

"Oh, that's my favorite movie!"

She rolls her faded blue eyes in my direction. "Oh, and you've watched it already."

"Of course. A hundred times."

She tosses back her mane of white hair and cackles. "You're funny, Irene. No wonder my brother loves you. Now you're not going to stand Coot up again are you?"

I give up. And really, what is it going to hurt for me to pretend a little? "Stand him up? When I've been dying to see *Gone with the Wind*?"

She gives a sweet little grin. "Now that's more like it." She tiptoes across the room like she's sneaking out, settles onto her hospital bed in front of the window and pats the space next to her. "Here's a seat. The boys should be here any second."

I know I shouldn't sit down on the job, but she has her heart set on watching this movie together. How can I say no?

The nurse comes into the room before the opening credits play across the old woman's memory.

"Miss Teffra, are you and Irene watching *Gone with the Wind* again?"

Note to self: remember Teffra.

"What are you talking about, you dumb crow? Do I look like I'm watching a movie?"

Sheesh, all of a sudden Teffra turned mean.

The "crow" doesn't seem a bit bothered by it. She wheels a medicine cart across the room. "Time for your medication, Miss Teffra."

The elderly woman clamps her lips together and presses her palms tight across her mouth.

"Now, Miss Teffra. You know if you won't take it by mouth, we're going to have to give it to you through a needle in your arm. Do you remember what an IV is?"

"Of course I remember. Do I look that dense to you?" She tosses me a glance. "They treat me like a child. I wish you'd tell someone how I'm being abused."

I send her a wink. "I'll see what I can do."

The nurse's lips twitch. Amusement, I hope.

I grab the cleaner off my cart and duck into the bathroom while Miss Teffra is occupied with her medicines.

I finish up the bathroom and leave, but first I peek in and note the old woman has drifted peacefully to sleep.

The nurse looks up and smiles and we leave the room together. "So you had the auspicious honor of playing the part of Irene today."

My cheeks warm. "I guess I shouldn't have played into it."

"Don't be silly. Of course you should have. Too many of the workers in here treat the residents like Miss Teffra as if they have no feelings. Her memories are all she has left."

I grin. "Sounds like she had a lot of fun when she was a young woman."

"Stick around, honey. You ain't seen nothin' yet."

Thanksgiving Day. The true start of the holiday season. I awaken early, excited to start my cooking for the day, nervous to be cooking for so many people. All right, if you want the truth, not only is Mom bringing a whole ham, but she'll be here any second to essentially cook the dinner because, as already indicated, cooking doesn't normally win me any awards. Still, I am allowed to fix the salad, warm the rolls, and mix things together, provided my mother is looking over my shoulder.

I push away the covers and swing my legs over the side of the bed. Yawn. Stretch. Smile. Holidays are pretty much the only days I don't mind waking up early. They're over so quickly, I want to savor every moment possible, even if that means rising early in order to pilfer a few extra minutes out of the day.

Within thirty minutes I've showered and I'm cutting through the package on the turkey so Mom can get to work as soon as she makes it over here.

While I prepare the turkey, per Mom's late-night instructions, I think ahead to the coming hours. I look forward to having everyone here. Jerry and Miss Lou, John Wells, Mom and Eli, Greg, his mom, and Sadie. The only sad part of today is that the kids will be with their dad. Last Christmas, his first married to Darcy, he decided it was time to exercise his right to every other Christmas, Thanksgiving, and Easter—staggered, of course. So this year he gets them. I console myself with the knowledge that I'll at least have Christmas.

Rick and Darcy arrive at nine, just as the turkey is starting to fill the house with its heavenly aroma.

Darcy's uncharacteristic lack of sunshiny brightness concerns me. For the first time I can remember, I'm the one to initiate a hug. Her response is lackluster at best. I'd almost call it cold, but I'm trying to keep a positive attitude since it *is* a holiday.

"Happy Thanksgiving, Darce."

I pull back and tweak Lydia's button nose. The baby launches herself at me with an adorable grin. Baby warmth covers the front of me and I almost close my eyes as I drink in the soft scent of Baby Magic. A sense of longing, much like the one I experienced in the nursery at Shepherd Falls, washes over me. When I open my eyes, Darcy's expression has softened considerably.

"She's so sweet, Darcy."

Darcy's eyes well with tears. "She is, isn't she?" The tears spill over and slip down her cheeks.

Oh, shoot! No! No meltdowns on Thanksgiving. I almost wish she had stayed aloof. But no. Darcy must be going through a lot right now for her to be gloomy on Thanksgiving.

Rick stands helplessly by, his gaze averted like he just wants to forget the whole thing. I pass the baby over to him. At least he's useful for something.

"Come on, Darcy. Tell me what's bothering you."

"Why didn't you invite us?" She snatches a Kleenex from the end table.

"Invite you where, Darce?" I'm truly confused. That is, until she looks past me to the kitchen, where Mom is whistling to the golden oldies radio station.

"What? For dinner?"

She sniffs, swipes at her perky little *Bewitched* nose, and nods.

Floundering for words, I glance at Rick. His shoulders lift in a shrug.

"Well, why would you want to come? This is Rick's Thanksgiving with the kids. I just assumed you would be doing a fancy dinner."

"You invited tons of other people. People who aren't even family."

Okay, I know Darcy is suffering from hormone and chemical imbalances. But she's really starting to get on my nerves.

"Good grief, Claire. There's going to be enough food to feed an army." I turn to the sound of my mother's admonishment. "Just invite them."

"We wouldn't want to put anyone out," Darcy mumbles.

Yeah, right. But the wonderful thing about it is that I can keep my kids close today. The bad thing is that I'm sharing the day with my ex-husband, my boyfriend, and a guy I find oddly attractive despite all the ways he irritates me.

By the time one o'clock rolls around, the house is packed with guests. I have no idea how to fit sixteen people and a baby around a table that holds six. I instruct the kids to run up to the attic and bring down the TV trays.

Jerry Calloway provides a much bigger challenge than simple logistics. He seems to have bonded with Tommy. From the moment I introduced them, Jerry looked Tommy over with fond amusement. A knowing look that says, "Hey, kid, it's no big deal." Now I'm not so sure I want Tommy to get any signals that in any way refute the concerns his dad and I have shared. So far it seems harmless enough, at least. Football and the occasional laugh or pat on the back. Apparently, they're rooting for the same team.

Neither Greg nor Rick seems all that pleased with Jerry's presence. But I think it might be good for more than one reason. Namely, Greg's been glued to my side all day and I have to admit, I'm enjoying the attention. The touches, the stolen kisses, the hugs from behind . . .

Dinnertime. Finally. I insist that the TV goes off.

"Mo-om! You're kidding me!" Tommy, of course, who isn't exactly on my happy list right now, so he'd better not mess with me and my Thanksgiving dinner.

Rick stands next to his son and claps him on the shoulder in a macho-man sort of way. "Come on, Claire, give the kid a break. It's not like we're all going to fit around the table anyway." A blatant attempt at trying to get back on Tommy's good side at my expense.

"Rick's got a point, sweetheart." Greg receives a scathing glare from me, but I'm aware he's trying to take points away from Jerry, so I nod.

"All right, but please stay in here for the blessing."

So the TV stays on. Fine. Big deal. Who cares? The kids "call" getting to eat in the living room, which according to Sadie and Jake is just "cool!"

The adults squeeze in around the table. All ten of us. It's a tight fit, but we manage. After all, it is a holiday. Time for togetherness. Right? Conversation is as you might expect. We discuss Eli's upcoming trip to Florida, where he'll reluctantly spend the rest of the winter. Poor Mom. I can see the thought makes her miserable. Next, the topic of Rick's probable deployment comes up, and for a few minutes a lively debate about the merits of the war versus the costs raises the level of tension from minor to major. Jerry obviously doesn't support the war. Neither, apparently, does John Wells. I can tell Rick is getting steamed. Time for a little intervention.

"Okay," I finally say when I've had enough of Jerry versus Rick. "Can we please change the subject?"

"I'm being rude, aren't I?" Jerry says, his mouth twitching in a manner I've come to recognize as a bit of mockery.

"Yes, you are. Very." I don't cut him slack just because he's a guest. I mean, come on, Rick's about to go over to Kuwait to serve his country. The least the guy could do is keep his antiwar sentiments to himself.

"My apologies to everyone." Could he be any more sarcastic?

"Oh, give it a rest."

He gives me a two-fingered salute. "So, Greg." He turns to my fiancé, and suddenly I have a premonition that leaves me wishing I'd let him continue his antiwar diatribe.

Greg swallows a sip of iced tea. "Yeah?"

"Claire tells me you two are tying the knot in a few months."

Taking my hand in a territorial move, Greg nods. "That's right."

"Congratulations. You're a lucky man."

My lungs start burning, and I realize I'm holding my breath.

"If you'll excuse me," John says, placing his napkin on the table and standing. "I believe I'll go keep the children company."

"I'll go with you." I've never seen Eli move so fast. Apparently, the older men are in no mood to see the younger men go at it like a couple of high school boys.

Jerry waits until the men are gone, then grins. "As I was saying, you're a lucky man."

"Thanks. I'd prefer to say I'm blessed." Greg's voice has taken on a defensive tone like he knows Jerry's baiting him.

"And I can most certainly see why." He just can't let it drop. Buttering a roll, Jerry continues his line of conversation, despite the fact that I'm staring him down. "So, where are you two lovebirds planning to go on your honeymoon? I hear Hawaii's popular with newlyweds."

How did he—then it dawns. I cut my gaze to Miss Lou, whose eyes have gone wide. She's staring intently at her son as though willing him to "hush, young man." I know beyond a doubt that she's shared with him a confidence I'd shared with her: that I'm being cheated out of a honeymoon in Hawaii. And I'm not one bit happy about it.

"We are planning on Hawaii." Greg clears his throat. Half-truths aren't easy for him.

"Oh? Good for you. How long will you be there? It really is a shame to stay less than two weeks."

Jerry winks at me! I can't believe it. The guy is absolutely baiting the man I love, and he has the audacity to wink at me.

I could just kick Jerry. Sort of. Another part of me is anxious to see how Greg will explain the actual honeymoon plans (the Shepherd Falls ones) to a man who is clearly flirting with me.

"Well—" Greg clears his throat "—we're not exactly going to take the trip right away."

"Oh, I'm sure. I know you'll be waiting until you get married." He gives me a conspiratorial laugh, and I swear if I were sitting next to him, he'd have given me an elbow jab. "Greg here *is* a preacher, after all. He's not likely to take a woman on a vacation unless he's married to her. Or are you?"

The muscle along Greg's jawline twitches as he bites down on his back teeth. He's fighting his irritation. We both know Jerry's alluding to the fact that we haven't slept together. And the way he's acting, it's like he's taunting Greg for not getting me into bed—or implying that there's no way we haven't—I'm not sure which. If only he knew how much we fight those physical urges. Greg keeps his cool. He's much more level-headed than I am. I want to tear into the guy. "Of course I wouldn't take her to Hawaii unless I married her first."

I guess I'd better come to his rescue. "Greg and I have decided to postpone our honeymoon so that Greg can help out a pastor whose health is failing."

"Oh, so it was your decision?" Jerry-the-Jerk.

I take in a breath, ready to lay it on thick. "As a matter of fact . . ." I open my mouth to lie about the whole thing, but somehow I can't. I just can't. It wasn't my decision. I only agreed to it because I felt guilted into it. That's the truth of the matter. And I've been hacked off at Greg ever since. It's not that I don't love him. But I'm mad. All eyes are on me to finish my sentence. Finish my defense of Greg. But I just avert my gaze and sip my Diet Pepsi.

"Of course it wasn't her decision," Greg's mom chimes in. "Greg goaded her into it."

Okay, I would have said "guilted," but "goaded" works. Helen has always been a bit of a hero to me.

"Well, it's not like she didn't agree to it, so she really has no right to complain." My mother, truly supportive. Thanks, Ma.

"Who's complaining?" I have to pipe in.

Jerry's eyes twinkle with unsuppressed mirth. I glare and stick out my tongue.

"Claire!" My mother is a traitor and therefore has no say-so in this matter.

"It's all right, Mrs. Everett. I deserved it. I must have inadvertently struck a chord here."

"Inadvertently, my eye!" I'm this close to yelling at the troublemaker. "Somehow you knew darned well I didn't want to spend my honeymoon in Shepherd Falls instead of Hawaii, and you intentionally tried to mess up my Thanksgiving dinner."

"Claire!" Mother again.

"Oh, dear." Miss Lou's voice trembles, and suddenly I feel about as low as a slug. "Maybe we should go, Jerry."

"No, Miss Lou. Please. I'm sorry. I overreacted to Jerry." (I think, *the jerk*, but don't say it.) "I want you to be here so badly. Please forgive my lack of manners. Besides, I made banana pudding for you."

Her eyes soften. "All right. We'll stay." She turns to Jerry. "Behave yourself."

I follow her gaze to her son, but he's not looking at his mother—he's looking at me. Once again with that look that is all at once tender and confused.

Greg's grip tightens on my hand. He sees the look, too.

I'm sweeping the hallway at Countryside when a dozen red roses arrive.

The nurse gives me a knowing grin as she hands them over. "Who's the guy?"

I grin. "Greg. My fiancé." Feeling proud and loved, I can't lose the cheesy grin as I slip the card out and read. My knees go weak with dread.

"Claire. You're white as a ghost. What's wrong? Did he break up with you over a dozen red roses?"

"What? No." I stare through her. "These aren't from Greg."

Her brow goes up and her mouth forms a silent O.

I don't want these roses. But I know someone who might. I stomp into Miss Teffra's room. "Miss Teffra, look at the wonderful roses Jimmy sent."

It's a risky move, because you never know if she's going to be in 1939 or present day. Luckily she's reliving her saucy glory days. "Irene! I told you he's going to pop the question tonight."

I smile. "I bet he will!"

She takes the roses and presses them to her face. "Don't tell Coot. I don't want him telling Mama before I get to."

"Cross my heart."

Miss Teffra reaches her tiny arms out to me and gives me a squeeze. "You're a good friend, Irene. The best."

I leave her to her girlhood memories. Once in the hall, I pull the card from my pocket and read it once more.

All is fair in love and war. I'm throwing my hat into the ring.

17

A week after Thanksgiving, my best friend Linda and I finally get a chance to drive the three hours to Kansas City to find me the perfect shoes to wear for the wedding. We've both been so busy, we've barely spoken in more than two weeks.

"Let me get this straight." Linda maneuvers her little Miata around Kansas City traffic like it's nothing. "You're telling me that Jerry-formerly-known-as-the-Jerk—"

"No, still a jerk."

"Okay, Jerry-the-Jerk came to dinner, needled your fiancé about everything from not having out-of-wedlock sex with you to postponing your honeymoon, and you didn't order him out of your house?"

"Well, Miss Lou was there too. I couldn't very well be rude." That's so lame. Good excuse, but still lame-o.

And Linda's not buying it. She takes her eyes off the road for a sec, just long enough to give me a look. "Last spring it was my brother."

"Your brother never came to my house for dinner and made Greg miserable."

"You know what I mean."

My defenses shoot up, along with the embarrassment that's scorching my cheeks. "Greg and I were split up when I dated Van—one time."

"Yeah, but the point is, every time Greg disappoints you, suddenly some other guy starts looking good."

"That's not true." That is about as far from reality as Oz.

"Uh, honey, yeah, it is. It's so true, you could be George Washington."

"What?"

She raises her right arm and deepens her voice, apparently channeling the first president. "I cannot tell a lie. I chopped down the cherry tree."

"Oh, brother."

"Yes, back to my brother. Last year, Greg first mentioned going to Bible college and becoming a pastor, and wham! All of a sudden you're thinking a man you would never have dated before is cute and you want to go out with him."

"Okay, first of all. It wasn't wham! It was a few weeks. And second of all, why do you think I wouldn't have ever dated him before?"

"He's five years younger than you are, for one thing."

"So what? Older women and younger men are the new thing. Look at Demi and Ashton."

"Oh, gee. Good point, Mrs. Robinson."

I can't help the laughter rising in me. "Shut up! Besides, I only went out with him once."

"And didn't even give the poor guy a little kiss at the end of the date."

"I couldn't. I was in love with Greg. It didn't feel right."

She whips the car into the turn lane and pulls onto the off-ramp. "Which is just my point. You get mad at Greg and decide you're attracted to someone else. But when push comes to shove, you don't feel at home in anyone else's arms."

"Linda!" I want to tell her she's completely wrong. So I do

my best, even though I know she's right about the "anyone else's arms" comment. "Greg and I were broken up. Van asked me out. But it was too soon, and I—okay, yes—I decided he was a little young for me when he took me to play putt-putt golf and eat chili dogs on our date. I couldn't kiss him. That's too special."

"That brother of mine." She shakes her head. "The last of the great Don Juans."

"Anyway, what does that have to do with Jerry?"

"He's the first guy you met after Greg took away your honeymoon."

"Greg didn't take it away." I hear the words, but I don't quite believe them myself. "He just postponed it."

"But you're angry. And you won't admit it." Linda pulls into a little shopping center. Ami's Shoes is dead center in a line of stores that look a little fancier than I'd have chosen. I mean, it's one thing to save for a great gown. But really, who is going to see the shoes? But Linda insists I have to find *the* perfect pair.

"You're right. I'm angry. And you know why? Because now I don't have an excuse to spend money on a tanning bed."

Now, see, normally Linda would have laughed at the clever way I diverted the focus of the conversation. But sheesh, she's like a bulldog with a juicy hambone. She just won't let it go. "Claire. I'm not kidding. You're going to have to deal with this issue, or you may as well not even buy that perfect wedding gown."

"What do you mean?"

She locks up the car, and we walk across the parking lot toward the shop. "I want you to be honest."

"I'm nothing if not honest, my girl." I raise my right hand. "I cannot tell a lie. I chopped down the cherry tree."

"Don't make jokes." That's the thing with best friends. They catch onto the crap factor pretty quickly. You can't get a thing past them.

"Fine. Be honest about what?"

"Are you one hundred percent sure you want to marry Greg?"

Never in a million years would I have expected that particular question. I'm taken aback. Outraged, really. I feel like someone's just accused me of using the mustard knife in the mayo jar. "Of course I'm sure! How can you even ask that? You know how much I love that man."

"You seem to have an awful hard time committing fully to him."

"I'm committed. What do you mean?" Now I'm honestly beginning to feel the emotional drain of the conversation. It's hitting below the belt, if you want the truth of it.

"Come on. The other guys?"

"I've never once cheated on Greg! How can you imply that?"

"I'm not talking about cheating. I'm talking about attraction."

"What attraction?"

"Oh, please."

The wedding march chimes as we open the door to the quaint little bridal boutique.

"Okay, fine." My defenses once again shoot to the surface. But I drop my tone considerably so as not to alert the entire store to our conversation—which has suddenly become a lot more personal. "Are you telling me you're never attracted to a man other than Mark?"

"I'm talking about entertaining attraction. Not split-second attraction."

"Haven't you ever heard that it's okay to window-shop as long as you don't buy the merchandise?"

The salesgirl closest to us gives me a sharp look as though I've just taken the name of shopping in vain. I send her a quick, reassuring smile. "Oh, don't worry. We're really looking for a pair of shoes for my wedding. I'm getting married in June."

"Maybe," Linda mutters.

"Stop it!"

"Let's get back to window-shopping. So that's all you were doing with Van and now Jerry?"

"Yes!" Ouch. "No!" It just sounds so wrong. And I don't believe that saying at all anyway. But she's pushing me into it, and backing down is painful for me.

"Okay. I see."

"See what?"

"Nothing." She sits on the leather loveseat the salesgirl motions to. Crossing her legs, she places her hands in her lap.

"You're driving me nuts here. You know that?" I flop down less than gracefully beside her. "What do you see?"

She turns to me slowly, and I can see in her eyes she's trying to find the right way to say this. "Claire, you need to talk to Greg. Let him know how you feel. You're so angry at him that you're building a wall. That's why it was so easy for Jerry to crash through your defenses. I think you actually like the guy."

"At least he doesn't think a guy ought to stick a woman in

a place called Shepherd Falls for her honeymoon. On Sunday morning, they're all going to know what we were doing the night before!"

Linda opens her mouth, then closes it and peers at me a bit closer. "Is that what's bothering you?"

"Partly."

"But no one cares about that. Half of them will have done it the night before too!"

"I know, but it's embarrassing to think of Greg up there preaching while all anyone can think about is what the newlyweds did last night in the parsonage."

"Ew. I see your point. Still, I think you're focusing on a detour to keep your mind off the real problem."

"Which is?"

"That you don't know for sure if you want to marry Greg."

For the next two weeks, all I can think about is that stupid comment. During my extra-early walks with the twins, I think about it. When I'm sitting on the couch with Ollie's big head in my lap, watching a movie, I'm distracted by Linda's words.

While I'm Christmas shopping, I wonder, *Is she right? Do I want to marry Greg?* Then guilt edges through me. I love him. How can I even consider that Linda might be right? But all of those doubts from last year seem to be creeping in again. Surely this isn't just about a dumb trip to Hawaii. I don't know. I just don't know.

"All right, Claire. Time to spill the beans." Miss Lou wheels herself up to the Christmas tree I'm putting together for the sitting room, a beautiful room with vaulted ceilings and a wall-length fireplace. It's my day off, but I thought it might do the kids some good to think about someone else at this time of year. I'd never realized how many old folks get stashed away and hardly ever visited, if at all, by their families.

"What do you mean? Spill the beans about what?"

"You haven't been yourself lately, and I'm tired of waiting around for you to open up on your own."

I slide another branch into the fake trunk. "Just a lot to think about with this wedding."

"Hmmm."

I decide it's best to just let that comment go.

Miss Lou seems to be enjoying her new home at Countryside. She has a downstairs efficiency apartment and is able to cook for herself if she chooses. Of course, she also has Jerry. And he has been visiting pretty consistently.

Sidebar: I've been doing my best to ignore him. But it's not so easy. He calls; he sends cards. He makes me laugh.

And I am wondering if maybe he's behind Miss Lou's question. I hate to be suspicious, but she's made no secret of the fact that she'd like Jerry to come out the victor in this little triangle we seem to be caught in.

Anyway, back to my kids, the elderly, and Christmas. The kids and I are spending the Saturday before Christmas helping the residents decorate their Christmas tree and fill out Christmas cards. Many of them don't have anyone to send a card to. Neither have they received Christmas cards in years.

So we—well, Ari, really—devised a plan. The girls at the teen pregnancy center are sending cards to the residents of Countryside, and the residents are sending cards, too. And that's where we come in. Many of the elderly men and women have trouble seeing small print or writing cards. So we've divided into teams. Jake, Sadie, Tommy (yes, even Tommy), and Shawn are here with me, and we've assigned them partners among the residents. Ari and the girls are over at the teen pregnancy center, filling out their cards.

"Look at that crazy woman!"

I focus my attention on Miss Teffra. "Look at who?" And isn't Miss Teffra calling anyone "crazy" sort of like the pot calling the kettle black?

Miss Lou and Miss Teffra are sitting at a little card table that's been set up in the sitting room. Miss Lou is helping Miss Teffra with her cards. Most days, Miss Lou does okay, although sometimes she has trouble with memory since the coma.

Miss Teffra smirks toward Miss Georgia Anderson. The plump African American woman never wears her dentures. And she perpetually talks to her dead husband, Will. She shuffles over to us and gives me her toothless grin. "Can you believe it's Christmastime again?"

Without waiting for an answer, she whips around to her left. "Well, if you don't like it, you don't have to stay in here. I want to help decorate the tree."

"Is Will giving you a hard time again, Miss Georgia?"

"Oh, you know that man never has liked Christmas." She gives an affectionate shake of her head and stares toward the doorway as if watching him leave the room.

Miss Teffra grins and winks at me. I suppress a giggle. It's been a couple of days since she's called me Irene, and I sort of miss the adventures we share together. Last time it was the county fair with who else but Jimmy and Coot.

Sadie and Jake enter the room, and the ladies light up.

"We're done with cards, Claire," Greg's daughter says. "Can we help you?"

"You sure can. Where are the other two boys?"

"Talking to Mr. Bridges."

Mr. Bridges is a Korean War vet and spins the kinds of tales about real life that I should be so lucky to write about. I'm glad the boys are taking an interest.

"Here, you can put the last two branches in." I hand each of the kids a branch, thankful there are two left. Sadie takes it grudgingly. She's trying. I know that. But sometimes she just doesn't know if she likes me or not. To be honest, I see Sadie far too little. She and Greg's mother often stay in Tulsa when he visits because Sadie has music and dance on Saturdays. This is Christmas vacation, though, so they're all home for the week. I asked Greg to let her stay with us some this week. It's been hard to really forge a relationship with the little girl, and last year we had our troubles. She still resents me, I know, for dividing Greg's love and loyalty. But she'll learn soon enough that no one takes the place of Daddy's little girl. And she is getting better. I nod at the beautiful child.

"Okay, now you two can help me by holding onto the lights and following me around the tree so they don't get tangled."

"Lights are my department." I glance up at the sound of Greg's voice, and my heart jumps. He sheds his leather jacket and holds out his hands. "Hand them over, woman, and let a man do his job."

I lift my face for his kiss. "Gladly. But first, meet the ladies."

He gives them a grin. "Hello, ladies."

"This is Miss Georgia."

She ducks her head shyly. "Pleased to meet you, Greg. I sure wish you could have met my William. He just left."

"Maybe next time." Greg smiles tenderly and pats the woman on the arm. I've given him the lowdown on all the residents, so he knows William is in Georgia's mind.

"This is Miss Teffra."

She puts her hands firmly on her hips and shakes her head. "Good grief, Irene. I think I know my own brother. Coot, does Mama know you're at the dance?"

Greg's face registers surprise only for a second. He sends her a conspiratorial wink. "You going to tell her?"

The wonderful old lady howls with laughter. "I won't tell on you if you don't tell on me."

"It's a deal."

"Good. Now leave me alone before someone thinks you're my date. There are too many soldiers to pick from for you to hang around."

"Where's Jimmy?" Curious, I step up.

She glowers. "As if you didn't know. How can you be so mean?"

"I'm sorry, Teffra." Oh good grief, what have I done?

She shakes her head. "Oh, no. I'm the one who's sorry. I know it's hard to remember that he's gone sometimes."

I swallow hard. Jimmy, gone? So young?

"This war." She spits the words with venom. "We'd have gotten married if only the war hadn't killed him."

Oh, my goodness. I toss a glance to Greg. We're so blessed to be in love and together. Nothing can tear us apart. I can't help but think of Rick and Darcy. With Rick preparing to go to Kuwait after the first of the year, I know Darcy's frantic with worry and sorrow.

"Daddy! Are you going to string the lights?" Sadie's insistent voice breaks through the tension and I'm grateful for the distraction. Her child's voice snaps Teffra out of it, too. She reaches out and pats Sadie's cheek. "Darling child." Then she raises her eyes to Greg and holds out her frail, veiny hand. "I don't believe we've met. I'm Teffra."

Later that night, staring at me from across the booth in Red Lobster, our favorite spot, Greg smiles and takes my hand. "It's nice to have a few minutes alone."

"Just think. In a few months we'll be together all the time."

He nods. "I felt so sorry for Miss Teffra today."

"I've been learning her story in sequence. It feels odd to know that Jimmy's gone. Weird as it seems, I feel the loss."

From the corner of my eye, I'm aware someone has stopped next to our table. I glance up, fully prepared to refuse another glass of Diet Coke. Instead, I look into the humor-filled eyes of Jerry Calloway.

"Look at you two, holding hands across the table. You're just as cute as two peas in a pod."

Greg's posture straightens, but he keeps a firm grip on my hands. The hands-off body lingo is cute, but it means I'm leaning a little bit forward and having to maneuver to keep my shirt from ending up in the buttery sauce from my shrimp scampi.

"Jerry." I swallow back a biting comment about stalking laws and force a polite smile. "Nice to see you."

"Here, allow me." He reaches down and takes my dish, scooting it out of harm's way.

Greg realizes he almost pulled me into the butter and lets go of my hands, his face a little bit red.

"So, Jerry. What are you doing?"

"I'm waiting for my date to come back from the ladies' room." A boyish grin plays at the corners of his lips. I try not to stare. "Amazing what driving a Jag does for a man's love life."

I can't help but smile at him. That self-deprecating humor of his hits its mark every time.

His amused gaze peruses my face. Greg shifts, and I know he's fuming.

"There you are, Jerry." A husky female voice invades my space. I tense before I even follow the voice to her. "I was looking for you."

And there she is. Just the kind of woman you'd expect Jerry to date. Tall, leggy, stacked like a can of Pringles, and wearing a tight shirt that is so low-cut that it doesn't leave much to the imagination.

Jerry's hand slides across her back and encircles her tiny waist. "Claire, Greg, this is Maizy."

Well, of course she is. I smile. "Nice to meet you, Maizy." Nice to meet her, my foot. And I'm not jealous, either.

"You too," she says with unconcealed boredom before turning her attention to Jerry. "Should we go back to our seat so our waitress doesn't think we left?"

"I suppose so. It was nice seeing you two."

"Nice seeing you."

I turn to Greg. He's staring at Maizy all right. But obviously sensing my movement, he quickly averts his gaze.

A jolt of jealousy slices through me. I know it's hypocritical, considering that Jerry's forcing a triangle in this relationship, but I'm powerless against it. I don't want Greg looking at any other women. No window-shopping for my man.

"Are you ready to go?"

Greg nods. Slipping a few bills into the black folder our server left on the table, Greg slides out of the booth. With a jerky movement, he grabs my coat and waits while I slide my arms through. All of a sudden, he's acting angry. *He's* angry? If anyone has a right to be mad, it's me, after the way he was gawking at Jerry's date.

He ushers me through the restaurant, his body language full of attitude. Once we get outside, he whips around. "What is going on with you and that guy?"

"Nothing."

"Don't give me that, Claire. He couldn't keep his eyes off of you, and you were jealous of that woman he was with."

"Of course I was jealous. Because *you* were gawking at her, you ignoramus."

And suddenly I realize how true that statement is. I couldn't care less if Jerry goes out with anyone. He can date Angelina Jolie, for all I care. The anger has sifted from me. I step closer to Greg and put my arms around his waist.

"Jerry can date all the Maizys in the world. I only want you, Greg."

He lowers his head, and right there in the parking lot of Red Lobster, while the cars whiz by on the busy street, Greg kisses me, taking my breath away and firmly ridding my mind of anyone but him.

18

Christmas Eve blows in with a few flurries. Not like last year when we had major snow. I'll always treasure last Christmas in my heart, for a couple of reasons: I forgave Rick for his part in the breakup of our marriage. And I got my first kiss from Greg.

Technically the kids should be spending Christmas Day with me this year, but we all agree that since Rick is going to be gone for up to eighteen months, I should be the bigger person and give up Christmas Day with the kids, especially since I got the unexpected fun of having them for Thanksgiving (even if Darcy and Rick came too). Giving Rick this holiday is the least I can do—this is Lyddie's first Christmas, and it's important to all of them to be together. I feel the pain of it. But it's the right thing.

So here we are . . . Greg, Sadie, Ari, Tommy, Shawn, Jake, and me, getting ready to have our Christmas together before Rick comes over and picks them up. We've just finished a nice gumbo dinner, and now the kids are popping with excitement as they sit around the tree. They'll each open two gifts tonight. And one extra little gift I always buy for each—an ornament to hang on the tree. This is Ari's eighteenth ornament. Every year I watch the kids line their ornaments up before they hang them on the tree, starting with each Baby's First Christmas. I always cry when I see those.

This year is extra special because Greg and Sadie are with us. And I've bought Sadie her first annual ornament.

And so the unwrapping begins.

"Thanks, Mom!" Jake is thrilled to get his new Shrek ornament.

Everyone is happy, and I pass out hooks so they can do as they traditionally do: hang the new ornament.

I pass Sadie her hook, but she shakes her head. "I'll wait and hang it on my tree at home."

A little pain clutches my heart. I truly wanted her to accept the gesture as my way of welcoming her as my child. "But I thought you'd like to hang it on this tree."

She shakes her head. I'm confused. I saw her face when she opened the princess fairy. Awe and joy. So what's the deal?

Greg clears his throat, and I expect him to back me up. Instead, when I meet his gaze, I discover he is shaking his head at *me*.

Well, I'm not happy, but I'm not going to make an issue of it on Christmas.

"Oh, just put it on the tree." Tommy always speaks to her like he'd like to smack her.

"I don't have to," Sadie shoots back, scowling fiercely.

"My mom shouldn't have ever gotten you one, you ungrateful brat."

"Tommy!" No matter if I sort of agree, I can't sit back and allow the insults to start flying.

"Well, she is. I know you had that stupid thing special ordered with her name on it just so she'd know you want her in the family."

Greg's face softens toward me. "Sadie, maybe you could hang it on Claire's tree."

She clutches the box to her chest. "I want to show Grammy," she whispers. "She's never seen one like this with wings."

My heart lifts. So she does like the ornament. "Greg, it's okay. Let her take it. Next year we'll all be a family and she can put it on our tree."

The doorbell rings just as the kids are finishing up their three-gift maximum for Christmas Eve. Still, I'm not ready to let them go. "That can't be Rick yet. He wasn't supposed to come for another couple of hours."

Ari stands and heads for the door. "It's Paddy. We're going to his parents' for a little Christmas get-together."

"What? You didn't ask permission."

"Dad said I could be late to his house so that I could spend a little time with Paddy. I didn't think you'd mind. We're finished here, aren't we?"

Doesn't she realize that this is her last Christmas as a high school girl? That this is our last Christmas as the five musketeers?

"Please, Mom?"

"But you're going to miss watching *White Christmas* with us."

"I know, but . . ."

One look into her pleading eyes and I'm beaten. She's a young woman in love, and her first thoughts aren't going to be of her mom and my traditions anymore.

"Fine." I grab her in a hug and she hugs me back tightly. "Have fun."

"Thanks, Mom. Paddy's going to drop me off at Daddy's. Will you make sure Daddy takes my bag?"

"Just put it by the door."

I stand by the door as she leaves. Greg encircles me from behind. "You handled that like a real grownup."

I can't help but laugh.

"You ready to open your present from me?"

I grin. "I thought you'd never ask."

Turns out my gift from Greg is wonderful. The kids are nearly popping with excitement as he lifts it from against a wall behind the tree.

I tear into gold Christmas wrap. My breath catches in my throat as the paper slips away revealing the masterpiece inside. "Oh, Greg. It's perfect."

"You didn't guess?" Shawn asks. "Really?"

"I had no idea." I am staring at a beautiful framed painting of my children . . . all of them, including Sadie. I turn to Greg. "How did you pull this off without my knowing?"

"I can't tell you all my secrets now, can I?"

In spite of our audience, I slip my arms around him and pull him close. "As long as your secrets are nice and fuzzy, like this one, I look forward to unwrapping them one by one."

It's an evening to remember. But as Christmas always does, it ends much too soon, leaving just a tiny feeling of letdown.

I stare at the painting long after Greg and Sadie go home. Long after Rick comes to retrieve our children. Once again, unbidden and definitely unwelcome, doubt scrambles my brain. Why doesn't the painting seem right?

On January 15, Rick's unit was officially called up to active duty. He's gone now, staying at Fort Leonard Wood, an army base thirty miles from our hometown. He'll be there two weeks for training and squaring things away medically, and should have one weekend at home before shipping out to

Texas, where he'll train for another couple of weeks before deploying to Kuwait for eighteen months.

Darcy finally went to the doctor and is taking medicine to help with postpartum depression. I'm happy for her. Glad that she took that step and got help. But it does sort of create a problem for me. She's happy again, so she wants to come out and play. Or in this case, run my wedding.

"Are you paying attention, Claire?"

Her voice cuts through my thoughts, and I force my gaze away from the window, where the snow is just beginning to fall outside. "I'm listening. Rhonda Barker's dress was made by someone in Springfield, and I should have mine made, too."

"That's right."

"I saw that dress, Darce. It looked like something out of a bad Civil War movie."

"For heaven's sake. It did not."

I give her a raised-eyebrow look.

"Okay, maybe it did a little. But it's a lot cheaper than the one you want. And you could quit dog walking and working at the old folks' home. You need to start concentrating on your wedding or you're not going to get everything done in time."

"I like my jobs, believe it or not. And I almost have enough paid down to start making the alterations."

"Well, let's at least go look at guest books and cake servers."

"Not today. I'm expecting a call from Bonnie."

"Claire. You promised I could help."

"No, seriously. A publisher is talking about my proposal, and Bonnie thinks we'll know if they want to buy it by the end of the day."

She lights up. "That's wonderful! Congratulations."

"Well, it's nothing to congratulate me for just yet." But maybe if God still loves me . . .

"It will be."

"So how are you holding up with Rick being gone?"

With a shrug, she attempts bravado. But Darcy's no good at concealing her emotions, and her lip quivers. "Oh, Claire. I don't think I can manage on my own."

"What? Of course you can. I did."

Practically before the words are out, I know I shouldn't have said them.

"Rick isn't leaving me because he wants to. He's being forced to."

Doesn't she realize how that stings? How even though I don't love him and have moved on with my life, the fact that he grew tired of me and moved on to someone else still makes me feel worthless?

"Well, you're not going to be any less alone than I was," I snap.

"I'm sorry, Claire. I didn't mean to be insensitive. I just mean I won't have anger to keep me strong."

"You'll have Lydia. Honestly, Darce. My so-called strength wasn't from anger as much as it was from a need to take care of the kids. Also, don't forget: I wasn't a Christian for the first couple of years after our divorce. You have God to be your strength."

"And I have you and the kids."

"That's right. We'll all be here for you."

"And I'll be there for the kids. Maybe we'll finally have something in common."

Something in her tone alerts my senses. "What do you mean? You get along great with the kids."

"I know. They're respectful. But you know they don't really like me."

"Oh, Darcy. Of course they like you. They love you."

"You think so?"

Um. Maybe. They don't really say anything against her. More like they just don't talk about her much. "Honestly, every kid wants their parents to be together. But they care a lot about you. You're good to them."

"Thanks, Claire." She sounds dubious, but I guess decides to let it go.

Ollie walks into the room and plops his enormous head on my lap.

"Need to go out? Go get your leash while I get my coat."

Darcy shakes her head in amazement. "I can't believe how smart that dog is. Maybe I should get a dog to keep us safe while Rick's away."

Now that she mentions it, I have felt a lot safer since bringing Ollie into the family.

"Might not hurt." I clip Ollie's leash and pat his head. "Mastiffs are great family dogs, and they don't have to be aggressive because people are intimidated by their sheer size."

"I don't suppose you want to get rid of Ollie."

"Not a chance." I grin. "First of all, he belongs to Miss Lou. And even though it's unlikely she'll ever be able to keep him again, I take him to see her once a week. She needs the illusion of still owning him."

"I understand." Resting her elbow on the table, she jams her chin into her hand. "I wonder where I can get one."

Apparently Darcy has no intention of leaving just because I have go out for awhile to walk Ollie. I glance at her with more fondness than I ever thought possible. "We won't be long with the snow falling. Ollie might be intimidating, but he's a big baby when it comes to weather."

We return twenty minutes later, and Darcy is talking on my phone. When I open the door, she whips around and frantically motions me over. "Wait, here she is now." She shoves the phone into my hand and snatches Ollie's leash.

"Hello?"

"Claire? It's Bonnie."

My stomach flops.

"Hi, Bonnie." I wait. I don't say, so how are you? Because we both know she didn't call to shoot the breeze. Finally I cut to the chase. "So?"

"Good news."

Amazing how much power two little words can have. Darcy is standing there, still holding onto Ollie's leash. "Well?" she whispers.

I give her the thumbs-up and don't bother to try to hide my smile.

"Hallelujah!" she whisper-shouts.

My agent talks about all the excitement for the project at my new publishing house. Then she lays out the terms of the contract that will be forthcoming if I agree to the financial aspect, which is in the upper five figures for three books. Three times as much as I've ever gotten for a book, to be honest. Methinks I'm taking the kids out for pizza and a movie tonight! I glance at my number-one cheerleader. I guess I'll invite her to go along too. After all, she *is* family.

And you know, she really is.

I'm finishing up my shift when Jerry shows up at Countryside. My stomach does a flip-flop. I'm almost sure it has more to do with my determination to avoid him than the actual sight of him. I have successfully evaded him since the night Greg and I saw him at Red Lobster three weeks ago. But there's no getting out of it this time. I'm trapped.

I slip my cart into the janitorial closet and head down the hall as he's coming up.

"Ah, what luck. You're off work."

"Hi, Jerry." I'm trying hard not to notice how great he looks and smells.

"How about letting me take you out to dinner?"

"My fiancé may not like that."

"Come on, Claire. A harmless little dinner. You pick the place."

"No thanks." Man, why am I so tempted?

He pulls me aside as the resident sweethearts shuffle past, so deep in conversation they don't even notice we're there. Kitty and Lewis Bridges are one of those couples who have weathered just about every storm life has to blow. They were married before he went to Korea. They survived war and out-lived half a dozen kids. And I've never seen two people more in love.

"Aren't they something?" Jerry asks, a quirky grin curving his lips.

"They sure are."

"What do you think are the odds of someone actually find-ing what they have together in today's world?"

I smile after them. "I think the odds are pretty much the same as back then. It depends on commitment, mutual love, and respect. He loves her more than I've ever seen a man love a woman. It's truly like something out of a romance novel."

"One of yours?" He grins.

I can't help but laugh. "Not even I could make up something so real and pure."

His face goes sober. "So where have you been? I haven't seen you around."

"I've been here." Hiding every time I know he's coming to visit Miss Lou.

"Hiding from me?" He stuffs his hands into the front pockets of his business slacks.

"Maybe." I press my lips together at the surprised expression that springs to his eyes.

"Why? What did I do?" He reaches out and captures my elbow. "Claire, what did I do?"

"Nothing. Let's just say I'm hoping I've found what Lewis and Miss Kitty have."

"With Greg?"

"Of course. Who else? You?"

"Maybe."

"Maizy might have something to say about that."

"Oh, come on. You know she was just a date. And boring. I almost fell asleep before my lobster arrived."

"Well, I don't suppose you asked her out for the dinner conversation, did you?"

"Okay, enough about Maizy. I want to talk about us."

"Us?" I give him a laugh, trying for a tone that's mocking and slightly condescending. Instead it comes out a little shrill—a telltale sign he's making me nervous.

He towers above me, so close I can feel the warmth of him, smell the musky scent of aftershave. Reaching out, he touches his index finger to the bottom of my throat. "Your breathing has picked up. Don't tell me there is no 'us.'"

"Don't mistake physical attraction for the real thing, Jerry."

"Physical attraction works for me." He dips his head, and I have half a second to make a decision.

I duck and move away just in time to avoid his kiss. "It doesn't work for me."

"You'd rather be with a man who doesn't love you enough to make sure you have a honeymoon?"

"That's none of your business!"

Stepping close to me again, he wraps his hands around my upper arms and stares down into my eyes. "I don't leave for Japan for a full month. Come to Hawaii with me. It wouldn't be a honeymoon, but I could show you a good time. Who knows what it could turn into? I know you feel the same attraction for me that I feel for you."

"Jerry," I pull away from him. "I'd rather have a sure thing with Greg in Shepherd Falls than what you're proposing in a tropical paradise."

"You didn't deny feeling the attraction."

"Remember Lewis and Miss Kitty?"

An amused frown crosses his face. "Okay, I'll bite. Yes, I remember them."

"Do you think they've been married sixty-five years and have never felt drawn to anyone else?"

"I don't know. Want me to call them back here and find out?"

Mr. Sarcastic. "Very funny."

"I'm sorry. Please continue."

"My point is that while I do find you more than a little bit attractive, I'm in love with Greg. And I would never do anything to jeopardize my relationship with him. Not for a whole year in Hawaii."

"Point taken."

"Good." Finally. Relief floods me. "I'm going to go see your mother, and then I'm going home. Greg is coming tonight and we have plans."

"Oh, you're going to see my mom?"

"Yes, she's not feeling well."

"Nothing serious?"

"A cold, I think."

"I'll walk with you to her room."

I send him a sideways glance.

"No objections to that, I hope?" he says, total innocence.

"Why? Should there be?"

"Yes. I can think of a very good reason there should be objections." He grins.

"And what's that?"

"There's still a month before I leave, and I don't give up very easily."

19

Jerry's not kidding. By the next afternoon, my house is filled with flowers. Tropical flowers that probably cost him a mint. A nice sight in January, but disconcerting when he sends them every day for two weeks. He's determined that I not forget about him.

As if I could. As often as he can swing the time, he shows up at work just as I'm leaving for the day. He follows me around while I gather my things and then walks me to the car. I admit it's flattering to be pursued, but I'm starting to feel like a rat for finding enjoyment in the whole thing.

"I mean it, Jerry. I'm marrying Greg, and he's going to be awfully ticked if you don't stop sending me flowers."

"Going to be?" Humor zings from his voice. "I'd have been ticked a long time ago."

I can't help but smile. "Well, he has been."

"Is he going to come after me?" Jerry shifts his gaze around like a B actor in a C horror flick.

Normally, I'd have smacked his arm. But I have a strict hands-off policy where Jerry is concerned, and hitting in jest can become a form of foreplay. "Idiot. I mean it. No more flowers. I won't accept them."

Next day, a package arrives with chocolates in a heart-shaped box.

The card: *Okay, no more flowers.*

Greg's not a bit happy about the situation, but the kids are on a major sugar high.

Linda isn't amused. She really isn't. We're sitting in Churchill's with our mocha lattes and blueberry muffins, and she's frowning as I tell her all about the third day of chocolates. "I swear, Linda, if Jerry doesn't stop with the chocolates, I'm going to be so fat he won't want me anyway."

"Who cares what Jerry wants? What's Greg saying about all of this?"

"Not much." Which upsets me a little. I mean, if a woman was going after him, I'd be all over her like white on rice. I would. She'd know right away to get her claws out of my guy. "I mean, he calls every night to see if I got something else from Jerry. And I can tell he's not happy about it, but all he's ever asked me is 'Does he know we're engaged?' Which he does."

"Does Greg realize the extent of Jerry's pursuit?"

I shrug and sip my coffee.

"Well? Does he?"

"All right. Probably not. But that's his fault for not being more curious about it."

"Maybe he just trusts you."

"Maybe."

"You *did* tell him about Jerry inviting you to Hawaii, didn't you?"

Heat rushes to my cheeks, and I look away at a fascinating little leaf printed on the tablecloth.

"Claire! Oh my gosh. How could you keep that from your fiancé? No wonder he isn't any more concerned than he is. He doesn't know Jerry's trying to steal you away."

"Then he's about the biggest ignoramus that ever walked

the face of the earth," I explode back, "because the guy is sending me flowers and candy. Hello? What does that say? Romance!"

"Well, you're going to have to put a stop to it before you lose the man you love." She peers closer at me. "Unless Jerry is the man you love and not Greg anymore."

"Don't be ridiculous."

Her red eyebrow lifts. (Linda's the only natural redhead I've ever known besides her brother, Van, whose hair was actually more auburn.) "Are you enjoying this attention a little too much?"

How can she even ask such a thing? Or is she right? No! I firmly push the thought aside. "I'm in love with Greg. I'm marrying Greg. It's just not fair that Jerry is the one pursuing me like a man on a mission."

"I was going to say a dog after a juicy steak."

"Thanks. Anyway, what I meant was it's not fair that he's being so attentive and Greg hardly remembers to call except to ask if Jerry sent me more chocolates."

"Isn't he working hard trying to finish up the semester so he can marry you and take over at the church for the summer?"

"Yes. And I know he's busy. You don't have to remind me. I'm just lonesome for some attention from him."

"Look, Claire. Love isn't always going to be about being pursued. You already let Greg catch you. Now are you going to let him keep you, or is he going to have to fight for you every time some guy thinks you're cute?"

"So it's my fault now that Jerry won't cut it out?"

"Is it?"

Anger at the injustice of her accusation shoots through me like a jolt of electricity.

"Are you saying I'm sending 'come hither, Jerry' signals?"

"Don't be mad. Just think about it honestly."

"I've told him a hundred times to stop. He's relentless."

"And you like it."

"Oh, all right. Sheesh. It's flattering, and I'm flattered. Wouldn't you be?"

Linda falls silent as our server takes our empty plates. We smile at the perky brunette, then go all serious again as soon as she walks away.

"I might be flattered, Claire. But I wouldn't be sending out the message that I want him to keep it up."

"I'm not." Methinks the lady doth protest too much.

"Look, girlie. Unless this Jerry guy is a stalker and dangerous, you can make him stop. Most people will see reason if you're serious about reasoning with them. The question you have to answer is: Do you really want him to stop?"

When the weekend arrives, I'm more than ready to prove to Greg that I love him and only him. The kids are with Darcy for the weekend, helping her cope with loneliness and giving me some time to spend alone with Greg. I order in Chinese and we rent *The Quiet Man.*

Over coffee, I confess Jerry's relentless pursuit. The one thing I leave out is Jerry's proposition and invitation to Hawaii—only because I don't want Greg to feel bad about the honeymoon.

Even without that revelation, his face reddens and his eyes flash with anger. "He's still sending you gifts and flowers?"

"Mostly candy these days."

"Are you interested in this guy?"

My shoulders rise and fall. "The attention is flattering. Can I admit that without you going ballistic?"

He scowls. "Do you know how hard it is being so far away and knowing some guy is pursing the woman I love?"

"I didn't think you cared that much." My lip quivers and I feel myself about to cry.

"I don't care?" He grips my hand. "I've had to put it out of my mind because it drives me crazy. How can I compete with a guy like that? I just have to trust that you love me."

He stands and puts a CD in the player. Louis Armstrong's timeless voice fills the room in his classic "I Only Have Eyes for You." Greg holds out his hand.

"Are you kidding me?" I ask. We've never danced before. Never.

A smile tips the corners of his sensuous lips as though he's read my mind. "It's time, don't you think?"

Without breaking the gaze, I slip my hand into his and he pulls me to my feet. The second his arm goes around me, I feel the weight leave my shoulders. Closing my eyes, I rest my head against his chest as he moves me to the music.

"You never told me you could dance," I whisper.

"You never asked."

His lips brush the top of my head. I could definitely stay here forever, with the pressure of the world firmly pushed from my mind and my ears tuned only to the sound of Greg's heartbeat.

"So, this Jerry guy. Am I going to have to punch him out to get him to stop wooing you?"

20

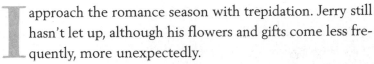

I approach the romance season with trepidation. Jerry still hasn't let up, although his flowers and gifts come less frequently, more unexpectedly.

My routine goes something like this: get up, get the kids off to school, walk Ollie, pray, and have devotions. Mondays are spent with the writing group (and I say "writing group" loosely) at Countryside. The rest of the week, I write on my newly contracted book.

I tackle the new book, *Brandi's World*, with renewed vigor and zeal, an excitement I haven't experienced in quite some time. I have to recognize that God took me through that dry time writing-wise to teach me to rely on Him. I guess I'd reached the point where I was cranking out the same-old, same-old just to make a living, instead of allowing words of life to flow from God's heart to my hands to the reader's life.

Don't you think sometimes we want the easy way out? And even though "easy" is nice in the short-term, the long-term lessons are so much more valuable. They make us tougher, more real. Battle scars prove we've been in the fight and survived. As a writer, the battle makes me more able to relate to the struggles of my readers. To paraphrase the words of the magnificent Maya Angelou, "I wouldn't trade my journey."

I drive out to Countryside on Monday, February 13, full of

nervous expectation. Jerry leaves for Japan on Friday, so I know this is my last chance to see him.

As much as I hate to admit it, I'm looking for that gorgeous black Jag as I pull into the drive. In its absence, I try to convince myself that I'm not disappointed. But it's no use. I can't even drum up a good denial. I'm definitely bummed.

I stop in to see Miss Lou during my coffee break about mid-morning. I bend and kiss her cheek. Her hip is fully healed now—has been for a while—but she's stopped hinting at moving home. I think, all in all, she's enjoying her life at Countryside. "Have you heard from Jerry?" I have to pat myself on the back. I actually sound pretty nonchalant.

Miss Lou looks up sharply. Okay, maybe not so nonchalant. "He's busy today. I'm not expecting to see him before Thursday evening. That company of his has him running hither and yon, making sure everything is all set for him to go to Japan. I don't know how they think they'll get by without him." Said like a true proud mama.

Thursday evening. After I'm gone for the day. I know it's for the best. Part of me is extremely relieved that all this will soon be over. "I see. Well, tell him I said good-bye, will you?"

"I sure will, hon."

My break is just about over when Annie, the day nurse, walks in carrying something that looks suspiciously like a box of flowers. I hold my breath, and my heart picks up. I recognize the name of the flower shop. Did Jerry—?

"Miss Lou, you have a secret admirer."

Disappointment. That's the wretched emotion coursing through me as Annie hands the old woman the box that should have been mine!

Miss Lou lifts her glasses from where they hang from a

chain around her neck. She reads and chuckles. Then she hands the card over to me.

Red roses for the woman in my life. I love you, Mom. Jerry.

Oh, yes. That sounds sweet, doesn't it? Until the P.S: *Tell Claire not to be jealous. Hers will be at home when she arrives.*

"Jealous?" Outraged, I hop to my feet and head for the door. After all, I have work to do. "I'll have you know, I have a perfectly wonderful fiancé who is . . . perfect."

"Don't take it to heart so. Jerry's nothing but a big tease, Claire." Miss Lou pats my hand to calm me. The action only adds to my humiliation and discomfiture.

I gather a steadying breath and smile. How could such a jerk have a mom like Lou? She must have spoiled him. "I'm all right. I know he's just teasing, but you have no idea how he's turned my life upside down."

"He's crazy about you." She speaks softly, and I jerk my head around. Her gray head inclines. "He told me a week ago."

"I'm engaged to be married, Miss Lou. To the man of my dreams."

"I know, honey. My Jerry isn't the man for you."

She's right about that!

"He isn't ready to settle down." She grins. "But you're the first woman he's told me anything about in ten years."

And who was that other woman?

Never mind. I don't give a rip.

"Lisa. I don't recall her last name right off. Oh, darn my memory. I used to know her name."

"It's all right, Miss Lou. You don't have to tell me her last name. This Lisa . . . he loved her?"

"Who?"

Poor Miss Lou. Her lapses of memory are getting more and

more frequent. I motion for Annie, who is standing at the door.

"Don't forget your flowers, Miss Lou."

"Oh, are these mine? How lovely."

Okay, when Jerry said, "Claire's are at home," I pictured the same flowers he sent his mom. The toying-with-Claire flowers. I was in no way prepared for the sight that greets me when I pull into my drive. Baskets and baskets of flowers fill my porch and line my front walk. I have everything from roses to lilies to one lone basket of beautiful orchids—my favorites.

But enough is enough!

I yank out my cell phone. I'm calling him and putting an end to all of this madness.

My fingers sting with the force of my number punching. Ring. Ring. Ring. Darn it. Voice mail.

"This is Jerry. Leave a message—or don't. I couldn't care less."

Figures, he has a stupid sarcastic voice mail message.

"Jerry, I hate every single flower. Leave me alone. I'm marrying Greg, and that's all there is to it. And if you don't stop sending me flowers I'm going to get a restraining order. Which I probably should have done weeks ago. I don't know what you're trying to prove—"

My time runs out. Shoot.

I stomp upstairs to my office and tackle my book with a vengeance, a perfect outlet for my stress. By the time the kids arrive home from school at three thirty, I've figured out what to do with my flowers.

"Ari, will you and the boys load up my van with those flowers, please?"

"I take it they're not from Greg?"

"What do you think?"

Her rosebud lips twist into a smile she's trying to hide. "That Jerry must really like you."

"He just wants to annoy me."

"Yeah, Mom," Tommy pipes in. "I know when I really want to tick a girl off, I just send her a few hundred flowers and that usually gets rid of her."

"Oh, sure, you have all the answers, don't you? After all, you *are* fifteen now."

"Do I have to help?" Jake asks. My youngest son is on his knees in front of the entertainment center, reaching for the shelf with his Xbox.

"Yes, you have to help. Where's Shawn?"

"At Mr. Wells's."

"Oh, yeah." Mondays after school are when Shawn has his private lessons with John Wells.

In no time, the flowers are loaded.

"Ari, stay with Jakey, will you? Tommy and I are going to take these over to the teen pregnancy center."

Her eyes light. "Good idea, Mom. They're going to love that."

"Come on, Toms." I toss him the keys. "Here, do you want to drive?"

We slide in and I buckle extra tight.

The girls are flush with excitement as we unload the van. They run out and begin to help.

"Look at all of these!"

"Well, I couldn't think of letting Valentine's Day pass without all of you getting some lovely flowers."

The director steps forward with a twinkly-eyed grin. Susan

Fine is a cute, plump, motherly woman of forty-five who has never been married, never had children, but has more of a heart for these girls than their own parents. "Ari called to let me know you were coming. I can't even imagine having a man line my walk with flowers. Why aren't you more excited?"

My face warms. I need to have another talk with Ari about telling family secrets. The last one was when she was five and told her teacher all about the fight she overheard about Daddy's girlfriend. Her teacher was extremely sympathetic with me—as were the rest of the teachers in the school—the ones Ari's teacher had spread my humiliation to.

I set down a basket of lilies and turn to her with a dubious smile. "Wrong man."

21

Remember how it doesn't usually bother me to wake up early on holidays because I want to squeeze every extra minute from the day? Well, it *does* bother me to wake up at all this Valentine's Day, and I wake up wishing it were just over. Greg can't make it home from Tulsa because he has school, so no romantic dinner out for me. The alarm buzzes in my ear, and I'm royally ticked off. I hate waking up mad. Even the smell of Folgers brewing downstairs doesn't give me a "best part of waking up" moment. I'm still grouchy. And I'm powerless to do anything about it. Until the phone rings a few minutes later—after I've poured my first cup of coffee and sat at the table to sip it while Ollie begs me with his eyes. He knows I'm not going anywhere without at least one strong cup of coffee coursing through my veins.

When the phone rings, he gives up and flops down in his spot at the corner of the kitchen.

"Hello?"

"Good morning, valentine."

My heart picks up at the sound of Greg's voice, and waves of relief wash over me. Relief that he's remembered today. That he called me and helped me start my day knowing I'm loved and wanted.

"'Morning, yourself. Happy Valentine's Day." Well, listen to me all perky and in the spirit of the holiday of love.

"Did my flowers arrive yesterday?"

"Flowers?" Oh, Lord. Don't tell me all those were from Greg and not Jerry.

"A basket of orchids." He groans. "Don't tell me they didn't come and I ruined the surprise. The flower shop must be backed up with orders because of Valentine's Day."

My mind steals back over the baskets and baskets of flowers to the lone bouquet of orchids. "No, they did arrive. And they were lovely. Thank you, Greg."

"I know they don't make up for us not getting to spend the evening together. But I promise I'll make it up to you in the years to come. We'll have every Valentine's Day together for the rest of our lives."

"I know we will, sweetheart." My throat clogs. "I can't wait."

"I had another reason for calling," he says, slightly hesitant.

"Oh?"

"One of the board members from Shepherd Falls called and asked if I can preach again this weekend. They're having a special dinner for Pastor's birthday and would like for us to come and be part of it."

"Us?"

"Yeah. Do you mind?"

"No. That'll be fine. I'd be happy to go." Anything to spend a few more hours with Greg.

We solidify our plans, and just before we hang up, Greg says, "What are you planning to do tonight?"

"I don't know. I thought I might spend the evening at Countryside with Miss Lou and Lewis and Kitty. Lewis arranged for a special dinner for Miss Kitty. Isn't that sweet?"

"I could take some lessons from that guy."

"You got that right, bub!" I laugh. "Anyway, I haven't decided for sure. Rick's all done with the training here in Missouri and leaves the day after tomorrow for Kuwait, so Darcy and the kids are driving down to Fort Bliss to see him off."

"That's going to be hard on them. I'm glad Darcy asked them to go along."

"Yes. A lot of stepmoms might have been stingy about that. But not Darcy. You know how she is."

"Listen, about tonight. I have a surprise for you, so why don't you stay home?"

"A surprise?"

"Yes, and don't press me for hints. You'll just have to wait and see."

"You know I hate surprises."

"I think you'll like this one."

With the kids driving down to Texas with Darcy, I'm alone to obsess about what Greg has planned for me. When the doorbell rings at four o'clock, I rush down the steps and fling the door open. A delivery boy hands me a corsage box and a note:

Put on a dress. Limo will pick you up at six.

My heart absolutely leaps for joy. I rush to the bathroom and run a tub of bubble bath. Then head to my closet and find the little black number I know Greg loves. I dig at the bottom of my closet and find the black, strappy high-heeled sandals that go with the dress. I'm ready by five thirty. At a quarter to six, I slip on my wrist corsage of red rosebuds and baby's breath.

This is it. The night I put Jerry completely out of my mind.

I stand in front of the mirror, lookin' good, I must say, and I'm thrilled that all this is for Greg.

Jerry Calloway, you're out of my life forever.

I smile at my reflection. And when the doorbell chimes at six o'clock on the dot, I know I've come to grips with my attraction to Jerry and I've recommitted to Greg in my heart and in my mind.

A driver, complete with black chauffeur's suit and hat, stands on my front step. I hope Greg isn't spending too much on this. The driver opens the door and I get in, expecting Greg to be there waiting for me, but the limo is empty except for a single red rose on the seat. My heart thrills to this romantic gesture. Greg's gone all out. I knock on the partition glass, expecting to have it roll down like in all the movies. Instead, a voice comes through an intercom. "Yes?"

"Where's my date?"

"I was told to drive you to the lake. That's all I know."

"The lake? That's forty-five miles."

"Yes, ma'am."

"Okay. Thank you."

I fall silent. I suppose I should lean back and enjoy the ride. But I'd be enjoying it a lot more if I were with Greg.

The forty-minute drive feels like two hours. Finally, I recognize the lights across the water. A romantic dinner in one of the restaurants on the lake. I fight butterflies as the car crunches to a stop on the gravel next to the boat docks. The driver opens my door and points to a boat lit up with a string of lights. "That's you."

I'm starting to get the feeling I'm in a spooky Stephen King movie.

"That's not a boat—it's a flippin' yacht."

"Someone must think you're pretty special."

"I guess," I murmur, still trying to take it all in and being careful not to twist an ankle in my four-inch heels. Whose bright idea was it to make the parking area gravel, anyway?

Somehow I make it to the yacht without breaking a bone and slip onto the boat. "Hello?"

Still no sign of life. "Greg? Are you here?"

Rose petals strewn across the deck mark a trail leading to the open door that I assume will take me to Greg. All I have to say is that if it leads to a petal-covered bed, I'm doomed. I follow the trail to the open door and down a length of narrow stairs. "Greg . . ."

I see a pair of legs before I'm all the way down the steps. "This is amazing! I can't believe you blew off classes."

He turns to greet me . . . only . . . it's not Greg.

Jerry stands there holding two glasses of wine, smiling as though we're sharing a secret. "Sorry to disappoint you."

"Jerry! What the heck are you doing? Why didn't you tell me it was you?"

"I thought this was romantic." He gives me a sheepish grin. "Never dreamed you'd think it was Greg. He doesn't strike me as the romantic type of guy. But then, maybe you know something I don't know about him."

"I know a lot about him that you don't know."

He holds out a glass to me, and I shake my head. "I don't drink."

"Not even wine?"

"Not with you."

He lifts the glass to his lips and drains it. "No sense letting it go to waste."

"You mean like all the money you spent on this little deception?" Anger burns through me. I feel like a big stupe. For two reasons. First, because I honestly believed Greg had suddenly become Mr. Romance, and second, because the real Mr. Romance isn't Greg.

"Don't be so sure it was a waste. You never know what the night holds for us."

"Get that from a romance novel?"

He grins. "Hallmark card."

Okay, I can't help but smile at that. Still . . .

"I'm out of here." I whip around and head back toward the ladder.

Jerry laughs. "Claire. The only way you're getting off this boat is to swim."

"What?"

"As soon as you stepped onto the deck, the crew got us moving."

"We can't be that far out."

"See for yourself."

I climb back up the steps, and my heart sinks as I spy land—not that far, but definitely too far for me to swim. I inch back down the ladder. "Turn it around, Jerry."

He winks. "In good time."

Well, now he's just being stubborn. I'll wear him down, and he'll be begging to get away from me.

My feet are killing me. I plop down on a dining chair. And for the first time I notice the table. It's spread with elegant dishes covered with silver. Candle rings made of fresh flowers circle two long flickering candles. I have to hand it to him, Jerry knows how to make a girl feel special. Still, he knows I love Greg. Knows I'm marrying Greg.

"What exactly did you expect to accomplish with this little Valentine's Day surprise?" I gasp.

Surprise?? Greg's surprise! And I'm not there! "I have to go home right now, Jerry."

"Claire, we've pulled away from the dock. We're halfway across the lake by now."

"Who's driving?" Jerry sets a glass on the table and moves around behind me. My heart speeds up a bit and warning bells go off in my head at his soft puff of breath, warm against my ear. "The crew, of course. Who did you think was going to *drive?*" He strokes the side of my neck with his finger.

It dawns on me. This is a seduction. Maybe I'm not the sharpest knife in the drawer when it comes to men. But I never thought Jerry would try this.

I whip around to face him. "Turn the boat around. I want to go home."

His face is inches from mine. He gives me a slow smile and places his hands on my waist, pulling me closer. "Come on. You don't mean that. If you didn't want to be here, you would have run away the second you realized it was me and not your lover boy, Greg."

"This is storybook romance. It's not real. You did all this just to get me in your bed."

"What are you talking about?"

"Oh, come on! What do you mean, what am I talking about? The rose petals, the candlelight, the limo to the lake. You want a romp before you go find yourself a geisha."

"Claire, that isn't what this is about at all." He leans his forehead against mine. "Remember, I asked you to go to Hawaii with me."

I pull back as hysterical laughter rips from my throat. "Yes, so you could have all the benefits of the honeymoon without the love, commitment, and marriage."

Jerry's lips twist downward. "Are you kidding me? All that no-sex-before-marriage garbage is real?"

"Of course it is."

"Then you and Greg have never . . . ?"

"Not even once."

The guy looks shell-shocked. I feel sorry for him in a way. He's bought into the lie that marriage is nothing more than a piece of paper.

"Jerry, there's only one man who could possibly seduce me, and that's Greg."

"So you would give it up for him?" The guy actually seems offended by this.

"The point is, he wouldn't ask. He is willing to wait for me even though it's not easy for either one of us." I smile. "It's like not snacking on Thanksgiving so you save room for turkey. If you nibble while you're preparing the food, the meal's not nearly as good."

"How about a little something to hold you over until the main course says 'I do'?"

I know he's just kidding, and I allow a hint of a smile. "No thanks. I'm saving myself."

"For a turkey?"

"Not funny. And, Jerry, I really need to go home. Greg told me he had a surprise for me and asked me to stay home."

"Ah, so that's why you thought all of this was him."

Averting my gaze, I nod.

Jerry tips my chin with his finger. "Are you sure he's the one you want?"

"I've never been more sure of anything in my life."

"All right. Go up to the deck and I'll instruct the captain to turn us around."

The first thing I see is Greg's Avalanche when the limo driver opens the door and offers me his hand. "Good luck," the driver says. "That's the only time Mr. Calloway ever got shot down on the company yacht. It was kind of fun to watch the boat come back to dock within twenty minutes. Sort of wish I could have been a fly on the wall for that conversation."

My face warms. "So I'm not the first he's performed his little dog-and-pony act for, huh?"

"Not by a long shot. But I'd say you're the prettiest."

Methinks the driver is vying for a tip. So I oblige.

"Thanks for the ride back."

The house is dark, which makes me even more curious as I open the door. I move into the living room, and my heart turns to mush. Greg is stretched out on the couch, his head resting on a throw pillow. Next to him on the coffee table are a dozen red roses, glistening in candlelight. Candles that Greg must have brought to surprise me. A box of pizza and a DVD sit on the other end of the table. Pizza. My favorite. I pick up the movie box and smile. *The Mirror Has Two Faces*. Except for the flowers and candles, Greg was trying to recreate the first time he ever shared a meal with me. Pizza and the movie. I drop to the floor in front of the couch, tears stinging my eyes at the thought of the hours that were stolen from us. I lay my head on his shoulder.

"Where were you?" his sleepy voice asks.

"It doesn't matter. I'm sorry I wasn't here for you. How long have you been here?"

"What time is it?"

"Almost nine."

"I got here about eight."

"I missed a whole hour with you."

"How come you're all dressed up?" he asks.

"It's Valentine's Day. I wanted to look nice for you." And that's the truth. I honestly thought I was dressing up for Greg.

"Come here," he says softly.

He folds me into his arms and kisses me. Part of me wants to cry for the wasted hour. This man loves me enough to drive over two hundred miles just to spend a couple of hours with me. With Jerry pushed firmly to the back of my mind, I enjoy the next two hours with Greg, eating cold pizza and watching a movie. It's not on a yacht or in a limo, but it's the best Valentine's Day I've ever spent.

22

March blows in like a lion, and life becomes a flurry of activity. I've finally paid off the dress, and the alterations are finished. My job at the old folks' home is almost finished, but I keep letting Sandy talk me into working more days because I can't bear to leave the residents. I'm deep into rewriting *Brandi's World*, plus Ari is gearing up for graduation, and then I'm getting married.

A knock at the door gives me a welcome respite from my work this Saturday morning. My stomach jumps as I head to the door because I know what's waiting for me on the other side.

Linda stands there grinning when I open up. "Ta-da!" She holds up a garment bag.

I step back with a squeal and let her in. She's unzipping the bag before she's even all the way inside. "Oh, just look at it."

"Go put it on!" Linda urges.

A bubble of excitement floats into the air on a burst of laughter. "Okay."

I slip upstairs, and within a few minutes I'm standing barefoot wearing the gown I was born to wear as I walk down the aisle. Tears flow as I study my reflection in the full-length mirror. The gown was made for me. I think back to the day I first saw it. The dogs I walked and the filthy apartment I cleaned just to get the down payment. The halls I swept and beds I changed. Every backbreaking moment was worth it.

As I think of how I almost ruined everything because of Jerry, the tears of gratitude to God quickly become tears of remorse for my foolishness.

After a few minutes, Linda knocks on the door. "Claire, are you okay? Why are you crying? Doesn't it fit? You have time to drop five pounds, if that's it. Or we can have it altered again."

"Everything's fine. You can come in."

She opens the door. "Oh, Claire. Just look at you. You're absolutely gorgeous." Tears well in her eyes as she stands next to me and stares into the mirror.

"I can't believe I almost ruined it all."

"Yes, but you didn't. And Jerry Calloway is safely in Japan, where he can't do any more damage to your relationship."

"I'm totally over him anyway. Jerry was a player."

I suck in a breath and launch into a confession about Valentine's Day and the yacht.

"Well, you were smart to have gotten out of there. He might have been a crazy man, getting you out on the water just to have his way with you and then toss you overboard like the guy in *The Net*. Remember? Sandra Bullock is on vacation and she meets Mr. Right? Only he sets her up, sleeps with her, and is about to shoot her and toss her overboard when she finds the gun?"

"You watch too many movies."

"Maybe so, but you didn't know Jerry all that well. So you'd better thank your lucky stars that you're even still here to marry Greg in your Vera Wang."

"Here, unzip me." I turn. "The only thing in danger out there was my virtue. And my relationship with Greg."

"Speaking of Greg." She takes the gown from me while I dress. "What did he say about what Jerry did?"

Guilt floods me, like it has every day since the incident. I avert my gaze.

A gasp escapes my friend. "Are you saying you haven't told Greg? Didn't he ask where you were?"

"I woke him up when I got back to the house. I just wanted to spend time with him, enjoying the rest of our evening together. It just didn't seem like the right time to tell."

"And you haven't brought it back up?"

"Here's the thing. When he called me the morning of the yacht incident, I told him I'd probably go visit the residents at Countryside, and that's when he told me to stay home because he had a surprise for me. When I wasn't home, I think he just assumed I got tired of waiting and drove to see Miss Lou."

Walking to my closet, she hangs my gown. She fingers the material for a second, then turns to face me. "So basically you're saying you traded one lie for another."

"How can you say that? Like you said, Jerry's gone."

"Yes, but what would it hurt to tell Greg the truth? You ran away from Jerry. You didn't know he was the one luring you there. You thought you were going to be with Greg."

"I know, but think about it. Jerry's surprise was a limo, a yacht, a porch filled with flowers. I just don't want Greg to feel bad because his surprise was pizza and a movie."

"And him! He drove four hours to get here just to spend Valentine's Day with you and then drove back four hours so he could be on time for classes. Good grief, Claire. Don't ruin it with this guy over a non-lie you don't even have to tell."

Okay, I'm not sure what that means. But I get the gist of what she's saying.

"I just don't see any reason to borrow trouble. If Greg comes to me and says, 'Hey, Claire, you remember that night I was at your house and you came home late? Where were you?' then I'll tell him. But unless that happens, I see no point. You, me, Jerry, and the limo driver are the only four people who know. So I really don't think it's going to get back to him. Do you?"

"I think you're playing with fire. Seriously."

I shrug and head toward the door, my signal that the conversation is over.

I know she is only being concerned. But honestly. This isn't the same situation at all. I've completely come to my senses. What good would it do to hurt Greg at this point?

As Easter approaches, I shove the entire incident with Jerry far to the back of my mind, and Linda finally lets it rest. I've finished rewriting the first draft of *Brandi's World*. I'm diving into edits and plan to have it on my new editor's desk by the first of May so I can enjoy the last two weeks of Ari's high school days: senior prom, graduation. My little girl is almost grown up.

With Rick gone, Darcy has thrown herself into helping me plan the wedding. And "helping" is putting it mildly. She's taken on the responsibility of being sure everyone makes fittings for the matron of honor, bridesmaid, and flower-girl gowns. She's relentless in bringing me bridal magazines to show me everything from place settings to flower arrangements.

Now, as we sit in my kitchen watching Lydia pull herself up by hanging onto Ollie's fur, Darcy's planning my bridal shower.

And this is where I think we might hit an impasse. Truthfully, I've been pretty satisfied to let her take care of things, as long as I have creative control and final word. A shower is not something I ever counted on. I never agreed to it, and I have no intention of surrendering to one.

As I inform Darcy of this fact, she stares at me, disbelief and horror combining in her expressive face. "You have to have a bridal shower. It's tradition."

It's not my tradition. "I'm not a young bride. I have everything I need."

"That's not the point."

Then what exactly does she think is the point? "Yes it is, Darce. Young brides have showers so they'll get the things they need to set up a household. I don't need anything. Good grief—I have more stuff than I need as it is. And Greg is the same."

"But—"

"I mean it, Darcy. It will embarrass me if you ask people to buy gifts."

A frown puckers her brow. "But that's just silly. You're not asking people to bring gifts. People want to. They love you. Claire, you're supposed to have a shower. People are supposed to send gifts. It's tradition!"

"You said that."

A pout forms across her china-doll features. Then her eyes go wide. "I know!"

Oh boy. "What?"

"Remember when Michael Douglas and Catherine Zeta-Jones got married?"

"Okay." Not sure where she's going, but I can humor her for a second. Oops, Lydia is chewing on Ollie's ear. That can't be good. I get up, grateful for an excuse to move across the room. I snatch the baby and goo-goo at her for a second before I retake my seat. Lydia is just as happy with her new game: slapping the table with her chubby hands and blowing spit bubbles.

Darcy grins at her girl and wipes the teething drool from her chin. "Don't want to get a rash, do we, Lyddie?" She turns her attention back to me. "Okay, the Douglases. They told people to write checks for charity instead of getting them gifts!"

"Well, I guess so. They're richer than King Midas."

"Anyway, don't you see? What if we have your shower and tell people to bring a baby gift?"

"What? Are you nuts? I'm not having a baby!"

"Well, I know that. Good grief. I mean for the teen home. That could be your charity."

"Why not just do a fundraiser?"

"Because people are already in the mood to buy gifts for you and Greg. People who might not otherwise buy gifts, and definitely not for pregnant teens."

"Oh, well, that makes sense. I guess it would be okay. But, Darcy, I want it to be clearly understood that the baby gifts are for the teen house. I don't want anyone thinking this is a shotgun wedding."

Amusement twitches her lips. "I'll be sure to clarify that you've asked that people not buy gifts for you and Greg, but rather that they buy gifts for the babies instead." Her eyes flood with tears. "Oh, Claire, you're just wonderful, and so unselfish."

"Good grief, Darcy. It was your idea."

Sheesh. I'll be glad when she's off the hormone therapy.

23

Ap200ril showers rain down from the sky this Sunday morning, washing away the winter's gloom and promising fresh green grass and vibrant buds.

Greg, the kids, and I are all driving to Shepherd Falls for another service. The congregation seems to love him. He takes at least one Sunday every month and drives down. I've been with him the last two months, but this will be the kids' first time. They're all attached to our church, so they're not exactly happy to have to leave. It's like it's just clicking in their brains that they'll be spending the summer with Greg, Sadie, and me in Shepherd Falls, since their dad is away.

And no one is acting too swell about it, either. That's the thing about my family. We don't have a problem expressing how we feel.

Rick e-mails often. The kids hear from him at least every other day. But his absence is affecting them. They miss him deeply. Ari laments that he won't be there for her graduation. Tommy just needs his dad, you know? What fifteen-year-old boy doesn't? Rick is missing Shawn's plays. And Jakey has taken up golf in his doctor-father's honor.

We're greeted warmly as we all step into the church thirty minutes before service is scheduled to start. The people know us now. They are beginning to trust us—especially Greg. His preaching has been right on, and today is no exception as he encourages the congregation that no matter what kind of past they've had, their best days are still to come.

I get teary-eyed as he preaches. I think about those first few months after Rick's infidelity, when I honestly thought my life was over. But God saved me, gave me a career I love, and then led me to this wonderful wonder of a man who, for some reason, seems to love me.

We stand together at the door after service so we can shake hands with members as they exit the building.

"Great sermon, Pastor." Albert March, a fiftysomething man I recognize as a church elder, pumps Greg's hand, his fat face scrunched into a jovial smile. "Much as we hate to lose Pastor Miller, you're just what this church needs to replace him."

The next few people shake hands, compliment the sermon. Then another elder approaches. I can tell Greg's a bit nervous, and he speaks up before the other man can say anything. "Ted, how's your son's track season shaping up?"

The man's face lights up like a Christmas tree at the mention of his boy. They talk track for a few minutes until the man shakes Greg's hand again. "See you next time, Pastor. Be glad when you're here for good. We have some ideas for sprucing up the youth program."

"Greg?" After the fourth elder approaches and makes similar statements, I'm starting to get an uneasy feeling in the pit of my stomach. A feeling that there's something going on and I'm not exactly in the loop. "What's going on?"

He gives me a grin and a wink. "We're shaking hands. Get used to it. We'll have to do it every week."

"Through the summer. You mean, every week through the summer."

A blush creeps up his face. "Sure, yeah. That's what I mean."

Oh, my gosh! I don't believe this. What's going on with him?

"Greg! You're a terrible liar. Stop trying to keep something from me."

"Wait until we get into the van."

It seems like an eternity until we're the only ones left in the church except for the pastor and his wife. We're following them to their house for lunch. So once we're in the van, I waylay him. "All right, bub. Spill it."

"Not here." He jerks his head toward the kids.

"Yes, here! They have a right to know what you're planning, too." Somewhere in the back of my mind I know that's not fair, but my fairness gauge is a little off due to being lambasted by something completely unexpected. "Out with it," I command. "Whatever it is, it seems like I'm the last to know."

Greg gathers a full breath and scowls at me. "The church has voted me in as their new pastor. If I want the job, I can start on salary in June instead of as interim pastor."

"What? Are they nuts? It's one thing for us to stay here for the summer, but surely they realize you're not looking for a full-time pastoral position. You have your teaching at the school and the associate pastor position in our own church."

He's awfully quiet. And that just makes me antsy. My stomach growls in response—a nervous habit. "Hey—you told them thanks, but no thanks, right?"

"I'm not moving to this hick town," Tommy pipes up.

"None of us is moving to this hick town," I reply. But as I study Greg's face, waiting for him to concur, he swallows hard. Realization suddenly dawns on me, and I can't stifle a gasp. Two and two come together and make a perfect equation. One that amounts to this: Greg's honestly considering accepting the position. "Wait! You didn't stop those men when they started talking about your pastoring this church like it's a done deal. Is there something I should know?"

"I've been praying about it for awhile."

"Since when?" I'm starting to get PO'ed.

"They approached me a couple of months ago."

"And just when were you planning to tell me?"

He attempts a grin, but it falls short of his lips. "I just did."

Does he honestly think he's funny? I glare at him, and he turns his attention back to driving the van.

"Have you or have you not given these people an answer?"

"Not yet. I wouldn't do that without discussing it with you first."

"If you move here, I'm moving in with Dad." Tommy's heated comment stills my heart. At fifteen, he can easily choose which parent to live with. Actually, he could have at age twelve.

"Tommy, you're not helping matters." Greg's stern voice remains even, but carries with authority all the way to the back.

"I'm just saying . . ."

The kid has to have the last word, doesn't he?

"Do they have a kids' theater in Shepherd Falls, Mom?"

"I'd say that's highly unlikely, Shawn. But I know the church does productions. I'm sure they'd love to have someone with your experience in the drama group."

"Oh."

My heart goes out to him. I know it wouldn't be easy. For any of us. But probably mostly for Shawn. His interests are community-related. Tommy can skateboard anywhere, and

Jake can definitely play video games anywhere. And Ari will be going to college.

"Don't worry, guys," I say as we pull in behind the Millers. "Everything will work out just like it's supposed to."

Mrs. Miller sets out a huge spread of pot roast, fried chicken, mashed potatoes and gravy, baked beans, several vegetable selections, and salad. The meal is topped off with a three-layer chocolate cake light enough to float down the river.

After lunch the men and kids head outside to play badminton while I help Mrs. Miller clean up.

"Everything was just wonderful. I don't know how you do it."

She smiles and slips a covered dish into the refrigerator. "People are always good to help when they know the pastors are having guest ministers for dinner. The only part of that meal I made was the salad. And I bought a bag already mixed."

"Really?"

"Uh-huh. I'm no Superwoman."

"That's a relief." Maybe there really is hope for me.

As I plunge my hands into a sinkful of hot suds, I can feel Mrs. Miller's perusal. "How are you holding up with all of this?"

"This? Do you mean the board offering Greg the church?"

She nods and gives a little laugh. "It's the first unanimous vote in the history of this church. So, needless to say, my husband and I are delighted and fully convinced that God must be in it. Unity isn't the board's strong suit. Not that they bicker," she hurries on, as though afraid I'll run away. "It's just that these men are used to having their own way. Compromise is a learning process. But Greg slid right in. First vote. Unanimous. Like God just had control over the voting."

I'm flattered on Greg's behalf, but a dull ache clenches my heart at the thought of what such a move would mean for the kids. Would I lose Tommy? Could I really do that?

We switch to idle chitchat while we finish up the dishes. I'm just drying off my hands when Mrs. Miller asks, "How would you like a tour of the parsonage?"

I fold the towel and set it on the counter. "I'd love it."

Mrs. Miller takes me through the two-story, five-bedroom farmhouse. She slides loving fingers along the banister as we walk upstairs, and a wistful sort of sigh leaves her slight form. "The house was built just after the Great Depression. We restored much of the original woodwork when we bought it."

"And this belongs to the church?"

"Technically, it's ours. The church gives us a housing allowance, but when we move we're deeding it to the church, provided they keep it for ministry." Her eyes mist, and she sniffs as though fighting back tears. "When my husband's health started going downhill and it was obvious we were going to have to turn the church over to someone new, I started praying for a new pastor with a young family."

"You did?" So it's all her fault God led Greg here!

"Your wonderful little family will fit in perfectly around here. And we need the energy of youth."

Does she think I have energy? Ha! I could take a nap right now.

I'm just about to ask her how she can be so sure we're the right ones to take over, when the phone rings. Mrs. Miller hurries down the steps ahead of me, and I hear her pick up the phone as I continue a leisurely walk into the living room.

I love this house. I really do. And to be honest, I can see our family living here. The thought of pastoring these people isn't completely unappealing, but I worry about my children. I can't lose Tommy. I love Greg, but my son needs me more.

"Hang on. Let me ask." Mrs. Miller slips her hand over the mouthpiece of the receiver. "This is our youth pastor. They want to know, since it's spring break, if you want to let your teenagers go to a Christian concert in Branson with our youth group."

"Southern gospel?" The kids hate that.

"No. It's a two-day concert with several Christian rock and worship bands. They started yesterday."

"I'll go ask."

"There's going to be a cookout and games at the church for the younger kids, so Jake and Shawn and Sadie will have somewhere to go as well."

"Okay, let's see what Greg thinks."

Excitement is building in me for some reason. I know Greg's classes are out this week, too. My stomach drops when I see Greg sitting in a lawn chair. Pastor Miller is playing with the kids, but Greg's head is resting on his palm, his elbow propped on the arm of the chair. Poor guy is exhausted. I'm sure he wants to go home.

As though sensing my presence, he opens his eyes, smiles, and straightens. He reaches for me and I go to him, taking his hand.

I relay the message. Tommy and Ari look hopefully at Greg. For the first time I see the tender paternal decision-making process slide across his face. He cares about my kids! He's going to say yes out of love for them.

"You kids have fun." And then the real test comes. Greg

drops my hand, stands up, reaches into his billfold, and pulls out several bills. I open my mouth to stop him, but a hand on my arm halts my forward motion.

I turn to see Pastor Miller shaking his head. "Let him."

Mrs. Miller stands at the door, the phone still in her hand. "Should I tell him yes?"

I turn to her with an affirming nod.

"I'll get the guest rooms ready for you."

"Oh, don't put yourself out." I never even thought about what we'd do in the meantime. "We can wait for the kids and drive back."

"Don't be silly," she says with a wave of her hand. "It'll be at least midnight when they get home. We have plenty of room."

"Grace is right," Pastor Miller says. "Unless there's a reason you need to be home?"

I look at Greg. He's staring at me with question. No begging, no demanding. Just a simple question. *Are you willing to walk into the life God is directing?*

Suddenly my love for this man shoots through the love-o-meter and I nod. "All right. We'll stay."

"Wonderful! I'll put out a call for clothes."

"Clothes?"

"From the congregation. They can't have their new pastor's family staying the night with no clothes to wear tomorrow."

An hour later, Tommy and Ari are on their way to Branson, which is an hour's drive. I always get a little nervous when the kids go on school field trips or church youth outings. I've had to completely roll those cares onto the Lord more times than I can count.

Pastor Miller and Greg settle into the living room with a chessboard, and Mrs. Miller and I decide to drive twenty minutes to the closest Wal-Mart so I can buy underwear and pj's.

The thing I regret most is that even if we do accept the position at Shepherd Falls, Mrs. Miller won't be there. I have found that I really like the older woman.

As we walk through Wal-Mart, I watch her interaction with other customers, stockers, cashiers. She's warm and friendly, and people respond to her kindness. Suddenly I wonder how on earth I'll ever fill the shoes of this lovable little ball of energy.

And later, after the younger boys and Sadie are back from their cookout at the church and tucked into bed upstairs, Mrs. Miller pulls out her scrapbooks that reflect all their years pastoring in Shepherd Falls. We haven't made it through four album pages before I'm convinced I'll never measure up. I see a young Susan Miller with her family. In the first pictures, there's only one child. Then photos emerge of enormous glasses and Farrah Fawcett hair with one baby on her hip, an obvious pregnant belly, and another baby clinging to her leg. Pastor Miller sports the Burt Reynolds mustache.

The photos also show the way the church has grown, changed. I recognize younger versions of many of the people I've met over the last couple of months.

"How can you bear to leave it, Mrs. Miller?"

"Call me Susan. And it's time. God is moving us on. He had to take Moses so Joshua could get his chance to lead in the direction God wanted Israel to go."

"It must be so hard."

Her eyes mist, and I feel just horrible for bringing it up. "It is. And when your time comes to pass it along to the next generation, it will be hard for you too. But you'll also rejoice, because you know that God is going to lead in a new direction and bring even greater glory to His name."

Without bothering to hold back a grin, I look her in the eyes. "You seem pretty sure we'll accept."

"I'm pretty sure God brought you here."

"You don't know me, though. I'm not sure I can do justice to the job." I turn a page and point to a photo of her teaching a ladies' meeting. "This is the kind of thing I'm worried about. These ladies will discover pretty quickly that I'm disorganized, I'm not a very good cook, and I often don't clean my house for weeks, especially if I'm on deadline."

"Those things can change. And, Claire, there's nothing wrong with hiring someone to clean for you once a week."

Yeah. The last time I tried that, my cleaning lady drank all my Diet Coke and still didn't get the house all that clean. But I suppose to help Greg build a successful ministry and not embarrass him, I can try.

"Well, my dear." Mrs. Miller stands. "I believe I'll gather up my husband and we'll head for bed. It's getting a little late for me."

I glance at my watch in surprise. It's after eleven already. We've been going over these photos for two hours. I stack up the albums.

"I'll put those away tomorrow," Susan says, a yawn stretching her mouth.

We walk into the living room together. "Well, would you look at that?" Susan's lips twist in amusement. I follow her gaze and can't resist a little laugh of my own.

Both men are sound asleep.

Greg is stretched out on the couch, snoring lightly, his

shoes resting neatly beside the couch. Pastor Miller is in his La-Z-Boy, reclining with his Bible face down on his slightly protruding gut.

Without waking Greg, Susan masterfully rouses her husband and guides him upstairs. I take over his seat since he's not going to be needing it any more tonight. And I watch Greg, imagining us living together in this house, building the kinds of memories the Millers have built over the last thirty years.

He stirs in his sleep, and my pulse rises from sheer love for this man. I can't wait to spend the rest of my life with him.

Despite Tommy's threats, I have to believe that God is going to work it all out.

Greg's stirring becomes consciousness. He glances over at me. "Hi. How long have I been asleep?"

"I'm not sure. We were looking at photos for a couple of hours."

"Fascinating," he drawls. He sits up and pats the cushion next to him.

"As a matter of fact," I say, as I stand up and accept his invitation, "it was a very nice two hours, and it helped me come to a conclusion."

He threads his fingers through mine. "What conclusion?"

"I think this is where God wants us to build our life and ministry."

His beautiful brown eyes widen and shine with excitement. "Are you sure? I don't want you to do anything you're not sure about."

I reach up and rest my palm against his cheek. "I'm sure. Very sure."

"What about your *Father of the Bride* house?"

"I love this one."

"We could build one like Mom's."

"Let's just play that part by ear. For now, I'd like to start out in this one."

"What about your kids?"

"I've already started praying."

We spend the next hour making plans about the wedding, the church, the merging of our two families. And somehow as I become caught up in the exciting possibilities, that Hawaiian honeymoon doesn't seem quite as important.

At twelve fifteen, I'm relieved to hear the crunch of gravel and then two car doors close.

"Think we should tell them tonight?"

"We can."

Thankfully, Tommy seems to be in a good mood when the two of them come in. I press my forefinger to my lips to quiet them down. "The Millers are in bed. Have fun?"

A shrug lifts his thin shoulders. "I guess."

"You guess." Ari chortles.

"What?"

"Tommy met someone."

Rather than the belligerence I've come to expect from Tommy when he's teased about girls, the boy actually blushes.

"What's her name?"

"Dakota."

"Pretty."

He gives me that impish grin of his that never fails to melt me. One I haven't seen in way too long. "So is she."

"I'm glad you two had a good time. Let's go upstairs. I'll show you where you're sleeping. Ari, you're with me. Tommy, you're with Greg."

"So," Tommy whispers as we start turning off lights and making sure doors are locked.

"So what, son?"

"If we move here, is this going to be our house?"

And all I can say is, "Thank you, Lord, for Dakota."

24

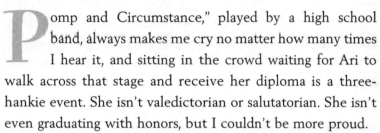

"Pomp and Circumstance," played by a high school band, always makes me cry no matter how many times I hear it, and sitting in the crowd waiting for Ari to walk across that stage and receive her diploma is a three-hankie event. She isn't valedictorian or salutatorian. She isn't even graduating with honors, but I couldn't be more proud.

My daughter has blossomed into a capable, self-confident, God-loving young woman. Someone who is truly kind and compassionate, with a bright future ahead of her. I lean forward slightly and turn to look at Patrick's face. The love written there is undeniable.

They're so young. My heart beats with anticipation to watch as their love blossoms and matures. But a little bit of dread, too. Am I ready to lose my little girl?

Darcy has the video camera and is filming every second of the ceremony so Rick won't miss anything. She sends him a new DVD every week. He's lucky to have her. I'm definitely not that organized. I have enough trouble remembering to give the kids lunch money.

"Arianna Everett Frank."

I want to stand—she deserves a standing ovation. *Come on, people!* I want to shout. *Don't you know what an amazing young woman my daughter is?* Oh, well. I know. I know that a year ago, she was sneaking out of the house and couldn't commit to a boyfriend.

Ari fought against the guy who was so right for her. They were sort of on-again, off-again for a year. Patrick cared about her; he waited for her. They did some heavy-duty making out that I had to put a stop to in the beginning, but in the long run, she made the right choice, and these two have been in a steady relationship since her birthday in October. I just pray they keep their resolve to wait until after college to marry.

She hasn't grown up *that* much! And she definitely isn't ready for marriage.

We sit through the rest of the ceremony, and then the music plays again and they file out.

I wade through students in black graduation gowns until I find her. She's in Patrick's arms, tears streaming down her face. My heart lurches. I'm torn. Should I go to her? Is something wrong or is this a case of emotions run amuck? Okay, I *am* her mother and this is a once-in-a-lifetime night for both of us. I'm interrupting.

Ari sees me coming and pulls away, wiping her cheeks with the sleeve of her gown. And this is why I say she's still a little girl in so many ways.

Her eyes are shining as she moves into my open arms. I hold her close and suddenly she's a newborn. I'm scared to death because I'm a new mom and I have no idea how to be a mom to a baby girl.

When I pull back and hold her at arm's length, I realize we've come full circle. I have no idea how to be a mother to a grown woman. "I'm so proud of you, Ari."

"I'm just so relieved to be done with school."

I grin. "For three months. Then it's back to the books, young lady."

A look passes between Patrick and Ari. A look that leaves me a bit uneasy, if you want to know the truth.

Patrick clears his throat. "We'd better go. My parents are meeting us at the restaurant."

I wanted to throw her a graduation party, but Ari didn't feel right having a party when her dad is serving in the war. So we compromised with a nice dinner for twenty-five of our closest friends and family. Even my brother, Charley, brought his family from Texas to visit. His wife, Marie, homeschools the children, so the family is free to pick up and travel during the school year.

Charley has confided that he wants to have a heart-to-heart with me. I'm bracing myself. I think it must have something to do with Mom. And he can barely even speak civilly to Eli. I know he must think Eli's taking advantage of Mom in some way. But that's too bad. Mom's made it pretty clear that the old guy is around for as long as she says he is. And what's it hurting? She really does seem to care about him.

Anyway, I'll deal with all that later. Right now I'm anxious to get to the dinner in my daughter's honor. "All right. You two go on to the restaurant while I round up the family." Ari slips out of her graduation gown and hands it to me. I can't get over how pretty she looks in the black dress we splurged on with part of the check I received from signing my new book contract.

I watch them leave, Patrick's hand spanning the small of her back in that possessive manner I observed at Thanksgiving. I can't help but wonder if I should have pressed for her to go away to college instead of registering at the same one Paddy attends. Maybe we're just asking for trouble.

"Ready to go?" Darcy pulls me from my thoughts as she approaches, leading the pack.

"Yeah, Patrick's parents are meeting us there."

Darcy frowns at the graduation gown in my hands. "Ari took off her graduation gown? Why'd she do that when we haven't taken pictures?"

You know, she has a point.

"We'll make her put it back on as soon as we get to the restaurant."

Darcy smiles. "That's a relief. Rick's going to want to see her in her gown."

"Of course. I'm just sorry Greg couldn't make it." He's taking finals and is staying in Tulsa to pack everything up in the apartment he's been sharing with his mom and Sadie for the last year and a half.

As a matter of fact, I'm not going to see him until three days before our wedding, when he will be home for good. Our wedding. Two weeks from tomorrow.

"You have that smile on your face again," Darcy says as we walk toward the door. "You must be thinking about your wedding."

"You sure you want to take that plunge again, sis?" Charley baits just like he did when we were kids, and just like back then, my ire shoots up.

"I think I'll take my chances."

He flips the bottom of my hair, because he knows I hate it. "I'm just kidding. When do I get to meet this Greg guy anyway?"

"He won't be home for a week and a half."

"Why? Is he afraid of meeting the man of the family?"

"Yeah, Charley. That must be it." Sarcasm has always been my strong suit. Why do I always revert to my childhood when my brother shows up, flashing those dimples, making Mom laugh?

"Now, don't you two start it." I bet Mom just loved saying that again. I haven't even seen Charley in a year and a half. Now, in less than two days since his arrival, Mom gets to break us up. I can't help but laugh. "Yes, Mother."

The single table in the back room at Jack's Family Dining is filling up with our family and Paddy's parents when we arrive. To my relief, Ari opted to keep the guest list simple. I hand her back her graduation gown and she slips it on for pictures.

During dinner, Ari seems very nervous. I'm watching her like a hawk, trying to figure it out. I lean over to Darcy. "Hey, what do you think is going on with Ari?"

"Besides graduating?" Sheesh, Darcy's distracted too. She keeps glancing at her watch.

"This is about more than graduation." It's more than just I'm-the-center-of-attention nerves.

"I hadn't really noticed. She seems fine to me."

"Well, she doesn't to me."

Ari looks up from her plate and catches my gaze. I lift my brow in question and her face goes white. I'm about to confront her when finally she pushes back her chair and stands.

"Told you," I whisper to Darcy.

"Huh?"

I give an exasperated sigh. "Ari is about to make a speech of some kind."

"Oh, shoot. She can't."

"Do you know what it is? Why am I being kept in the dark?"

"I don't have the faintest idea what she's doing. I have another surprise I'm waiting for." She draws in a sharp breath.

"I have an announcement to make," Ari says.

"Can it wait until your daddy gets a chance to hug his little girl?"

Every head in the room turns to the sound of Rick's voice. He's in desert fatigues.

"Daddy!" Ari abandons her announcement and flings herself into her dad's arms.

Tears are flowing down Darcy's cheeks, but she hangs back, allowing Ari this time.

"So you knew about this and kept it secret?"

She gives a weepy laugh. "Hard to believe, huh?"

"Yes. How long have you known?"

"A few weeks. He wasn't sure when he'd get his flight out for his R and R, so he didn't want Ari to get her hopes up that he'd get to be here for graduation."

Ari finally lets go, and Rick gathers up the boys one at a time.

Darcy is clearly conflicted.

"Darcy, take Lyddie to him and kiss your husband."

Their reunion is sweet, I have to admit. Rick's crying as hard as Darcy is when he sees how much the baby has changed. She doesn't even know him.

It's a good thirty minutes before things settle down and everyone resumes their seat at the table. We order another plate for Rick.

"What's this announcement you were going to make before I walked in?" Rick asks Ari.

"Oh, i-it can wait."

Oh, no. She's not doing that to me after she had me on pins and needles all evening leading up to that point.

"Get up and give your announcement, sweetheart," I nudge.

"Come on," Charley calls. "Don't keep us in suspense."

Drawing a deep breath, Ari rises slowly.

Paddy takes her hand and stands up next to her.

Ari begins with trembling hands. "You know that minister from the School of Missions in Dallas?"

"What about him?"

Cut to the chase, already. I get nervous when people hem-haw.

"Okay, Paddy and I have been praying about this for a few months."

Her voice is shrill, hesitant. I can tell I am not going to like what she's about to say. And judging from the looks on Patrick's parents' faces, I'd venture to guess they aren't going to be too thrilled, either.

She squares her shoulders, a sign she's gearing up for a fight, and launches in. "Paddy and I are going to get married and go to that school."

It must be the shock. But the first thing that pops into my head is: *Why would you want to go to Texas when you're so young?*

I know. Makes no sense. I think I had ten questions all rolled up into one and my mouth got ahead of my brain.

Patrick's father stands and clears his throat.

Yeah, tear into them, Pastor! You go!

"I know you said you've prayed about this, but are you sure

you're not just hearing the answer you want to hear? Nineteen is pretty young to be getting married, son."

Okay, a little calmer than I had expected. I glance at Rick. He looks confused. Like he's not sure if he's still in the plane or if he's actually with his family. I don't think he'll be much help. I honestly think he believes he's dreaming.

"Dad," Patrick says calmly. Forced calm that happens despite knocking knees and trembling hands. "Ari and I love each other. We know God brought us together, and we don't want to waste our time pursuing careers that won't take us in the right direction."

Is this kid serious? I stare her down while I collect my thoughts. *Reason. Reason with her. Don't yell.* "Look, you two have plenty of time to get yourselves degrees from the university and then get married, and *then* go to mission school."

"I told you she wouldn't understand."

Okay, now my brain and tongue are starting to work together. I jerk my head to my daughter. "You want to know what I don't understand, little girl?" Fuming now. This will help me ignore those enormous tears welling up in my daughter's eyes.

"Calm down, Claire," Rick says.

"Stop! I have a right to be—" I'm too overwhelmed to think "—whatever the opposite of calm is!"

He holds up his hands in surrender. "Fine."

I focus back on Ari. "What I really don't understand is why you think you're going to get married when you're only seventeen years old. You're not legally an adult until October."

"We—uh—were planning a November wedding."

At least she knew better than to ask for a signature.

"Well—uh," I say, drawing on my rapier wit and effective sarcasm. "Think again. You're going to college, and that's that."

"Claire . . ." Rick again?

"You mind your own business, *soldier.*"

"Mom!" Ari is shaking so hard, I almost feel bad. "Stop attacking Dad. I don't mean to be disrespectful, but at eighteen, I'll be an adult."

"No! You'll be legal. You will *not* be an adult."

Darcy reaches out and touches my arm. "Claire, you're starting to sound a bit . . . irrational."

"Irrational? You of all people are talking about *irrational?*"

She jerks her hand back as though I'm a blistering flame. "What's that supposed to mean?"

"Mom! Darcy! Focus." Ari is getting her spunk back. "The bottom line is that Patrick and I have made our decision. And that pretty much ends the discussion."

Okay, if she thinks the discussion is over just because she says so, little Miss Missionary Bride is sorely mistaken. I have just begun to fight. "Oh? And how do you plan to pay for this school and take care of yourselves?"

"I have a college fund. I know it has at least twenty thousand dollars in it. You told me last year."

"You're right about that. And it's for *college.* You can't touch it until you're twenty-five unless I give the okay."

She blanches. "Are you telling me you're not giving me my money if I don't do what you want me to do? That money would pay tuition for both of us for the entire year, plus pay most of our bills."

Mr. and Mrs. Silent Devine over there finally start to stir and I'm thinking, *Great, a little support here.*

Pastor stands. "Paddy also has money left in a college

fund—not nearly as much as his future bride, but enough to pay his own tuition to the School of Missions, and part of Ari's."

"And we can get part-time jobs," Ari says, her face shining with love and the eager light of youth.

Rick clears his throat. "And Darcy and I can help too. We have some stocks for each of the kids, and Ari's part comes to several thousand dollars."

Ari's eyes spill over with tears. "Thank you, Daddy."

I look around the table, and I don't even recognize these idiots. "What are you people talking about? Giving them money to throw their lives away? Are you nuts?"

Patrick's mother looks at me, and I see in her eyes the same concern I feel. Her lips tip upward in a compassionate smile. "They're going to do this. Let's ease the way so they don't have the struggles most people face."

Dead in my tracks. That's where her words stop me.

I stare at my daughter and the young man she's chosen. I see all the hopes, the dreams I had for her. And I realize that God didn't give her to me. He shared her with me. For seventeen beautiful and sometimes heartbreaking years. She's beautiful, talented, and knows where she stands. Knows where she's going.

I'm not crazy about this. I'm not. But if this is where God is leading them . . . my shoulders slump, and I look at my daughter. She looks back at me, her eyes questioning, pleading, hoping.

"Honey, are you sure this is what you want?"

"I am, Mom. I know we're young, but we'll make it. I know we will."

Spoken like a truly wide-eyed young woman in love.

"Claire, don't make her pay because we didn't make it." Rick's voice startles me. "Patrick isn't me. He's not going to do to her what I did to you."

I don't know why, but hearing that reassures me somehow. Maybe it's just that I'm cooling off. I turn my gaze to Patrick. He nods as though he's in the know about our family history. Ari must have told him about Rick's infidelity. "I love her, Ms. Everett."

"Please, Mom."

I turn once again to my daughter. "Okay. I'm not going to keep the money from you. I just hope you don't regret it."

"I won't." She launches into my arms. "Thank you, Mama. Thank you so much."

25

A week and a half flies by and drags, all at the same time. Suddenly it's three days before my wedding and Greg is home from Tulsa for good. As a matter of fact, he's helping me move boxes into storage until we decide what we're merging and what we're getting rid of when we move to Shepherd Falls. We'll have plenty of time to figure all that out later on. A lifetime.

With a fat black marking pen, I label my dishes KITCHEN STUFF—TAKE. Charley walks into the kitchen.

"Don't you knock?"

"Door was open. Greg said to come in."

"Oh, never mind anyway. Need something?"

Charley's been trying to nail me down for a chat for a week. But after Ari's little announcement, I've been preoccupied with things like trying to hang onto my sanity and trying not to change my mind and tight-fist that money until she comes to her senses. Things like that. The last thing on my mind has been having a chat with Charley.

Don't misunderstand. There isn't anything necessarily wrong with Charley—well, except maybe the new mustache that looks like a fake you buy with a Halloween costume, and the fact that he talks with a phony Texas drawl since he moved to the Lone Star State a few years ago—but all in all, he's a pretty good guy.

I nod toward the table. "Coffee?" I ask, holding up the pot and then remembering I packed all the cups. I'll have to unpack that box, darn it. Can't very well go three days without coffee.

He shakes his head. I find a mug and pour one for myself, then sit across from him. "What's up?"

"I'm a little worried about Mom."

"Mom? Why's that?"

"With you moving three hours away, I'm just worried that she'll be alone and—" he hesitates for a second as though trying to find the right word "—vulnerable."

I smirk. Charley can be such a dope. And he obviously doesn't know our mother well. "Have you ever known Mom to be vulnerable? She's as sharp as they come. No one is going to take advantage of her. So don't worry your little head about telephone scammers and pressure salesmen. Mom can take care of herself."

He reddens and averts his gaze until it rests longingly on my coffee.

"Look, do you want a cup or not?"

"No. I promised Marie we'd cut back on caffeine."

Oh, brother. This must be like the time they went on the macrobiotic diet. Poor Charley was miserable.

"Back to Mom," he says, tearing his eyes from my cup. "This Eli she's been hanging around with, for instance."

"Eli? What's he got to do with anything? Mom really likes him."

"I know, but have you had him checked out?"

"Checked out?" I give him that "you're crazy" look. "For what? Fleas?"

"You know what I mean. Make sure he's on the up-and-up."

"Who are you? Remington Steele?"

"Scoff if you want, but we knew a lady down home—" down home is Texas-talk for Texas "—who was swindled out of every red cent she had to her name."

"Well, I see no evidence that Eli is out to swindle anyone. If anything, I think Mom could refuse some of his gifts. He buys her anything he knows she wants. The guy has money coming out of his ears."

"Are you for sure about that?"

"He used to be in real estate. That's all I know."

"Anyway, I've decided to move back to Missouri."

"What?"

"I mean it. Marie and I agree that we want the kids to be raised around their grandmother. With Marie's folks both gone, Mom's all our kids have left."

"Wow, Charley. That's a huge surprise. What about your businesses?" Charley owns two new and used car and pickup dealerships. Both doing very, very well.

"I'm leaving them under management. And I plan to open another one right here."

"Have you told Mom?"

A grin splits his mouth. "She's about as happy as a pig in poop."

Okay, ew! "That's really gross, Charley."

"Sorry." No he's not, or he wouldn't still be grinning.

"Anyway, that's the main reason I came over."

"Not to help load boxes?"

"That too. But mainly, I want to make an offer on your house."

"You do? What for?" Charley and Marie can afford twice this house.

He shrugs. "We just like it, that's all. Good neighborhood. Mom's down the block. I don't know. It just feels right. Marie thinks so, too."

"Okay, make me an offer."

Just as my brother and I agree on a price, Greg walks in with a basket of flowers. He's frowning, and considering the tropical nature of the arrangement, I have a sinking suspicion who sent them.

"Who sent you these?"

Charley laughs. "Another guy sending your woman flowers three days before the wedding? Claire! I'm so ashamed."

So much for brotherly love. Time's up for him. "Get out of here, Charley, or so help me, I'll change my mind about selling you the house."

Greg's brow goes up, and he forgets to frown for a second. "Charley's buying your house?"

"Yeah, they're moving back so the kids can be close to Mom. And Charley's worried Eli might try to take her millions."

He gives a brief laugh then nods pointedly to the card.

Ugh. I don't want to look. But I do. And then . . . all you-know-what breaks loose.

> For the one that got away—
> My offer still stands. Say the word and I'll meet you in
> Hawaii.
> Jerry

Greg looks from the card to me and back at the card again. "Do you want to explain this?"

Um, nope. I'd rather swallow a thumbtack.

"Claire? I think it's pretty clear there was more going on with Jerry than you owned up to. Is there something I need to know before we get married?"

My eyes narrow. Indignation rises in my breast. "Are you implying I've had an affair?"

He swipes his hand through his thick dark hair and huffs out a breath. "I don't know what to think."

"Well, I wasn't cheating on you, if you want to know the truth!"

"Why does this guy think it's okay to send you flowers? And what is he talking about when he says he'll take you to Hawaii? As in a honeymoon?"

My lips twist in a wry smile. "Yeah, without the vows."

His face mottles with anger, eyes flashing. "I knew I should have decked him. I just never really thought he was serious with all the flowers and candy. You said he was kidding around."

"He kept after me because I'm the only woman who's ever turned him down." I try to lighten things with a smile, but Greg's not amused.

"About Hawaii. Was that a random thought?" He taps the card he's still holding. "Or does this comment have something to do with our trip being postponed?"

"It's directly related to us. He's baiting me."

"But why would he—"

"Miss Lou must have told him we weren't having a honeymoon."

"And Miss Lou was told because . . . ?"

"I had a weak moment, Greg. I was upset about Shepherd Falls and the dress being five thousand dollars and . . ."

"Five thousand dollars?" He looks aghast.

"Yes. And I earned every inch of it."

That elicits a smile from him. I relax, but not for long.

He shakes his head as though trying to take in all of this new information. "I guess I'm confused."

"I'm sorry, Greg. I'm sorry Jerry seems to take such pleasure in needling us."

"What I'm confused about," he continues as though I haven't spoken, "is why you were complaining to Miss Lou."

"I wasn't complaining. I just needed a friendly shoulder."

"And you didn't feel you could come to me with this?"

"What would you have done about it?" The question sounds more like an accusation. I know it's not fair. Especially since I came to grips with it a long time ago. "Greg, you wanted that position at Shepherd Falls. You would have been so disappointed if I'd taken that away from you. You would have resented every minute of Hawaii. It wasn't worth it to me."

"So you sacrificed for me, but you don't think I would have sacrificed for you?"

"There's no comparison. Of course your ministry is more important."

His expression softens. "Is there anything else I need to know about Jerry?"

Fear shoots through me as I think back to Valentine's Day. Nodding, I explain the entire situation.

"You're telling me you were lured to a boat on Valentine's Day by a man you admittedly had an attraction for?"

I feel like hanging my head in shame. But I need to see the expression on Greg's face. Even when it's filled with hurt and looming anger.

I nod. "I came home as soon as I realized it wasn't you."

"But you didn't tell me."

"I didn't know how. Things have been odd for me. The whole disappointment over the honeymoon . . . and then Shepherd Falls offering you the job permanently. And then my wedding dress costing so much I had to walk dogs to buy it. It was all so overwhelming."

"Why didn't you come to me with any of this?"

"I didn't want to lose you."

He stares at me for a long moment, then draws a short breath. "I need to go."

"What? We're in the middle of a discussion. You can't go."

"I'm sorry. I have to. If I don't, I'm going to . . . I just have to go, Claire." Greg sets the card on the table next to the flowers and walks away.

I step inside my church that night bewildered, wondering if I will need my gown after all. I haven't heard from Greg, nor have I tried to call him. I know he's upset. To him I've been duplicitous. Okay, that's a nice word for "liar." My church family is all abuzz when I arrive. There is talk of Ari and Patrick's engagement (which I'm still hoping will turn out to be for much longer than six months), Rick's impending return to Kuwait Saturday morning—the day of my wedding, hopefully—and of course there's talk of my wedding itself.

Once I would have considered it nosiness for these people to ask about my personal life, to discuss my family this way. But now I understand that church family is just that—family. I think about our upcoming move to Shepherd Falls (again, hopefully), and I just know I'm going to miss these people more than I ever thought possible.

Greg never shows up. Finally on Thursday morning, after I

walk Ollie, I get up the nerve, swallow my pride, and dial his mother.

"Helen, can you tell me where Greg is?"

"You don't know?" That definitely doesn't sound good.

"No. I haven't heard from him since yesterday morning."

"He's gone to Shepherd Falls. He didn't say why."

My heart sinks. Surely he wouldn't call off the wedding without letting me know.

"He's due back tonight. I'll have him call you, okay?"

"Thanks, Helen."

So that's that. I try not to worry. But I know there are things we need to clear up. Surely he won't ignore this and then show up on Saturday like nothing happened. Maybe he won't show up at all . . . or maybe he's planning a Dear Claire letter.

The next morning I awaken, determined to proceed with wedding plans as though nothing is amiss. Linda, Darcy, and I, with the kids' help, are transforming our church sanctuary into a little wedding chapel. Well, not so little. It'll hold four hundred people.

At three thirty, the sanctuary door opens, beaming light into the room. I look up and my heart fails a beat. "Greg."

"Can we talk?"

"We'll just be out doing . . . something else." Darcy grabs Linda, and the two of them hurry past Greg and through the door.

"You left."

Nodding, he walks toward me. "I'm sorry. I had to think."

"And did you?" I don't know how to react. I'm so relieved, I want to throw myself into his arms and beg him to marry me. But I keep my cool. Although begging is still an option if things go badly. "Your mom said you went to Shepherd Falls."

He nods. "I did. To turn down the offer."

I gasp, and suddenly disappointment twists inside me. "But I wanted you to accept, Greg. You know I did."

"I got a counteroffer that I think might interest you."

We're face-to-face now. Greg reaches out and takes my hand. "I met with the board and with the Millers and told them I couldn't start our marriage by disappointing you."

Tears form and my throat clogs.

"Mrs. Miller said, 'Finally! A man who gets where his wife should be in the lineup. You put her before the church. Otherwise the church itself won't be ordered right.' She made a motion to send us on our honeymoon to Hawaii as a signing bonus. And then give us two extra weeks to get everything wrapped up here. We don't officially take the office of pastor until the first Sunday in July."

I'm so surprised I can't speak. Joy rises, and I rush him, throwing my arms around his neck. He laughs and lifts me off my feet.

"I take it that's a yes?"

"Of course that's a yes."

Greg! Shepherd Falls. And Hawaii too!

Greg dips his head and catches my lips with his. "Let's get married."

And so we do. On Saturday afternoon, just like I hoped, dreamed, planned, I'm standing in front of my full-length mirror waiting for the limo to pick up the kids and me and drive us to the church, where I will join my life with the man I love. Charley will bring the mother of the bride, of course.

Ollie has been moping a bit. I haven't been showing him the kind of attention he's accustomed to, so I allow him in my bedroom while I get ready.

"What do you think, Ollie? Do I make a smashing bride, or what?"

His ears perk up at the sound of his name on my lips. Then he realizes I'm not offering him a banana Popsicle, and he flops his head back down on his paws. Totally bored.

A knock on my door is followed by Ari's face peeking through the small opening she made. "Need some help?"

"I'd appreciate it. Can you please zip me the rest of the way and fasten the hooks?"

She walks across the room, an absolute vision in her pale pink silk bridesmaid gown. Her blonde hair is swept up, with a few wispy curls caressing her neck. "No one is going to be looking at the bride today," I say, smiling at her through the reflection in the mirror.

"Don't bet on it." She fastens the last hook and steps to the side. "I've never seen you look so gorgeous, Mom. Greg's going to die when he sees you."

"I hope not." I feel my face glowing with joy and excitement.

"Let's slip on your veil," Ari says. She walks to the bed where I've laid the sheer veil and carefully brings it to me. I take it, sliding the combs into my hair to keep the circle at the top of my head in place. And my transformation from everyday woman to bride is complete. Ari and I stare silently, and in unison, our shoulders rise and fall with audible sighs. We look at each other and laugh just as the doorbell rings.

"I guess it's time to go," I say.

I grab the white beaded purse from my dresser and head toward the door.

"Mom."

I turn.

Ari laughs and holds out the satin shoes I bought to carry me down the aisle. "You might want to change out of your slippers."

Oh, yeah. My cheeks warm as I look down and spy my fuzzy leopard-spotted slippers. I slide my feet out of them and transfer to the satin slippers. As much as I love those old favorites, these definitely suit me better at this moment.

Jake, Shawn, and Tommy are standing at the bottom of the steps when I descend. All are wearing rented black tuxes and look so handsome, I once again have to fight back tears to keep my makeup from running.

"You look awesome, Mom," Shawn says. The other two boys just stare, as though they're not sure they're allowed to move.

"Ready to go?" I ask.

We bustle out the door. The driver is standing next to the limo, waiting to open up for us. The kids pile in, and I carefully slide into one of the leather seats.

As the driver pulls away from the curb, I take in the faces of my children. They've been through so much in the past six years. Just like I have. The thing about divorce is that it doesn't only affect the couple involved. My children suffered deeply when their father left.

This marriage affects them too, and though they've each given their blessing, I feel the need for some sort of closure on our old life. "So, how are you all feeling about things today?"

I guess it's a lame way to open the conversation. No one but Jake answers. "I have a sore throat."

"You do? Let me see."

He opens wide and sticks out his tongue—standard protocol that he no longer has to be coached in.

"Pink as a bunny's ear." I smile and hug him close, then realize I'm probably wrinkling my gown, so I gently set him from me and take his hand instead.

"What I meant was, are you really okay with how things are about to change? You know, Greg's going to be my husband. It's not like when we were just dating. He'll be part of the family, and I won't be making all the decisions around the house like I do now."

"We know, Mom." Tommy's voice squeaks—another sign he is passing from boy to man. Thankfully no one teases him, so I don't have to deal with a massive brawl in the limo on my wedding day.

Ari smiles. My daughter is a young woman with a growing sensitivity. "We've been part of a blended family since Dad married Darcy, Mom. We know the drill. We wish you and Daddy hadn't split up, but that's life. And we love Greg. We'll adjust."

"Greg's nice." Jake's two cents' worth. "And I can't wait for Sadie to live with us."

A collective groan emanates from the other three.

Seriously, I understand their dread of the situation, but still . . .

"Come on, guys. Let's give her the benefit of the doubt. Please?"

"We'll try." Ari smiles—I know it's fake, but pretend I don't.

"Thank you, honey."

"As long as she doesn't touch my stuff," Shawn says.

Tommy stares out the window. "Whatever."

I enter the church by a side door where Linda, Darcy, Charley's wife Marie, and my mother are waiting to escort me to the nursery room they've converted into the bride's room. It smells slightly of disinfectant and baby powder. And I once again have a second of longing for a baby to share with Greg. There isn't time to dwell on the thought, though, because I'm immediately swarmed by my attendants.

"Oh, Claire, you're just beautiful." Darcy's eyes shimmer with unshed tears. "I'm so happy for you."

Maybe it's the mood I'm in. Maybe it's that I'm a bride—I don't know. But suddenly, I'm overcome with affection for dear Darcy. I embrace her fully. My own eyes well with tears. "You're beautiful too, Darce."

Suddenly I wish I'd made her a bridesmaid. Who cares what people think?

"All right. No tears yet." Linda steps up with tissues, and we pull apart from each other. "Here, you're both ruining your makeup, and not even a bride looks beautiful with a runny nose."

The photographer arrives moments later to take shots of the faux preparations. Mom's eyes are watery when the photographer instructs her to raise my veil and kiss my cheek.

"Be happy, Claire," she whispers. "That's all I've ever wanted for my girl."

"I am. So happy."

The wedding coordinator steps into the room just as the photographer is packing up to head into the sanctuary. "Okay, the bride's attendants need to start lining up. It's almost time."

Sadie, my flower girl, takes her basket of flowers, but her heart isn't in it. She's stopped being mean to me—thanks, I'm sure, to threats of pain on her backside from her father. Still, she can't seem to hide her displeasure. Oh, well. Hopefully it won't be too obvious in the pictures.

My heart begins to race as I see the long white cloth that has been rolled from the stage, where I will stand and marry Greg, all the way back to me. A long walk down the aisle on a blanket of rose petals and I'll stand beside the man I love.

Beautiful Sadie moves forward like a trouper. She releases rose petals from the basket with grace, and my heart feels the familiar beat of maternal pride. This child will be mine in a few more minutes. I pray I can guide her into womanhood in a way that would please her biological mother. I know one thing—I will do my best.

As if in a dream, the music changes, signaling that the time has come. I look up at Charley and slip my hand through the crook of his arm. He grins. "You're on, sis." A surge of affection for my little brother hits me. For all the irritations and rivalry, Charley comes through pretty well.

We step together. Walking slowly, I almost feel suspended in time. My hands start to tremble as Greg comes into view. I keep my focus on him. All of the dreaming, planning, fantasizing, and praying hasn't prepared me for the adoration on his face. I walk slowly toward him, and he reaches for me before the preacher asks, "Who gives this bride?"

I take Greg's hand. That wonderful, warm, encompassing hand. His eyes never leave mine, even as Pastor Devine begins the ceremony.

A smile covers Greg's face. There's no denying by the tenderness in his eyes and the gentle caress of his thumb against the back of my hand that I am loved.

And much like the Velveteen Rabbit, the Vera Wang dress finally becomes a real live wedding gown.

Epilogue

So here we are, lying on the beach in Hawaii! We chose the island of Lanai for its relative remoteness compared to the other islands. As much isolation as possible.

"Mom! Tell Tommy to stop kicking sand all over me."

Didn't quite work out that way.

"Toms, stop kicking sand on your sister."

"Look, Mom—a shell. You can hear the ocean." Jake stands over me, dripping water onto my cooked flesh. He jams the shell to my ear. How relaxing. And such a romantic getaway.

"Yeah, Jake." The kid has the ocean in front of him and he's fascinated by a shell? I think he's not quite grasping that fact, though. I mean, we are from the Ozarks, after all, so we don't see much in the way of sandy beaches and seashells.

With Rick leaving to go back to Kuwait the day of the wedding, the kids were feeling the sad loss of separation from one parent. I couldn't leave them, too—even for a honeymoon. So here we are. The travel agent took pity on us and allowed us to trade in the tickets. We scored four nights, five days for all of us, instead of two full weeks for just Greg and me.

"Daddy, I have to go pee-pee."

And of course we couldn't very well leave our daughter Sadie behind.

Greg moans in the sun next to me.

I rise up on my elbow and bend to kiss my new husband's

red forehead. "I'll take her." I hop to my feet. "Come on, Sadie."

"I wanted Dad."

"I know, but I thought we could walk up there together." I smile down at the belligerent little girl. "I have to go, too."

"Okay," she shrugs, but doesn't take my proffered hand. So much for girl bonding over a bathroom run. The beach is virtually empty anyway, so I won't insist unless it picks up and I want to be sure she doesn't get lost. Or snatched.

It's about a hundred yards from the beach to the nearest bathroom, and I'm keenly aware that the silence could be extremely uncomfortable if I don't at least attempt small talk. Besides, no time like the present to start. "How do you like Hawaii?"

"It's pretty. I wish my mommy could have come with us."

My heart goes out to her. When she's being hateful, it's easy to forget how much she's hurting over losing the mother she doesn't even remember, but when she's sad, it tears me apart. "Oh, honey. The place your mommy is at is even prettier than Hawaii."

She looks up at me then, her beautiful brown eyes wide and gentle. "Heaven?"

"Yes."

"You think she's mad my dad got married to you?"

Oh, boy. I know I would be. No. Can't think in limited human terms. "You know what? I think your mommy is just glad your dad is happy and that you are going to have a big family to grow up in. A family who loves you."

"I guess I have brothers now, huh?"

"That's right. And you and Jake have been such good friends for a long time. You're happy about it, aren't you?"

Her head bobs, and she smiles shyly.

A group of laughing teenagers comes toward us in a pack. Before I can say a word, Sadie moves close and takes my hand. I close around the soft, chubby fingers and I realize that when I became Greg's wife, I truly did somehow become this little girl's mother. I'm under no illusions that it's always going to be easy to manage this spoiled, willful child, but who am I trying to kid? My kids are no picnic.

Greg is sitting up when we get back. He pulls me down to share his lounge chair. I lean back against him, resting in the V of his legs. "Did I see you and Sadie holding hands?"

"You did."

His chest rises and falls, and I realize he too has been nervous about how we'd get along. As we watch the sun sink along the horizon and the kids running and splashing along the water's edge, Greg's lips hover close to my ear.

"You sure you're okay with moving to Shepherd Falls?"

"Is there any doubt? After all, I sold my house and gave up my *Father of the Bride* house. Honestly, Greg. I'm anxious to start our life there."

His arms tighten around me. "I love you, Mrs. Lewis."

My ears thrill to the sound of my new name. "Everett-Lewis," I correct.

"Nope. You can be Everett to the rest of the world, but in my arms, you're Mrs. Lewis."

Greg doesn't often assert the macho alpha male lurking beneath the easygoing, laid-back guy he normally displays. But when he does, it does one of two things: really irritates me, or really gets my blood pumping.

I turn in his arms, and his lips claim mine.

And I can only say: I'm not one bit irritated.

READING GROUP GUIDE

1. Claire battles insecurity about Greg's love for her. Why do you think that is? Is it reasonable for a Christian woman engaged to a godly man to have such insecurities?

2. Claire has a lot of ideas about the way things should go and tends to resist any change of plans. Are you a roll-with-the-punches kind of person, or are you easily thrown for a loop? Read Proverbs 19:21. How does that verse apply to this kind of thinking?

3. Just when Claire's daughter is starting to straighten up her act, Claire's son is found to be hiding drugs. Do you think Claire handles Tommy's discipline properly? Why or why not? What would you have done differently?

4. Have you observed differences in the child-rearing strategies of single moms as opposed to married moms? How and why do those strategies differ? Is it about marital status? Personality differences?

5. Claire wants to make Greg happy, but she's not sure she can be an effective partner to him if he takes on a senior pastorate. Do you think she's being selfish, or is she genuinely concerned for his sake?

6. In Proverbs we find the "virtuous woman." Claire desperately wants to fill those shoes. What do you think are her biggest obstacles? Do you face any of the same obstacles? Is it even possible to be the kind of woman described in Proverbs 31?

7. Claire is far from perfect and has a stubborn streak that causes her to hang on to the ideal of the perfect wedding gown even if it means doing a job she hates in order to obtain it. Is this admirable? Explain.

8. Claire's daughter announces her decision to marry fresh out of high school and go to missions school with her fiancé. Claire is mortified but eventually gives in. Speaking from your own life experiences, what would you have done in that situation? Why?

9. Greg is portrayed as a good man who has his priorities in line. But when a job opportunity arises, he has no problem delaying the dream honeymoon he and Claire had planned. Is that selfishness on his part?

10. Claire ultimately reconciles with and even looks forward to the ministry aspect of her marriage. What are some challenges she might face as a pastor's wife and the mother in a blended family?

ABOUT THE AUTHOR

Tracey Bateman is the award-winning author of more than twenty-five books. Currently, she serves as president of American Christian Fiction Writers (ACFW), a one-thousand-member organization. Tracey enjoys playing and listening to music, and reading. She lives with her husband and their four children in beautiful southwest Missouri.

Tracey welcomes e-mail from her readers at tvbateman@aol.com.

Visit her Web site at www.traceybateman.com.